D0724513

904-797-3388

"YOU COULD'VE KNOCKED!"

The bedclothes had slipped down, and Colin jerked the covers up to his chin to hide the telltale rise in the blanket at his hips.

Annie tossed him a sassy grin. "You expect to be treated differently than anyone in my family?"

"You mean I can walk into your bedroom any time I want?"

Annie's eyes glittered mischievously, and her gaze roamed up and down Colin's hidden body. "Why not? I'm sure I don't have anything you haven't seen before."

Colin called her bluff and swung his feet to the floor, strategically keeping the blanket over his lap as he sat up.

Surprise flickered across Annie's face and she took two quick steps backward. "You wouldn't dare!"

Colin grinned. "Try me," he invited.

Annie spun around to the door, then faced him again, her eyes laughing. "You'd better be careful—one of these days I might not walk out of your bedroom."

The door closed with a soft click, and Colin stared at it for a long moment, wondering what he would do if that day ever came.

Other AVON ROMANCES

BEFORE THE DAWN *by Beverly Jenkins*
BELOVED PROTECTOR *by Linda O'Brien*
HEART OF NIGHT *by Taylor Chase*
AN INNOCENT MISTRESS: FOUR BRIDES
FOR FOUR BROTHERS *by Rebecca Wade*
THE MACGOWAN BETROTHAL:
HIGHLAND ROGUES *by Lois Greiman*
THE MAIDEN AND HER KNIGHT *by Margaret Moore*
SECRET VOWS *by Mary Reed McCall*

Coming Soon

THE BRIDE SALE *by Candice Hern*
A SEDUCTIVE OFFER *by Kathryn Smith*

And Don't Miss These
ROMANTIC TREASURES
from Avon Books

THE OUTLAW AND THE LADY *by Lorraine Heath*
THE SEDUCTION OF SARA *by Karen Hawkins*
SOMEONE IRRESISTIBLE *by Adele Ashworth*

ATTENTION: ORGANIZATIONS AND CORPORATIONS
Most Avon Books paperbacks are available at special quantity
discounts for bulk purchases for sales promotions, premiums, or
fund-raising. For information, please call or write:

Special Markets Department, HarperCollins Publishers, Inc.,
10 East 53rd Street, New York, N.Y. 10022–5299.
Telephone: (212) 207–7528. Fax: (212) 207-7222.

MAUREEN MCKADE

His Unexpected Wife

AVON BOOKS
An Imprint of HarperCollinsPublishers

This is a work of fiction. Names, characters, places, and incidents are products of the author's imagination or are used fictitiously and are not to be construed as real. Any resemblance to actual events, locales, organizations, or persons, living or dead, is entirely coincidental.

AVON BOOKS
An Imprint of HarperCollins*Publishers*
10 East 53rd Street
New York, New York 10022-5299

Copyright © 2001 by Maureen Webster
ISBN: 0-380-81567-2
www.avonromance.com

All rights reserved. No part of this book may be used or reproduced in any manner whatsoever without written permission, except in the case of brief quotations embodied in critical articles and reviews. For information address Avon Books, an Imprint of HarperCollins Publishers.

First Avon Books paperback printing: December 2001

Avon Trademark Reg. U.S. Pat. Off. and in Other Countries, Marca Registrada, Hecho en U.S.A.
HarperCollins ® is a trademark of HarperCollins Publishers Inc.

Printed in the U.S.A.

10 9 8 7 6 5 4 3 2 1

If you purchased this book without a cover, you should be aware that this book is stolen property. It was reported as "unsold and destroyed" to the publisher, and neither the author nor the publisher has received any payment for this "stripped book."

Chapter 1

September 1894
Denver, Colorado

Colin McBride set his scuffed portmanteau on the porch and straightened his stiff wool coat. The last time he had visited Trev and Kate Trevelyan had been ten years ago; he had all but forgotten them while he'd pursued his pot of gold.

But now he wanted to see them again, wanted to relive those early years when he had been young and naïve, and believed the world was his for the taking. He smiled to himself, imagining Trev and Kate's surprise to find him on their doorstep after so long—though he suspected Trev would have a few paternal comments to make about his long absence.

1

Colin raised his fist and knocked on the door.

The door swung open and a young man as tall as himself stood framed in the entrance. The years evaporated as he stared into the boy's midnight blue eyes—there was no doubt he was Trev's son. "Brynn?" he asked.

The boy nodded and regarded him curiously. "Who're you?"

Colin swallowed to ease the tightness in his throat. "Colin McBride, though you might remember me as Laddie."

Brynn's young face lit with a grin and his eyes sparkled. "You bought me chocolate ice cream."

Colin tried to reconcile the lively lad with chocolate smeared across his face with the young man in front of him. "You weren't more than five years old then."

"I was almost six."

Colin laughed and relaxed. "You're lookin' more and more like your da every day." His Irish accent, which he'd lost years ago, returned with the fond memories the boy evoked. He offered Brynn his hand and the young man shook it enthusiastically.

Brynn stepped aside. "Come on in. Are my folks expecting you?"

Colin shook his head and grinned wryly. "No. I'm hoping they still remember me." He stepped over the threshold with a slight wince. The one thing he wouldn't miss when he left Colorado were the cold winters, which played hell with the leg he had broken a few months previous.

"Laddie?"

Colin looked up to see Kate staring at him as if he were a ghost. She had no idea how close he had come to being just that.

She hurried toward him, her skirts bustling about her ankles, and affection flowed through him. He set his bag on the floor and Kate wrapped her arms around him, hugging him tightly. Colin reciprocated the embrace as memories inundated him. Although he had only been seventeen and life in the mining town of Orion, Colorado, had been difficult, he remembered those years fondly because of Kate, Trev, and their two children.

Colin took a step back and studied her face, surprised to see a few telltale lines at the corners of her eyes and on her brow. Where the hell had the years gone? "You're looking as beautiful as ever."

"And you still have the gift of blarney." She tucked her arm through the crook of his and led him across the spacious foyer. He tried not to limp, but knew he didn't succeed when she glanced at him quizzically. Colin ignored her unspoken question as she guided him into a high-ceilinged room that hummed with activity. Six children, ranging from barely walking to Brynn's fifteen years, talked and laughed and argued.

"Look who dropped in," Kate called above the din.

Trev, his thick black hair now a distinguished white, glanced up and his eyes widened. He disentangled himself from two of the younger children and strode to Colin with his right hand extended. They shook firmly, then Trev pulled Colin into a one-armed hug. "Damn, Laddie, it's good to see you."

"Same here, Trev." Colin slapped Trev's back and the two men drew apart. Colin's throat grew thick. He felt like the boy he'd been when he'd first met Trev and Kate fifteen years ago.

Trev eyed him closely and whistled low. "Nice suit. The railroad business must be treating you pretty well."

"I've done all right." Colin looked around the bright, airy room that overflowed with warmth and love. All the money in the world could never buy what his friends possessed. He tamped down the melancholy thought. "You and Kate haven't done bad yourselves."

Kate moved over to Trev, who wrapped an arm around her waist. The tender look they exchanged twisted Colin's stomach into a knot. He envied the love they obviously had for one another and sadly realized he'd never possess what Trev and Kate shared. He had resigned himself to finding a woman he could feel comfortable with and who would bear his children. He'd known married couples who possessed less. All he had to do was find that woman.

"So, what have you been up to the last few years? We were ready to give up on you," Trev said.

"Same old thing—putting holes through mountains," Colin replied.

Kate brushed a strand of her still rich chestnut

hair back from her forehead and her curious gaze swept down to his knee and back to his face. "What happened to your leg?"

Colin managed a nonchalant shrug. "An accident about three months back." He looked around at the children ringing them, determined to change the subject. "Now, I know Brynn and Lucy. But what about the other four?"

Kate moved out of Trev's affectionate hold and leaned over to pick up a dark-haired girl who appeared to be two or three years old. "This is Kathryn." She pointed to two identical looking boys about five. "That's Michael and Matthew, the twins, and there's Darcy, who was born right after your last visit."

"Darcy?" Colin asked, startled.

"You said you had a younger brother named Darcy, didn't you?" Kate asked softly.

Numbly, Colin nodded. The gesture touched him; it also sharpened his guilt for staying away for so long. "Thank you."

"How long are you in town?" Trev asked, seeming to understand Colin's awkwardness.

"A few days."

"I'll get a room ready," Kate said.

"Don't go to any bother, Kate. I'll stay in a hotel."

"Oh, no, you won't." She looked at her husband. "I expect you to convince him."

"Looks like you don't have a choice, Colin, because if you don't stay here, we'll both be staying at a hotel," Trev said with a grin.

Colin chuckled. "Then I guess I'd be a fool to turn down your invitation."

"Now that that's settled, let's go out on the porch and have a cigar," Trev suggested.

"I'll call you when dinner's ready," Kate said.

Colin followed Trev out onto the porch, accepting the thick cigar the older man handed to him. Trev lit Colin's, then his own, and a companionable silence rose as the hazy cigar smoke surrounded them.

Trev propped his shoulder against a support post and said in a quiet voice, "You've changed, Colin, grown harder."

The younger man took a deep breath and tension tightened his muscles. "Life has a way of doing that."

"Why didn't you stop by more often? I know you weren't that far away." Trev paused and added, "Kate and I worried about you, wondering whether you were alive or dead."

Exhaling a stream of bluish-gray smoke, Colin gazed across the city laid out beyond them. "I'm sorry, Trev. I had to make my fortune, make my da proud of me." The words came out with more bitterness than Colin intended. He turned his gaze to the door that led into the love-filled home. "You and Kate have a beautiful family, Trev."

"Why didn't you ever get hitched?" Trev shifted uncomfortably. "Kate used to worry it was because of her."

Colin's face warmed as he remembered how

infatuated he had been with Kate, but he had long ago gotten over that youthful notion. "No, it wasn't her. You know what it was like in the camps—the decent women were few and far between." He shrugged. "I just didn't make the time to meet someone. But now I have the time."

"Did you get a different job?"

"I quit my old one."

"What're you going to do now?"

"I'm going to find a wife, buy a place in California, and raise children and Andalusians."

Trev's mouth dropped open. "Anda-what?"

"Andalusians," Colin repeated with a grin. "They're horses. I met this man from Spain who had brought some of them with him. Beautiful animals, Trev. I'll be one of the first breeders in the country."

"But you don't know anything about horses. And where are you going to get the capital to start something like that?"

Colin shrugged. "I didn't know anything about making tunnels, either. I figure I'm not so old that I can't learn."

Trev chuckled. "Damn, Colin, you just might do it." He sobered and the furrows returned to his forehead. "Did you quit the railroad because of your leg?"

Colin's chest tightened with remembered anguish and he shoved aside the terror the memory awakened. "Partly. I'm lucky I wasn't killed."

Trev nodded, and his expression told Colin he understood what had been left unspoken. They'd both seen their share of injured miners in those early years.

"Are you still teaching?" Colin asked, needing to change the subject.

"I'm an administrator now. The mining school's growing so fast they need to hire more instructors." He paused thoughtfully. "I could use someone with your experience."

Startled, Colin shook his head. "No thanks, Trev. I don't want anything to do with mining anymore." He doubted he would ever overcome the intense fear of being underground again.

He couldn't dwell on it. As long as he stayed out of tunnels and caves, he didn't have any trouble. He shifted his attention to something less disturbing—Trev and Kate's children. "I haven't seen Annie yet."

Trev's gaze filled with concern. "She's out with some friends—probably at the theater." He began to pace the length of the porch. "She's got it in her head to become an actress."

Colin puffed on his cigar, trying to keep the astonishment from his expression. "A little young, isn't she?"

"She's twenty—should be married by now, but she's turned down every suitor in the last two years." Trev ran an impatient hand through his hair. "Kate says we shouldn't worry, that this acting is only a passing fancy, but I'm beginning to wonder. If she wanted to be anything other than an actress, I could accept it, but . . ."

Colin pictured the blond, blue-eyed scamp he

remembered and tried to imagine her as a woman of marriageable age. He couldn't do it. "Acting isn't a respectable profession for anyone, much less a young lady."

Trev halted his pacing. "That's exactly what I said, but Kate thinks she'll grow out of it. And Annie damn well better, because a daughter of mine is *not* going to be an actress."

Colin stepped over to his friend and laid a hand on his shoulder. "Relax, Trev. You and Kate raised her right—she'll come around."

"I hope so."

The sound of voices and laughter drew Colin's attention to the sidewalk. He watched as a group of young people walked toward the house. They paused in front of Trev's place, and one of the women waved good-bye while the rest continued on.

A long, hooded black cape covered her, and as she approached, Colin could see she was petite, not more than an inch or two over five feet. Whitish-blond hair peeked out of the hood and when the woman looked at him with bright blue eyes, Colin's heart lurched in his chest.

"Laddie!" Annie let out an unladylike whoop and launched herself into a startled Colin's arms.

Colin felt the fullness of her breasts against his chest, and the scent of lilacs sent Colin's senses spiraling as he hugged her back. This woman couldn't be little Annie—the girl who had demanded piggyback rides and pelted him with hundreds of questions.

"I'm so glad to see you, La—Colin." Annie drew away from him, smiling. "Last time you were here, you said you preferred being called Colin." She propped her hands on her hips and glared at him. "Of course, that was ten years ago."

Colin held up his hands in surrender. "I've already gotten a lecture from your parents; I don't need one from my little lassie, too." He eyed her up and down, trying not to linger on the curves that hadn't been there the last time he'd seen her. "You've grown up."

"That's what happens when you disappear for so long."

"I'm sorry, Annie. It just seemed like there was no time to get away."

Her mercurial smile returned, dazzling him with its brilliance. "I'll forgive you, but only if you promise not to stay away so long again."

"Were you at the theater?" Trev demanded.

Annie lifted her chin and met her father's strict gaze unflinchingly. "Yes. I told Kate where I was going."

Colin could feel the tension between the equally strong-willed individuals. When had they become adversaries? Trev used to dote on his beautiful blond daughter, yet here he was questioning her like a common criminal.

Annie pinned her baby blue eyes on Colin. "I bet you enjoy going to the theater."

Colin narrowed his gaze—what was the imp up to? "I've only been to a couple of shows."

"And I'll bet you liked them." Her smile could have melted a frozen mountain lake in the dead of winter.

He'd have to tread carefully—on one side was his best friend and the other a girl he loved like a sister. "They were all right, but I don't see why folks like to get up on a stage and pretend to be someone they're not."

Fire flashed in Annie's eyes and her cheeks blossomed with color. "You sound just like Papa. A performer wants to entertain; to make people laugh and cry; to help people forget their troubles for a little while."

Her passionate defense of the theater surprised Colin; Trev obviously hadn't exaggerated the problem.

The door opened, splashing a rectangle of light onto the porch, and Kate stuck her head out. "Dinner's ready." She noticed Annie and smiled. "Oh good, you're home. I see you've welcomed Laddie already."

"Colin." Annie winked at him like a fellow conspirator.

Kate smiled ruefully. "Right. Well, don't just stand there, come and get it before I throw it out."

Colin and Annie exchanged an amused look, but they followed Kate. Colin allowed the girl to precede him, his treasonous gaze following the delicious sway of her backside.

Trev came behind him and leaned over to whisper in his ear. "Be careful of Annie. She can wrap you around her finger without you ever knowing until it's too late."

Colin didn't doubt that. She'd done it often enough to him when she was a child. Now that Annie was a woman, he had a feeling she could charm the whiskers off a cougar if she put her mind to it. "Don't worry—I've known her too long for her tricks to work."

Trev shook his head in mock sympathy. "That's what I used to tell myself, too."

Annie overheard her father's warning to Colin and some of the happiness at seeing her friend faded. If only her father could understand why she wanted to act, she wouldn't have to resort to deceptions to get her way. She removed her cape, then took Colin's jacket. Her fingers brushed his and arrows of heat darted up her arm. Surprised, Annie glanced up to see him studying her.

His reddish hair had been muted by time, becoming brown with strands that caught the light's glow and reflected auburn tints. The curls she remembered had also disappeared, leaving his hair thick and wavy. A stray tendril had fallen across his forehead in devil-may-care fashion. Without thinking, Annie reached up to brush the errant strands back and Colin's forest green eyes flickered at her touch. The silky softness slid across her fingers and she was loath to draw her hand away.

"Come on, you two," Trev called.

Annie quickly retreated and hung up their coats, her face warm. The last time Colin had visited, she had developed an embarrassing crush on him. She'd only been ten at the time and Colin had treated her like he always did—as a little sister. For a whole day after he left, Annie had sworn her broken heart would never heal.

Colin held out his arm and after a moment's hesitation, Annie put her hand through the crook and rested her fingers on his forearm. As they walked into the dining room, she noticed his slight limp. "What happened to your leg?"

He shrugged. "It's nothing."

"Will it get better?"

"Yeah, but the doctor said it'll always ache in cold weather."

He said it so matter-of-factly that Annie felt oddly uncertain what to say or do.

Her family gathered around an eight-foot table which seemed to groan beneath the weight of the steaming food—a typical dinner for the Trevelyan clan. Without asking where Colin was to sit, Annie led him to the setting to the right of her usual place. He held her chair for her and sent her a wink that would have made her knees wobble if she had been standing. Then he lowered himself to the seat beside her, his arm brushing her breast so lightly it was almost nonexistent. Almost.

Her heart skipped a beat as her nipples hardened, and her bodice felt tighter than it had earlier. She had a difficult time catching her breath.

"Let's say grace," Kate said.

Everyone held hands, and the warmth of Colin's callused fingers across Annie's palm sent a shudder of excitement down her spine. She'd held hands with many men, and most of them had smooth, slender fingers that hadn't known a day of manual labor. They hadn't thrilled her like Colin's did.

Annie was barely aware of when the prayer ended. If Colin hadn't eased his hand out of her grip, she would have remained holding it throughout dinner—probably dessert, too.

Food was passed around the table amid affectionate banter.

"Maybe you should let Colin get some food first or there won't be any left," her father teased Brynn, who was a bottomless pit when it came to eating.

The smaller children laughed, while Lucy, who was on the verge of becoming a young lady, merely sniffed in disdain—a common reaction of late to the antics of her siblings.

Annie watched the familiar scene with a sense of sadness—she would miss this when she went to San Francisco. The love her father and stepmother shared enveloped each of their children like a fluffy blanket and their home echoed with laughter and affection. This was the only home Annie would ever have—she would never marry and have children. That was how her real mother had died, and Annie had too many things she wanted to do to risk dying so young.

"Is something wrong, Annie?" Colin asked quietly.

She glanced up to find his gaze on her. "No,

I'm fine," she lied. *No, not lied, acted.* That was how she had to look at this deception—as a role she must play in order to achieve her goal. "I suppose you aren't used to meals like this."

Colin's smile was familiar, but the tug on her heart wasn't. His teeth were white and straight, and his lips full and firm.

"To be honest, it's a nice change," he said.

Annie remembered the stories of faraway places he had told her when she was a child. They had enchanted her and given her imagination wings. They had carried her far beyond the dull monotony of her life and given her dreams to aspire to. They had convinced her she could do anything she set her mind to.

"Have you been to a lot of different places in the past ten years? Met a lot of important people?" she asked Colin.

He chuckled. "Still the same Annie—full of questions." He laid his fork down and propped his elbows on either side of his plate as he threaded his fingers together. "I've spent most of my time in the mountains, which would be depressingly dull for a young woman like yourself."

Annie's expression fell—she was so certain Colin would regale her with some new stories of his travels. "How long were you with the railroad?"

"Thirteen years." Colin's eyes glowed with inner fervor and his voice became animated. "In the beginning, we were the pioneers, determined to connect one side of the country with the other, even if it meant going through solid rock to do it. I wish I could tell you what it felt like to see a train pass through my first tunnel." He glanced down, and his face became shadowed with sadness and something else—something Annie couldn't identify. His smile was forced when he looked up again. "Well, that's all in the past. All I want to do now is settle down and have my own home and a family."

Annie wrinkled her nose. "That sounds boring."

Colin laughed. "I suppose it would, to someone who's young and has a world waiting to be discovered."

"You're not that old, Colin," Kate said. "Why, you're younger than Trev was when I first met him."

"Thanks, Kate, but to the children, I'm sure I seem as ancient as the hills."

Annie narrowed her eyes—she didn't consider Colin ancient. Gazing at his aquiline profile, high forehead, and strong chin, she definitely didn't see an old man. However, he wasn't the Laddie from her childhood, either—he no longer laughed easily and often. Troubled by her thoughts, Annie barely listened to what Kate was saying.

"It'll be so nice to have you nearby where we can see you more often."

Colin shook his head. "I won't be settling in Colorado, Kate. I'm headed west."

"To Utah or Nevada?"

"California."

Annie jerked her head up. *California*?

"I want to live someplace that's warm all year round," Colin explained.

"Near San Francisco?" Trev asked casually.

"Not that far north."

"Oh. I thought maybe if you were going that way, you could escort Annie to finishing school."

"You're sending Annie to a finishing school in San Francisco?" Colin asked, taken aback.

"That's right. It'll be good for her." Her father spoke as if she were a three-year-old child.

Annie narrowed her eyes, but all her arguments had been dismissed since her father had made the decision. She sighed dramatically. "I'm only going because it'll make you and Kate happy, Papa. But I'm going to miss everyone so much." She was surprised by the moisture that filled her eyes—she hadn't planned the tears. That would have been overplaying her role.

Colin took hold of her hand and gave it a squeeze. "I'll travel with you, Annie, if you'd like."

She glanced at him, noticing his long eyelashes and recalling the softness of his hair. Her heart did a somersault. "Yes, I'd like that, Colin."

"Good," her father said with a satisfied grin. "Colin will make sure you arrive safe and sound."

"I'll walk her right up to the front door of the school," Colin reassured him.

Panic leapt through Annie's veins. Colin's escort to the school would ruin her plans. "I'm not a little girl who needs her hand held."

Her father speared her with a measuring look. Annie had never been able to hide anything from him when he looked at her like that, but the stakes had never been this high. She returned his gaze without blinking, her chin jutting out stubbornly.

Kate laid a hand on her arm. "That's not what we meant, sweetheart. It's just that your father and I will rest easier knowing Colin is with you."

Her stepmother's obvious love and concern weakened Annie's resolve. She couldn't love Kate any more if she were her real mother. Well, Annie would accept Colin's company on the train, but as soon as they arrived in San Francisco, she would convince him she could get to the school by herself. She had a plan, and it didn't involve attending finishing school.

Annie Trevelyan was going to be an actress, and nobody—not even Colin—was going to stop her.

Chapter 2

Colin's nose twitched and he brushed a hand across his face. The comfortable mattress felt too good for him to open his eyes to see if the sun had risen yet. The annoying tickle came again and he frowned as he again swept aside whatever drifted across his nose—probably a feather from the fluffy pillow.

A distinct pair of giggles startled him. Who had gotten into his sleeper car? His eyes flashed open and he found a pair of mischievous blue eyes staring down at him. After a moment of bewilderment, he realized where he was—and who stood over his bed.

"Matthew?" he asked the young boy.

The grinning lad with a feather in one hand shook his head and pointed at a matching pair of blue eyes peering at Colin from the other side of the bed. "That's Matthew. I'm Michael."

A chuckle rose in Colin's throat.

"So how do I tell you two apart?" he asked, looking from one to the other of the chestnut-haired boys.

Michael pointed at his brother. "He's got bigger ears."

"Do not," Matthew shot back.

"Do too."

Colin pushed himself up to a sitting position and studied each boy with pointed scrutiny, taking special care to tilt his head and grunt a few times. "I have to agree with Michael. Matthew has bigger ears."

"Told ya!" Michael taunted.

The door burst open and Annie stood framed in the entrance, her hands propped on her hips. "So this is where you two ran off to. Your mother's been looking for you and she's not happy."

Matthew and Michael's wide eyes and gaping mouths mirrored one another as they both mumbled an "uh-oh." Then they raced out of the room, forcing Annie to turn sideways to allow the little tornadoes to escape. She shook her head and stepped into the bedroom. "They aren't used to company or closed doors."

Colin's gaze was captured by the sway of her hips as she approached the bed. She might be petite, but all her curves were in the right places—and she hadn't been shortchanged on them. She crossed her arms and his eyes followed them to their resting place below her full breasts. What God had taken away in height, He had given back in other places, and Colin breathed a silent amen.

"Are you going to sleep all day?" she asked with a smirk, reminding him this was Annie, the girl he had known since she was four years old.

His face burned as he realized he wasn't wearing anything but his long underwear, and the bedclothes had slipped down to his hips. A tell-tale rise in the blankets told him his body wasn't thinking of Annie as a little sister. He jerked the covers up to his chin and directed a glare at her. "You could've knocked."

She tossed him another sassy grin. "You expect to be treated differently from anyone else in the family?"

Colin scowled at the much too self-assured young woman. "You mean I can walk into your bedroom any time I want?"

Her smile faltered and a faint blush spread across her cheeks. Her embarrassment gave Colin more than a little smug satisfaction, but the uninvited vision of her dressed in nothing but a thin nightrail made it damned near impossible to remember why he thought of her as a sister.

Then Annie's blue eyes glittered mischievously, and once again she was Annie the imp, not Annie the woman. She took a step closer to the bed as her gaze roamed up and down the length of Colin's hidden body.

"Why not?" she asked with a husky voice. "I'm sure I don't have anything you haven't seen before." She drew the tip of her tongue along her lips, leaving them red and glistening.

Colin nearly groaned aloud as he tugged the blankets upward so his growing erection wasn't obvious. At least he hoped it wasn't.

He dragged his mesmerizing gaze away from her mouth to her familiar twinkling eyes. "Be careful, Annie. You're not too old to be put over my knee," he warned.

Her eyebrows hiked upward. "I'd like to see you try."

He called her bluff and swung his feet to the floor, strategically keeping the blanket over his lap as he sat up.

Surprise flickered across her face and she took two quick steps backward. Fire glittered in her eyes and gave each cheek a splotch of red. "You wouldn't dare!"

Colin grinned. "Try me."

She stared at him as if trying to decide if he was serious, then spun around and marched to the door. There she turned back to face him, her spine ramrod straight but her eyes laughing. "You'd better be careful, Colin—one of these days I may not walk out of your bedroom." She strolled out the door, closing it with a soft click behind her.

He stared after her for a long moment, wondering what he would do if that day ever came.

He threw off his blankets and suppressed a

groan. Mornings were always the worst—his leg stiffened up overnight, and it took an hour or two for it to loosen up enough that he could walk with only a slight limp.

After shaving and dressing in navy wool trousers, a white collarless shirt, and suspenders, Colin opened the bedroom door and headed down the stairs.

Years of eating railroad food had resigned Colin's taste buds to the bland meals the work crew's cook prepared. Now the smell of bacon, fresh coffee, and baking bread caused Colin's stomach to growl in anticipation. It was amazing that Trev hadn't gained a hundred pounds in the years he'd been married to Kate—Colin knew *he* would have.

Entering the dining room, Colin spotted little Kathryn in her high chair and the twins seated beside each other, arguing over the last piece of bacon. He sighed—tomorrow he would rise earlier.

Kate came through the swinging door leading to the kitchen and spotted him. "Good morning, Colin," she said with a welcoming smile. "Annie told me about your early morning visitors." She cast a stern frown at Matthew and Michael, who had abruptly stopped fighting when Kate entered the room. "What do you have to say to Colin, young men?"

They squirmed in their seats, then murmured as one, "I'm sorry."

Colin tamped down the smile tugging at his lips. He checked their ears, then said, "Apology accepted, Michael." He turned to the other twin. "And Matthew."

"I see you've figured out our secret."

"Aye. Actually, Michael let me in on it. He wants to make sure he doesn't get blamed for Matthew's shenanigans." He winked at the boys.

Kate laughed and lifted her youngest daughter out of the highchair. "Trev's left for work already and the older children are in school."

"What time does Trev get home?"

"No later than six, if he can help it. He said you're more than welcome to stop by his office today."

"I might just do that."

Annie breezed into the dining room, a steaming plate and cup in her hands. "I'll go with you," she offered as she set the food on the table. "But first eat before it gets cold."

Colin eyed the eggs, sausage, bacon, fried potatoes, and biscuits warily.

Annie towed him over to a chair. "Don't worry. Kate taught me how to cook."

Colin settled in his seat, looking to Kate for reassurance that the food was edible.

"Annie *can* cook when she wants to and she insisted on preparing your breakfast," the older woman assured.

He shifted his attention back to Annie, who studied him with a daring twinkle in her eyes. She drew her gaze from his and glanced at her stepmother. "I make the meals when you and Papa have an engagement to attend."

Kate, carrying Kathryn in one arm, put her other arm around her stepdaughter, who was nearly a foot shorter. "I know you do, sweetheart. I don't know what your father and I would do without you." She dropped a kiss on Annie's crown. "I'm going to take Kathryn and the twins for a walk in the park. Could you keep Colin company while we're gone?"

"Sure. It'll give us a chance to catch up."

Kate had arrived in Orion years ago as a mail-order bride, but her future husband had been killed in a cave-in the day she arrived. Trev had hired her to take care of his two children—Annie and Brynn—because his wife had died giving birth to the boy.

Only four at the time, Annie had stopped talking when her mother had died, and it was only her love for Kate that had brought her voice back. Colin often wondered how much Annie remembered of the day Brynn was born.

"Just don't talk his ear off, Annie," Kate warned with a smile. She turned to the twins. "Come on, boys, let's get our coats."

Matthew and Michael raced out with Kate, who shook her head in tolerant amusement as she followed in close pursuit.

Colin chuckled. "Where does Kate get all her energy?"

"I have no idea. Sometimes I get tired just watching her," Annie replied.

Colin picked up his fork and tasted the potatoes. Not bad. Then the eggs. "These are good."

Annie tilted a blond eyebrow upward. "You sound surprised."

"After our exchange in my bedroom, I thought you might add a little extra to the food."

"Ah, but you know what they say: 'Revenge is a dish best served cold.'"

Colin laughed at Annie's melodrama and continued to eat as she cleaned off the table. His gaze strayed to her as she piled the plates, bending at the waist gracefully and moving with an innate confidence that Colin had never noticed in a woman before. She had tied back her long whitish-blond hair with a ribbon at the base of her neck and the ponytail fell to her waist. He had a sudden urge to remove the ribbon, freeing those silky strands from their captivity so he could thread the soft tresses between his fingers.

"Are you done?"

Annie's voice broke into his musings and he blinked, startled. Afraid she might guess his not-so-brotherly thoughts if he met her eyes, Colin merely nodded and gazed at a painting of a waterfall. He imagined it was a very cold waterfall.

She picked up his plate and whisked it into the kitchen. After she wiped the table clean, she sat in the chair across from him and sipped a cup of coffee. "What would you like to do today besides visit my father at the school?"

Colin concentrated on the heat of the coffee as it slid down his throat—it was safer than the heat that raced through his veins at Annie's proximity. "I can't think of anything else. What about you?"

"How about going to the theater?" she asked.

Unease wound through Colin—he knew what Trev would say about that suggestion. Colin himself wasn't so keen on the idea, either. "Your father wouldn't like it."

"He doesn't like anything I do anymore." She leaned over the table and whispered, "Besides, what he doesn't know won't hurt him."

Trev had been right to be concerned about his daughter. It appeared she wasn't above using a little chicanery to do as she wished. "I won't go behind your father's back."

"What if I ask him?"

Colin's suspicions weren't that easily appeased, especially with a smile that could make an angel forget his halo, but he nodded slowly. "*If* he says it's all right."

She wrapped her smooth fingers around his hand. "Give me two minutes."

She jumped up and hurried out of the dining room.

Colin listened to her footsteps fade as she flew up the stairs. Trev's warning about Annie wrapping him around her finger echoed in his mind. Surely Trev had been exaggerating; she had given in to his request without even attempting to sway him.

Annie quickly shed her everyday skirt and blouse and tossed them on her bed. Grabbing a pale green dress from her armoire, she slid into it and nimbly buttoned each little pearl button up the bodice. She had learned how to make quick changes this past summer with the small theater group she had worked with, unbeknownst to her parents. Annie knew Kate would understand and had wanted to tell her, but suspected her step-mother would have told her father and he would have raised the roof. He barely tolerated her attending the theater. If he had found out about her acting on stage, he wouldn't have let her out of the house until she was old and gray. Or married. She rolled her eyes. When had he turned into such an old fusspot?

Annie was taking a chance with Colin, but she had shared many secrets with him in the past. She paused a moment, staring into the mirror at her wistful reflection. No matter how much she wished their years-old friendship could remain the same, she knew time had changed both of them. How much could she trust him now?

She drew a brush through her hair, then took a thick strand from each side, pulled them back, and tied them together with a light green ribbon. After pinching her cheeks for a little color, she went downstairs to rejoin Colin.

"Ready?" she asked brightly.

He glanced up from the dining room table and pushed himself to his feet.

She noticed his almost imperceptible shift of weight off his injured leg. "The school's half a mile away. Do you want to take the buggy?"

He sent her a sharp glance. "I'll be fine."

Annie nodded mutely as her cheeks warmed.

She hadn't meant to embarrass him. He reached for her cape and held it for her as she slipped her arms into it. Then he lifted her long hair out from beneath the cape, his fingertips brushing the nape of her neck. Heat rushed through her veins, coming to rest in her belly.

She glanced at Colin as he pulled on his jacket, but didn't see any sign of the turmoil that stormed through her. Chiding herself for her silly reaction, she quashed the odd feeling.

Side by side, they strolled to the mining school. Annie kept her pace slow and relaxed, partly out of consideration for Colin's limp, but more because she enjoyed his company and wanted to prolong their time together.

"How's the school doing?" Colin asked.

"Papa says it keeps on growing and," she lowered her voice to sound like her father's, " 'it's getting too damned big.' "

When Colin smiled crookedly, she noticed a dimple in his chin that she had never seen before. It gave him an endearingly boyish expression.

"Don't let your father catch you swearing like that," he warned.

Annie rolled her eyes heavenward and brought the back of her hand against her forehead in mock anguish. "He would confine me to my room until I'm old and gray; then I'd end up a spinster with five cats, condemned to playing the organ at Sunday service and always muttering about the foolishness of youth."

Colin chuckled. "You always did have a flair

for melodrama." He shook his head and asked curiously, "So what do you usually do during the day when you're not haunting the theater?"

"I help out at the public school or fill in for a teacher who's sick. Standing in front of a class of children is as close to acting as I can come without being on a stage."

"So why don't you become a teacher?"

"My heart wouldn't be in it. It's not where I belong."

"How can you be so sure?"

Annie whirled around and struck a pose, lifting a hand to the sky. " 'Sow an act, and you reap a habit. Sow a habit, and you reap a character. Sow a character, and you reap a destiny.' " She drew her arm back to her side and turned to Colin expectantly.

A smile flitted on the corners of his lips. "I don't think Charles Reade was referring to a character on stage."

Startled, Annie blinked and studied Colin as if she had never seen him before. "I had no idea you were so well read." Looking uncomfortable, Colin continued walking. Annie caught up to him and laid her hand on his arm, but he didn't look at her. "Did I say something wrong?"

"Not really, lass. Considerin' I didn't have any schoolin' to speak of, because the Irish weren't worth the ground they walked upon, I can understand yer surprise."

Colin's brogue had thickened and Annie knew she had hurt his feelings. Again.

"I'm sorry, Colin," she said. "But I didn't mean it the way it came out. Most 'educated' people don't know who Charles Reade is and I figured you were probably too busy with your job to do much reading." His muscles beneath her palm relaxed and she drew her hand away reluctantly.

"To be honest, after I was done working, the only things to do in the evening were play poker or read. Usually I read. Every trip into a town, I searched for somebody who would sell or lend me books."

"I can't even imagine what that was like. We had the library and books to read in school."

Colin's gaze turned inward. "I'm going to have a library in my house someday."

Annie smiled with understanding at the yearning in his face.

The sprawling school came into view. "Papa works in the administrative office now." She pointed to a three-story brick building that looked more like a mansion.

Colin whistled low and glanced at her with a teasing glint in his eyes. "Your father was right, it *is* getting 'too damned big.'"

Annie laughed, relieved and delighted their camaraderie had returned. They mounted the steps to the office building and he opened the door for her. She performed a quick curtsy and entered.

Inside, Annie led him down the hall to the last door and without knocking, went in. Her father looked up in annoyance at the interruption, but his expression quickly turned to pleasure.

Rising from behind his desk, Trev shook Colin's hand. "I see you have your own personal escort," he said fondly.

"Only to your office. You'll have to show him the rest," Annie said, her voice sharper than she had intended.

Some of her father's impatience returned, but Annie ignored it. Or tried to. She missed the closeness she had shared with him before she'd told him about her dream. Since then, he'd treated her as if she didn't have the brains God gave a jackrabbit.

"The school's grown," Colin said, drawing Trev's attention.

"That it has, Laddie. I'll show you around," he said. "Annie, would you like to come with us?"

About as much as I'd like to step into fresh horse droppings.

She planted a smile on her face and nodded. In order for her plan to work, she had to ask a question out of Colin's earshot, but where he could still see them—someplace along the tour.

An hour later Annie had run out of time and endurance. Rocks might be fascinating to Colin and her father, but Annie had worn out her smile muscles and her head was going to fall off if she had to nod one more time. When she had been a young girl, her papa's job had seemed wonderful and exciting, but now it was dull and boring.

As they finished the tour of the last building, Annie worried her lower lip between her teeth. She was fast running out of time to speak to her father alone. Outside the brick building, Colin paused to read a marker on the wall and Annie took the opportunity to draw her father away.

"What is it, Annie?" Trev asked.

"I was thinking of surprising everyone by making dinner tonight. Do you think that would be all right with Kate?"

Her father smiled widely. "I'm sure she'd welcome a night off from cooking. What do you have in mind?"

"How about a pot roast?"

"Good idea. Just stop by Heinemeyer's Meat Market on your way home. You'd better pick up two of the largest ones they have—Brynn can probably put one away himself."

He winked at her and this time Annie's smile was genuine. She still idolized him, and wished with all her heart he could accept and support her aspirations.

Annie unobtrusively glanced around her father and saw Colin approaching, reminding her of the deception she'd orchestrated. Her throat constricted with remorse, but she managed to say, "Thanks, Papa." She turned to Colin. "So what do you think of the changes?"

He shook his head in amazement. "I can't believe how large it is. Who would've thought there'd actually be a school that taught what I've been doing since I was six years old?"

Trev clapped him on the back. "We can really use experienced miners like yourself to teach the courses."

"No thanks, Trev. All I want now is my ranch."

Annie wrinkled her nose. Ranching seemed like a life sentence of drudgery.

After the two men spoke for a few more minutes, they shook hands. Her father turned to her and wrapped his arm around her shoulders, giving her a quick hug. "I should be home at the usual time, so you can have supper ready then."

Annie smiled warmly, wishing she and her father could get along this well all the time. "All right, Papa."

He headed back to his office and Annie allowed herself to relax. Colin hadn't asked her father about the theater. "Are you ready to go?"

"Weren't you going to ask your father if it was all right if you went to the theater?"

"You saw me asking him." Annie's heart thundered in her chest. She didn't like lying, but this was for a good cause. Well, for *her* good cause, anyhow.

"Is that what he was nodding about?"

Annie bobbed her head up and down, her heart pounding as if she were climbing the steps to the gallows.

He studied her a moment and she affected her best innocent expression—the one she'd been told was as good as Sarah Bernhardt's. Though Colin's eyes narrowed slightly, he didn't challenge her.

"How far is it?" he asked.

"About six blocks."

"Let's go, then."

As they started walking, Annie sent him a side-long glance, wondering if he suspected anything. Personally, she doubted Miss Bernhardt's performance would have been any better.

Relieved that her ruse had worked, she relaxed and reached out to take hold of Colin's hand. He shot her a startled glance and she smiled. After a moment, his strong fingers curved around hers like they used to when she had been a child. Only she wasn't a girl anymore, and the tremor that skated up her arm had everything to do with a woman's desire.

Chapter 3

Colin relished the feel of Annie's delicate hand in his. The light fall breeze occasionally teased him with her lilac scent—a distinct womanly fragrance. How could he have known she would grow up to become the proverbial swan? No, a hummingbird, with bubbling spirit and boundless energy packed into her petite body.

She made him wish he could recapture his own youth—this time he wouldn't waste it working eighteen hours a day, only to have it all come to an abrupt end in a moment of miscalculation.

"Is something wrong?" Annie's brow creased with concern.

Her perceptiveness surprised him, but he couldn't tell her about the darkness that had become his enemy, or of how time was a bandit that had robbed the last fifteen years of his life. All the energy Colin had invested in his work would now be used to find a suitable wife to bear his children, then he would begin his new enterprise.

Colin shook his head. "What could be wrong, lass? I'm enjoying the company of a beautiful young woman on a lovely fall day. Tell me about this theater we're going to."

Her expression brightened. "The troupe that's performing came to town about two months ago. Since I was familiar with the theater, I volunteered to help them with the stage and whatever else they needed."

"And your father doesn't mind?"

Annie's gaze slid away. "Not exactly."

"He doesn't know, does he?"

She stopped, forcing him to halt. "Papa doesn't understand. If it doesn't involve rocks or digging, he doesn't see much use to it."

"What about Kate and her stars? He's never made fun of her, has he?"

"That's different—Kate's his wife." Annie threw her head back in frustration. "But since I'm his daughter, I'm expected to follow his orders and find some dull man to marry. God forbid that I should fall in love with someone who could tell the difference between a Shakespearean drama and a Victor Hugo play."

Colin stiffened instinctively. He had felt the sting of his sparse education more times than he could recall. "You shouldn't judge a man by his education, lass."

She pressed her fists into her skirt folds and her cheeks colored. "And how should I judge a man—by how well he holds a pick axe? Or maybe by the amount of rock he can shovel in a day?"

Colin clenched his jaw. Annie was young and naïve. She had no idea that how a man did those things often gave telltale signs of his character—if he was honest or lazy or bullying. She didn't understand the ways of the world.

He bit back his temper. "I can't be tellin' you what you'll have to be learnin' on your own, Annie. All I can say is that life isn't black and white, and people change."

The spark in her eyes gentled to a soft glow. "Like you've changed?"

Colin nearly stumbled. "Like we *all* change."

They continued walking, keeping a buffer of silence and a foot of space between them. Colin could see the snow-capped mountains against the distant skyline. They had been his home for years; now he couldn't look at them without being reminded how he'd been buried alive.

Despite the warmth of the sun, Colin shivered and directed his gaze to his oddly subdued companion. He couldn't help but notice the sway of her hips beneath the long cape and her pursed lips, as if she were deep in thought. Her pensive expression seemed incongruous with the bubbly Annie of moments before.

He never knew how she would react, and that bothered him. The little Annie he had understood, but not this girl-woman who didn't follow the rules and kept throwing him off-balance.

They neared a shopping area with stores lining the street, and he noticed many women strolling about, parcels in their arms. He greeted a few of them and they smiled in return. He suddenly realized he should be taking advantage of his time in Denver to wife hunt.

"Come on." Annie tugged him into a confectionery shop. "It's lunch time."

As she leaned over to peer at the tempting candies that were displayed in trays behind glass, Colin studied the curve of her cheek and her eyes that sparkled with eagerness. In that moment, he saw his little lassie still remained within the woman.

"This isn't exactly what I'd call lunch food," he said wryly.

She straightened and crossed her arms. "Where in the rules of life does it say fudge isn't for lunch?"

He had followed the rules all his life and where had it gotten him? Maybe it was high time he started breaking a few. "All right. What do you suggest—milk or dark chocolate?"

Her curved, rosy lips framed dazzling white teeth. "Be daring—go for the milk chocolate."

Her husky voice and brilliant smile made Colin's heart stumble in his chest. "Milk chocolate, it is."

Minutes later they sat on a bench outside the shop, eating the sweet indulgence. Annie had been right—the milk chocolate was sinfully delicious and guilt nudged him for spending his money on something so frivolous.

He glanced at Annie and his breath caught in his throat at her unadulterated pleasure. Suddenly the cost of the fudge seemed insignificant compared to the innocent and genuine joy it brought to her. Dangerous thoughts flitted through his mind, even as he knew nothing could come of them. Annie wasn't the type of woman he wanted—she was too immature and too spoiled, and she had too many pipe dreams.

"Why haven't you ever married, Colin?" Annie suddenly asked.

"I never found the time to court a woman," he replied.

"Why not?"

"Because I was too busy working."

"Why?"

"You sound like this little girl I used to know. 'Why does the sun go away at night?' 'Why is the grass green?' 'Why do we walk on our feet and not our hands?' "

Her cheeks reddened. "Papa and Kate said I was an inquisitive child."

Colin laughed. "Inquisitive? More like insatiable. You used to drive us crazy with all your questions after you started talking again."

Annie's sheepish smile disappeared.

"What's wrong?" Colin asked.

"Nothing."

Annie's smooth brow furrowed and he wondered what had brought on the quicksilver change. Did she remember the day her mother died? Trev had told him about it, and about the melancholia his first wife had suffered. Colin had heard the talk about her, but he hadn't put much stock in the miners' gossip. However, it had turned out to be true.

Annie finished the last bite of her fudge and licked her fingers. Colin's gaze latched onto those slender fingers, wondering how they would taste. For a moment he considered indulging in his curiosity, then he quickly looked away.

"Have you ever seriously thought about getting married?" Annie asked.

He thought of Kate and his long-ago infatuation. "Once."

"Why didn't you marry her?"

"She was an older woman," he teased.

"That shouldn't make any difference," Annie stated with all the certainty of youth.

"That's only if the man is older than the woman."

"You're so old-fashioned."

Colin pressed his lips together in feigned indignation and turned to look at her. "I've been told I'm a progressive thinker."

"No reason to get your dander up. The world is changing. A girl doesn't have to get married, but if she does, she doesn't have to marry a man as old as—well, as old as you."

"Thank you, little girl." Annoyance lent sarcasm to his words. He wasn't *that* old. But maybe it wasn't the years, but the losses and experiences that aged a man. In that case, he *was* old.

Annie laid a hand on his arm and his body hummed with awareness. "All I meant is that a woman shouldn't be forced to marry a man a lot older than she is unless she loves him. And if a woman falls in love with a younger man, they should be able to marry without folks looking down their noses at them."

Colin didn't know if he should feel appeased or not. "So you don't think a man or woman should get married unless they love one another?"

Annie stared at him as if he'd just recited a sonnet in Portuguese. "That's the *only* reason two people should get married."

"What if the man wants a wife to have a family and carry on his name?"

"I'd say that man better step out of the dark ages."

Offended, Colin drew his shoulders back. He was merely being practical. "I know men and women who did that and the love came later. What about them?"

Annie shrugged. "Then they got lucky, but that doesn't happen with most people."

Their discussion was interrupted by a woman a few years older than Annie who paused in front of their bench. "Good afternoon, Annie," she greeted.

Colin stood and his irritation fled at the interruption when he looked into the arrival's warm brown eyes.

"Hello, Margaret," Annie said. "How are you?"

"I'm just so busy getting everything organized for our trip," the woman replied, excitement evident in her flushed cheeks. "I'm having a most difficult time packing for three weeks. I can't imagine packing for six months."

"I haven't even started yet," Annie said with a shrug.

The attractive woman drew back, the shock in her face almost comical. "Goodness, I would have begun months ago." Margaret's expression eased into a smile. "But then, you always were a bit unconventional. You are very fortunate your parents can afford to send you to a finishing school, especially one as prestigious as Miss Sally Langford's."

Annie smiled sardonically. "Yes, I am fortunate, aren't I?" She turned to Colin. "Margaret, I'd like you to meet an old friend of the family, Colin McBride. Colin, this is Mrs. Margaret Mopplewhite. She's my chaperone for the trip to San Francisco."

Colin took her soft hand in his, enjoying the light pressure of her fingers. "It's a pleasure to meet you, Mrs. Mopplewhite. Surely you're much too young to be married."

She giggled like a schoolgirl and Colin noticed Annie's muffled snort of disgust.

"I'm a widow, Mr. McBride. My husband, God rest his soul, died two years ago, though he left me well taken care of."

"That's good. It can be a burden for a woman without a man to take care of her."

Margaret nodded vehemently. "Yes, at least I don't have to worry about my future." She studied him with a part shy, part coquettish gaze. "Do you live here or are you only visiting our fair city?"

"I'm visiting. Annie's parents are friends of mine from when her father was a miner."

Annie watched as Colin studied Margaret's plain features a little too intently. She narrowed her eyes. What did he see in the mousy woman?

"Perhaps we'll see each other again before Annie and I must leave," Margaret said hopefully.

Colin smiled much too pleasantly. "I have a feeling we'll be seeing quite a bit of each other. You see, I'll be traveling to San Francisco with you and Annie."

Margaret's face lit up like old Mr. Dickers' after he'd had a few too many drinks. "That's wonderful. I'm sure we'll have a most enjoyable trip."

"I'm sure we will." Colin took her hand in his once more and pressed his lips to the back of it.

Annie nearly gagged. If Margaret giggled one more time, she was positive she would.

"I shall see you soon then, Mr. McBride." She raised a hand and waggled her gloved fingers. "Good-bye."

"Good-bye, Margaret," Annie said with forced cheerfulness, then added under her breath, "and good riddance."

Colin admired Margaret's generous sway as she strolled away, and Annie smacked his arm.

"Ow! What'd you do that for?" Colin rubbed the offended limb as he glared at her.

" 'I'm sure we will,' " Annie parroted. She scowled back at him. "Why didn't you just ask her to marry you and skip the preliminaries?"

"I would have, but first I wanted to ask you if anyone was courting her."

An odd feeling sliced through Annie. Was Colin serious? Did he actually like Margaret Mopplewhite? Not that Annie disliked her—it was just that she was . . . boring. "You're joking, right?"

"I want to have children before I'm too old to enjoy them, and for that I need a wife. And it would probably be easier to meet a woman here than find one after I'm settled on my ranch." He paused to grin. "Besides, Margaret and I will have a lot of time to get to know each other on the train."

Annie tossed her long blond hair over her shoulder. "If you like dull as a post."

"You sound jealous, lass."

If he thought she was actually jealous of someone like Margaret, he didn't know her at all. She'd prove to him that jealousy was the furthest thing from her mind. "Why don't you ask her out to dinner before we leave? I'm sure she'd be *thrilled*."

He cast her a disapproving frown. "You might take a few lessons in gentility from her."

Colin's censure stung, but she lifted her chin. "I can be just as refined as Mrs. Margaret Mopplewhite if I want to be. I just don't want to." She stomped away. "Come on, the theater's around the block."

If he liked Margaret so much, he was more than welcome to her. Why, she would even help the courting along. If Colin became involved with Margaret, he would be less inclined to keep a close eye on her.

Annie tapped her forefinger against her chin—she couldn't have come up with a better arrangement. She glanced at Colin, ignoring the strange little flutter in her chest. Yes, it was the perfect diversion. After all, it wasn't as if she had any designs on Colin.

Five minutes later, Annie announced, "Here it is."

Playbills heralding upcoming shows with their dates and times had been tacked to the door and walls of the theater. She pointed to one that showed a woman wearing a skirt that came to her knees, leaving her shapely calves and ankles covered only by dark stockings. Her blouse was loose and gapped above her abundant breasts, revealing an ample cleavage. "That's the production I've been helping with."

Colin's right eyebrow shot upward. "I see why your father doesn't want you doing this."

"Adah Menken wore less than that in the play 'Mazeppa' and she performed all over the world."

"Wasn't she also married four times, and didn't she die of consumption when she was only thirty-three?"

Annie blinked, disconcerted by his knowledge. "That's right. How did you know?"

"Like I said, I read a lot," he answered dryly. "Is that the kind of life you want?"

"I'm not going to marry at all, much less four times." She smiled smugly. "I'm just going to take an occasional lover."

Colin's mouth gaped.

"And if a role called for me to wear an outfit like that, I'd do it," she added, trying not to laugh at her friend's shocked expression. Annie grabbed his wrist and tugged him into the theater. "Come on."

She led him across a foyer, then through a door that opened to the theater. Pausing at the back of the tiered room, Annie breathed deeply of the heavy scents of greasepaint and musty curtains and damp wood—all the odors of the life she wanted so badly. The troupe was rehearsing and she leaned close to Colin. "We'll wait until they're done."

Annie guided him to the back row of seats and sat beside him. Essie and Percival were practicing the lines Annie could recite by memory. She also spotted Toby, a boy of nine going on forty, in the background beside Alexander, a huge giant of a man with the heart of a lamb and the mind of a child.

"What are they doing?" Colin asked.

His warm breath whispered across her cheek and brought gooseflesh to her arms, though she was far from cold. In fact, the room suddenly seemed too warm and she struggled to remove her cape. Colin reached around to help her and when his arm brushed her breast, Annie's bones almost melted.

"Thank you," she said with a breathy voice, unable to meet his gaze. Flustered by her reaction, she pointed to the stage. "They're rehearsing—perfecting their performances. Every speech nuance, every gesture has to have a reason. The actor has to become his or her character, so he or she knows how to react to dialogue."

"I thought they just had to memorize their lines."

"Most people think that, but there's much more to it. I like to know why a character behaves like she does—I want to become that person, find out what makes her do what she does. For just a little while, I want to *be* someone else."

She could feel Colin's intense gaze upon her in their shadowed alcove, but she kept her attention centered on the stage.

"Don't you like who *you* are?" he asked.

A dark, faint memory of her mother rolled through her, leaving her uneasy and anxious. She laughed nervously. "That's a silly question." Needing to change the subject, she asked, "Have you ever been on stage?"

He shook his head.

"It's the grandest feeling in the world—when

everyone applauds, it's like being embraced by a thousand people."

"How would you know?" Colin asked suspiciously.

Annie froze, her mind blank. In her eagerness, she had let her secret slip out. She noticed her friends were taking a break on the stage and jumped to her feet. "Come on."

She hurried down the steps to the platform, anxious to escape Colin's scrutiny.

"Hello, sweetie. What're you doing here?" Essie asked with a tobacco-roughened voice.

"I brought a friend." Annie glanced behind her and found Colin approaching at a more sedate pace. In her haste, she'd forgotten about his limp. Chastising herself, she waited for him to join them.

Self-conscious of his slowness, Colin came to stand by Annie and forced himself to smile at the motley group.

"Colin, I'd like you to meet Percival Fortunatas. He's the owner of the Fortunatas Traveling Stock Company," Annie introduced.

Colin sized up the man who was about the same height as himself, but carried a good twenty pounds less on his frame. When they shook hands, Fortunatas had a soft palm and loose grip. All his life, Colin had judged a man by his handshake, and Percival Fortunatas came up woefully short. The actor reminded Colin of the traveling medicine men he'd seen in many of the boomtowns. But for Annie's sake, he'd lay aside his prejudice this time—besides, judging by his standards was unfair to a man who probably hadn't done an ounce of physical labor in his life.

"Nice to meet you, Mr. Fortunatas," Colin said.

"Please call me Percival. All my friends do." The actor smoothed a hand over his black hair that was parted in the middle and slicked down with some fancy-smelling pomade. A large gold pinkie ring with a red stone glittered beneath the sparse stage lighting.

Colin nodded, uncertain how friendly he wanted to get with the fastidious man.

Annie drew his attention to a woman with bottle red hair and an hourglass figure. "And this is Miss Essie Charbonneau."

The woman on the playbill. His gaze swept to her breasts, which were hidden beneath a fancy blue dress. In person, she had less there than the playbill artist had sketched. He supposed a smaller bosom wouldn't attract as many male theatergoers. His attention shifted to her face, where the cynicism in her eyes said she'd seen more than her share in life.

"You're a handsome devil, aren't you?" Essie commented, her gaze roaming up and down his body with obvious approval.

Colin didn't know whether to be insulted or complimented by her blatant perusal. He chose the latter and gallantly kissed the back of her hand. "Thank you, Miss Charbonneau."

Essie leaned close to Annie and spoke in a

stage whisper, clearly intending Colin to over-
hear. "Tell me this one isn't taken, darling."

Annie's eyes twinkled. "Not yet, but I heard
he's looking."

Colin glowered at Annie, which only made her
flutter flirtatiously. He ought to send her to her
room for behaving as brazenly as . . . an actress.
The uninvited image of Annie dressed in the
skimpy outfit on the playbill stampeded the
blood through his veins. The artist wouldn't have
to embellish Annie's lush figure.

Looking for a diversion, Colin turned to the
tow-headed boy who stared up at him curiously.

"And who are you, son?" Colin asked, leaning
toward the lad.

The young boy approached him, stopping only
when his toes nearly touched Colin's. He planted
small fists on his hips. "First off, I'm not your son.
Secondly, my name is Toby."

Taken aback by the boy's belligerence, Colin
straightened.

"I expected better manners from you, Toby,"
Annie scolded. "Colin is my friend."

Toby's fists uncurled, but suspicion remained
in his eyes. "He's not one of them do-gooders, is
he?"

Annie's lips twitched. "No, he's not going to
take you to an orphanage."

The wariness faded and he shrugged. "All
right, then." He stuck out his hand. "Nice to meet
you, Colin."

Toby's handshake was stronger than Fortunatas'—he'd best keep an eye on this one.

"Same here."

The boy stepped over to a large man who stood silently. "And this is Alexander," Toby said, laying a hand on the monster's massive arm.

Colin extended a hand, but Alexander merely stared at it.

"It's all right," Toby assured the monstrous man. "He's not going to hurt you."

The big man's hand enveloped his and Colin had to clench his teeth to withstand the powerful grip. Somebody should have warned him that Alexander might hurt *him*.

"Alexander isn't real smart, but he's strong," Toby said in a voice too mature for a boy of nine.

"I noticed," Colin said wryly.

"Colin is in Denver visiting for a few days," Annie said.

Essie sidled up to him and rubbed her shoulder provocatively against his chest. "I sure hope you're bringing him to the performance this evening."

Colin's male reaction shouldn't have surprised him. He hadn't visited a sporting gal in months and being around Annie for the last twenty-four hours had been an exercise in restraint.

He reluctantly stepped away from the woman who was probably ten years older than himself. She was the type he would have spent a lusty evening with a few years ago, but now he was looking for a respectable wife. Besides, Annie was staring at him like he was a stranger. For a woman who could shamelessly talk about taking a lover, Annie was surprisingly naïve.

"We can't come this evening," Annie spoke up firmly, moving to stand beside Colin.

Her possessive maneuver amused Colin, but he didn't dare smile. He glanced at Essie, who drew her tongue along her ruby red lips as her gaze moved languidly down his chest to his groin, where it lingered, then back up to his face.

The part of his anatomy that had been fairly aloof for the last few months was definitely becoming more sociable.

Annie pressed against Colin and he nearly groaned. If she got any closer, they would be sharing the same shirt.

"I thought I'd bring him to the show tomorrow evening," she said.

"Wonderful. I'll leave two tickets for you at the window," Percival said.

"Could you make that four?" she asked.

"Why four?" Colin asked her.

"I thought you might like to escort Margaret, and I could ask a friend of mine to escort me."

Surprised by her suggestion, he wondered just what kind of friend she meant and nodded warily. "All right."

"I'll have four tickets waiting for you, Annie," Percival promised.

"Thank you." Annie turned to Colin. "We should get back."

"It was nice meeting you all," Colin said as Annie tugged him toward the steps. "I look forward to seeing you again."

"Me, too, honey," Essie called out, throwing him a kiss.

Outside, Annie abruptly released him and strode down the street.

Puzzled, Colin hurried after her. "Slow down, Annie."

He saw her shoulders stiffen, then she stopped and whirled around to face him. "You should be ashamed of yourself."

Coming to an abrupt halt, Colin realized what was bothering her. He smiled slow and easy. "Why?"

"For letting Essie think you might be interested in her."

Colin swallowed back his chuckle. "How do you know I'm not?"

Annie's eyes widened. "She's older than you."

He crossed his arms and couldn't help but tease her. "Didn't you say earlier that age difference doesn't matter?"

Annie fairly sputtered. "I thought you liked dull women like Margaret."

"A man likes variety in his women, lass."

She studied him, then her expression changed and deviltry glinted in her eyes. "So it's variety you want. All right; I'll see what I can do."

Puzzled and a little concerned, Colin wondered if he'd pushed too far. "What do you mean?"

She didn't answer, but turned and strolled

down the street, whistling a merry tune and looking dangerously pleased with herself. Colin followed, more than a little worried about what the imp had up her sleeve.

But not so worried that he couldn't enjoy the pleasant view of Annie's backside as she sashayed away from him.

Chapter 4

On the way home, Annie took Colin into a butcher shop where it was obvious the Trevelyan family was well known.

"Afternoon, Miss Annie," the round-faced man called out from behind the counter.

"Hello Mr. Heinemeyer," Annie returned fondly. "We have a good friend visiting and I thought he might like a pot roast tonight. And since you *are* the best butcher in town . . ." She batted her eyelashes flirtatiously.

Colin kept his lips pressed together to keep from chuckling.

Heinemeyer smiled and teased back, "You're shameless, Miss Annie, flattering an old man like myself."

A genuine smile replaced her coy one. "You're not old, merely mature."

He laughed, his ample belly quivering. "You're a handful, young lady."

He didn't know the half of it.

Annie introduced the two men.

"Any friend of the Trevelyans is a friend of mine," Heinemeyer said with a slight German accent. "Especially when he brings the lovely Miss Annie into my shop."

"Now who's the flatterer?" she shot back playfully.

It seemed Annie didn't even have to work at charming anyone; it merely came naturally. He should have known—he'd seen her get her way often enough as a child with huge blue eyes set in a deceptively angelic face.

"Would you be wanting one or two roasts?" Heinemeyer asked.

"Make it two. You know how much Brynn can eat." Annie rolled her eyes. "I swear, I don't know where it goes."

"I can always count on your brother to keep me in business. Just give me a couple minutes, Miss Annie."

The butcher went into the back of the shop.

"Ugh." Annie pointed to a tray of meat behind the counter. "How can anyone eat a cow's tongue?"

Colin shrugged. "I hear it's a delicacy in some countries, just like caviar is here in the United States."

"What's caviar?"

"Fish eggs."

Annie gagged eloquently. "That's even worse than tongues!"

"If you plan on becoming a famous actress, you'll have to get used to it. I hear all those wealthy folks eat caviar with crackers and champagne."

Annie wrinkled her nose. "If I'm rich and famous, I won't have to eat what I don't want to." She shuddered. "Yuck."

Colin laughed at her disgusted expression. "So how long have you known Mr. Heinemeyer?" he asked.

"We've been getting our meat here for as long as I can remember," Annie said.

"I've never lived any place long enough for anyone to get to know me." How different would his life have been had he decided to work with Trev at the school instead of working for the railroad? "They say a rolling stone doesn't gather any moss, but it also rolls over a lot of things in its path and never looks back."

Annie's brow furrowed. "Do you have regrets, Colin?"

Startled, Colin realized he'd spoken aloud. It was a habit he had fallen into while working alone so often. He shrugged with forced casualness. "A man can't live for long without having some regrets, lass, but there comes a point when he has to decide if he wants to continue gathering them."

She was quiet for a long moment, making Colin nervous. He'd already discovered that a quiet Annie was a dangerous Annie.

"I'm sorry I acted like a child," she finally said. "If you want to have an affair with Essie, I don't mind. In fact, when we go to the show tomorrow night, you don't have to take Margaret. After the performance, you can invite Essie out for a drink. I know she'll agree because she likes you, and then she'll take you to her place and the two of you can fornicate. I can walk home by myself," she finished in a flurry, her cheeks high with embarrassed color.

If Colin had been prone to apoplectic fits, he would've had one right then and there. He managed to take a deep, steady breath, then spoke in a normal voice—or what he hoped was a normal voice. "First off, you will not be walking after dark unescorted. Second, I happen to be looking for a wife, not a mistress—"

"Courtesan," Annie interrupted.

"Excuse me?"

"I prefer the word courtesan to mistress. It sounds more mysterious. Exotic."

Heat filled Colin's face and he wondered how in the world he'd lost control of the conversation so quickly. "Do Kate and Trev know about your, uh, extensive vocabulary?"

Her eyes held a sassy sparkle. "They call me precocious."

Too damned precocious.

"Maybe we should just start this conversation

over," Colin said deliberately. "Thank you for thinking of me, but I don't need your assistance in finding a casual female acquaintance. I would prefer to attend the theater with a proper woman like Mrs. Margaret Mopplewhite, as you originally suggested."

"Have you ever thought of becoming an actor?"

Before Colin could figure out whether he'd been insulted or not, Heinemeyer returned from the back room bearing two packages.

"Here you go, Miss Annie."

Colin stepped forward to take them from the butcher. "How much do I owe you?"

Heinemeyer blinked in surprise. "I just put them on the Trevelyans' bill."

Annie took the smaller of the two roasts from Colin's arms and tucked it against her side. "That's right. Papa would be upset if you paid for them, Colin. You're our guest."

Although Trev had a good position at the school, Colin suspected that with the size of his family, money was short. Colin had more than enough and vowed to come back later to pay the Trevelyans' bill before he left Denver. It was a gift he could easily afford, and he owed Trev far more than he could ever repay.

He nodded, then turned to Heinemeyer. "It was nice to meet you."

"Same here, Mr. McBride."

Colin ushered Annie out of the shop with a light hand against her back. The afternoon sunshine slanted across his shoulders and he enjoyed the warm rays that seeped into him. There were so many things he'd taken for granted in the past—the sun's cheery brightness was one of them.

"We can stop at Margaret's house and you can ask her if she'd like to accompany you tomorrow evening," Annie said.

Did he really want to ask the woman? He would have enough time to get to know her on the long train ride to San Francisco. His other option was having Annie with her quick wit and easy laughter all to himself.

Tempting as that was, it was foolish. Annie already had some young man in mind to go with. Besides, Margaret could be *the* woman he was searching for, and he might regret wasting a precious minute courting her.

In a pig's eye.

Colin shushed the sarcastic voice that sounded too much like Annie in his mind. "Is her place far from here?"

She pointed to a side street. "It's over there."

"Let the hunt begin," he murmured.

Annie quirked an eyebrow upward, but didn't ask. It was a good thing she didn't, because Colin wasn't sure why he had said the words with a cynical twist.

The widow had been ecstatic to have Colin ask her to the theater. In fact, it had been almost embarrassing to watch her chin quiver and her cheeks redden after Colin had requested her company. A person would have thought Colin had popped *the* question.

"Mrs. Mopplewhite seemed very enthusiastic about joining me," Colin said as he guided Annie around a broken board on the walkway.

"Calling her enthusiastic would be like calling Papa mild-mannered," Annie said.

"All right, lass, I get the hint." He shifted the roast from one arm to the other. "So who is the lucky fellow who will escort you to the theater?"

Annie's mouth dropped open in mock astonishment. "Why Colin, I do believe you sound jealous."

"I am not jealous. I'm only concerned that the young man behave like a proper gentleman."

"Oh, he'll behave or he'll get a knee in a very sensitive area."

Colin nearly stumbled. "Where in the world did you learn that?"

"From Papa. When I turned sixteen, he taught me some important details about a man's anatomy and how to protect myself if a man did something I didn't like."

Colin cleared his throat and Annie stifled a giggle. He was so easy to fluster; it was boyishly endearing.

"A woman should, uh, know how to protect herself."

"Don't worry, Colin. As long as you behave yourself, I won't be forced to take action."

Colin growled something under his breath, but

Annie wisely didn't ask him what it was he said. She glanced up at the cloudless deep blue sky which backed up against the mountains to the west. The pockets of yellow on the slopes told her the aspens were already turning. It wouldn't be long before the leaves fell and they would see the drab reddish-gray rocks that remained as sentinels, overlooking their kingdom. Though it was only the middle of September, snow had already fallen on the highest peaks and it didn't look like it would be leaving before next spring.

Suddenly it struck her that for the first time in fifteen years, she wouldn't see the mountains lose their white mantle. Although Annie was anxious for her first glimpse of the Pacific Ocean, San Francisco didn't have mountains—and even if it did, they wouldn't be *her* mountains.

A cool breeze tickled a strand of hair across her forehead and she paused to close her eyes and inhale the autumn air—with its scents of damp loam and smoky curls of burning leaves. She listened to the sounds of women laughing, men boasting, children shouting, cable cars clanging, and horses neighing. The city's resonance would be the same in San Francisco, but the rhythm would be different. She didn't know how she knew, only that she did.

"Annie?"

The voice broke through her sensory banquet and she opened her eyes to find Colin's worried gaze aimed in her direction.

"What're you doin' stoppin' in the middle of

the street like that, lass?" he asked, his brogue more obvious.

Annie glanced around, surprised to see she was indeed standing smack dab in the center of a side street. Fortunately, it was devoid of traffic. "I was trying to memorize all of this."

"I don't understand."

It suddenly seemed important that he did understand. "In three days I'm leaving here. I may never return." Her eyes stung with moisture. "I don't want to forget this."

"You're not going away forever, lass." He smiled gently. "And you'll be so busy making new friends and seeing new places you won't even miss this."

When her father learned what she had done, he would probably disown her. But she couldn't confide in Colin—in anyone. She had to hold her dream close to her heart and hope it had the power to sustain her in the months ahead.

She smiled brightly. "I guess you think I'm being pretty silly. By the time you were my age, you had been on your own for quite a few years already, right?"

"Aye, but it wasn't something I would've chosen, Annie. You've been blessed with a family who loves you. Don't ever forget that."

The sadness in his eyes mesmerized Annie and she clasped his hand. "I won't," she promised.

The dark of his eyes grew until it nearly covered the hazel irises and his expression turned to something hot and sultry. Her palms dampened and her belly tightened under the intensity of his gaze.

"Annie, lass, why did you have to grow up to be such a beautiful woman?" His husky voice sent desire spiraling through her veins.

His lips were mere inches from hers, a temptation she didn't want to resist. She had to feel his mouth on hers or she was certain she would die. Raising up on her tiptoes, she released his hand and reached up to lay her hands on his shoulders.

The next thing she knew she found herself enfolded in his arms and rolling across the road horizontally. Horses' hooves and large wheels barely missed them as a wagon raced past. Her heart hammered in her chest and broken gasps slipped past her dry lips.

The weight against her side shifted and she was able to breathe a little easier.

"Annie, are you all right?" Colin's voice trembled.

She couldn't speak, and just nodded.

Colin's jaw muscle clenched as he helped her to her feet carefully. A wave of vertigo washed across her and she swayed.

"Lass?"

She swallowed and managed to croak out a reply. "I'm fine. J-just a little shook up." As she drew in deep draughts of air, Annie's head cleared as her body started to complain about her bruises. "What happened?"

"A reckless driver. I don't know how he didn't see us," Colin replied. Anger radiated from his taut body and fisted hands. "He could've killed you."

Annie's heart skipped a beat. "And you, too."

Colin blinked as if it hadn't occurred to him. He forced a weak smile. "Trev and Kate may kill me yet, for not keeping a closer eye on you."

"I'm not a little girl anymore, Colin," Annie refuted, her fear transformed to annoyance. "If you recall, it was me who was stupid enough to stand in the middle of the street in the first place."

Colin brushed ineffectually at the dust on his trousers. "Now that you mention it, you're right."

"You could've argued."

"Why? I'm man enough to admit when a woman is right." He shrugged. "Even though it's a rare occasion."

"Why, you—"

Colin raised his hands. "Temper, temper, Annie."

She glared at him, but found she couldn't stay angry. Shaking her head, she searched for the roasts and found them about six feet away. Fortunately, they had been wrapped well and the wagon's wheels had missed turning the roasts into hamburger.

She picked them up and turned around to see Colin scowling as he gazed down the street. Returning to his side, she asked, "What's wrong?"

"Are drivers usually so careless?"

She shrugged. "Some are. Don't worry about it, Colin."

His scowl eased, but the suspicion in his eyes

didn't abate. "Here, let me take that." He reached for the larger of the roasts.

They began to walk again and Annie noticed Colin's limp had become more pronounced. She glanced at his face and spotted white lines near the corners of his mouth. Remembering how sensitive he was about his leg, she clamped her mouth shut.

She slowed her pace subtly until the pain lines eased and Colin wasn't limping quite so badly. What would have happened if the recklessly driven wagon hadn't interrupted them? Would Colin have kissed her? She had seen the desire in his eyes, but would he have allowed himself to?

If only they had kissed, then she would know for certain how she felt about him. For as long as she could remember, Colin had been her best friend. Even when he wasn't around, she would talk to him in her head, telling him about her day and what had happened and how she felt about things. But the boy she'd silently conversed with for years no longer existed and she swallowed back the unexpected grief at the realization.

Feeling foolish about the irrational emotion, Annie took a deep breath and grimaced at the soreness of her ribs. If she was this tender, she wondered how Colin could even stand, since he had cushioned her, taking the brunt of the ground's force.

But then that was Colin. He had always protected her, heedless of the cost to himself.

That hadn't changed.

* * *

Colin retreated to his room as soon as they arrived back at the Trevelyans' home. He sank onto his bed, his torso aching almost as badly as his leg. He considered soaking in a hot bath, but decided against it. Too many questions might be asked and he didn't want them to know how much he hurt.

He lay back against his pillow and closed his eyes, only to see the wagon bearing down on them. His eyes flashed open immediately. He and Annie had been in plain sight—how had the driver missed seeing them? Or hadn't he cared if he ran down two strangers?

No, he couldn't imagine someone deliberately doing such a thing . . . unless someone was out to get them. Why? Annie couldn't have done anything deserving that kind of retribution.

What about himself? He had made two or three enemies while working with the railroad, but none of them would do anything this drastic. Would they?

It had to have been merely an accident, a nearly tragic accident. The fear he had felt for Annie's life when the wagon had borne down on them had nearly stolen his breath away. He trembled with the sharp memory, remembering too clearly how he had wrapped his arms around her and how the wagon had rumbled past them, so close Colin could feel the vibrations of the horses' hooves on the ground. Then there had been the paralyzing fear when he wasn't certain if Annie had been hurt by the very action that had saved her life.

Colin reminded himself she was unharmed and safe. Holding onto that reassurance, he thought about what had nearly transpired right before he had seen the wagon.

He was certain Annie was going to kiss him, and he had been more than willing to participate. Her face flushed with the cool breeze and her blue eyes reflecting the sky had stolen away his common sense. The knowledge that Trev might blacken his eye for touching his little girl hadn't even halted him.

There was no doubt about it—he'd been thinking with something other than his brain. He scrubbed his palms across his face. It seemed like only yesterday he was giving his little lass a ride on his shoulders. Now the image of the grown-up Annie riding him sent blood rushing to his groin.

Groaning, Colin banished the picture from his mind and sat up. There was no way in hell he was going to have that image scampering through his thoughts, especially when he was under the same roof as the luscious imp.

"Buck up, McBride. You're lookin' for a wife, and Annie Trevelyan is too young and too high-spirited for an old man like yourself," he muttered.

So why did thoughts of Annie make him feel anything but old?

* * *

Annie checked the roasts, then closed the oven, satisfied they would be done at six thirty as planned. She leaned against a counter and shifted slightly as a bruise made itself known. Colin had disappeared up to his room when they'd arrived back at the house and she hadn't seen him since. Maybe he had been hurt more seriously than he'd admitted.

Then laughter drifted in from the front room, and Colin's full-throated chuckle reassured her that he was fine. Listening closely, she could pick up his masculine tone as he visited with her father and Kate. Actors took pride in their rich deep voices, but theirs had never caressed her from the inside out as Colin's did. Maybe it was because it was familiar and made her feel secure and safe.

No, not secure and safe . . . he made her feel like she was on the edge of a precipice, eager to dive off, yet knowing she might not survive the fall.

Her heart picked up its beat and she listened to it echo in her ears, comparing it to the heartbeat she had listened to while she and Colin lay on the street, his body atop hers. The memory of their position made her wonder about the women he had made love to; had he cared about their pleasure? Essie had told her what men and women did in private, and she couldn't help but imagine her and Colin doing those things Essie had described.

She pressed her palms to her warm cheeks and blamed the oven's heat. Time to think other, less dangerous thoughts.

Since Colin was taking Margaret to the theater, Annie had to find somebody to accompany her. In spite of her brazen words, she had never let a man do more than kiss her. Except for Jonathan, who had touched her breast. Her body reacted as she imagined Colin taking that liberty.

Not liking where her thoughts were returning her to, Annie considered her male friends. Maybe Thomas. He was nice looking and gallant, and they were good friends. There wouldn't be any danger of him trying to kiss her. Or vice versa, she thought with a devilish smile.

"How's dinner coming?"

Annie glanced up to see Kate enter the kitchen. "I just basted the roasts, and the carrots and potatoes will be ready the same time as the meat."

"Is there anything I can help you with?" Kate asked.

Annie shook her head. "Everything's under control."

Kate studied her a moment. "Is it?"

"What do you mean?"

"Colin told me you stopped by the theater this afternoon."

Annie turned to check the roasts in the oven again so her stepmother wouldn't see the guilty flush in her face. "Does Papa know?"

"No. You know what your father would say."

Annie let the oven door slam shut. Staring up at Kate, she wished she didn't have such a disadvantage with her height. It made her feel like a child and she didn't like that one bit. "Papa is so unreasonable."

Kate gently clasped her stepdaughter's shoulders and gazed down at her, affection clearly evident. "Your father loves you and worries about you."

The compassion in Kate's face made Annie feel even more guilty. "I know he does, but he just makes me so angry sometimes. When he was my age he didn't have anybody telling him what he could and couldn't do."

"That's because he didn't have any family left."

Annie didn't want to hear this. She wanted to be able to be angry and feel justified in her indignation. Pulling out of Kate's hold, she picked up a knife and began to slice the two loaves of bread sitting on the counter. "If you'd like to help, you can set the table. If not, I'll take care of it."

She felt Kate's censuring gaze on her back, but refused to turn around.

"In less than three days you'll be leaving for San Francisco—don't turn those days into bitter memories," Kate said softly.

Annie forced herself to continue her task until she heard her stepmother retreat. Moving mechanically, she picked up the bread slices and piled them on a plate. A splash of moisture on the back of her hand surprised her and she quickly blinked.

If anybody made the next three days hellish, it would be her father, with his rigid rules. No, it would definitely not be her fault if her leave-taking was unpleasant.

Chapter 5

Annie picked at her food, wondering who was going to tell her father about the unapproved visit to the theater—Colin or Kate. Maybe she should just tell him herself and end the torment. She pressed the thought aside—as much as she considered herself to be strong and independent, she was pretty much of a coward regarding her father's temper. There was no doubt he would hit the roof when he found out about her transgression. Especially after he had adamantly forbidden her to go there.

However, the meal passed with lively conversations about past days when Colin had worked with her father in the now ghost camp of Orion. In spite of herself she listened to the stories, her lively imagination vividly painting the pictures in her mind. She had heard the story about Colin saving her father's life numerous times, and every time she couldn't help but feel an overwhelming pride in Colin's courage.

"Tell us about the tommyknockers," Darcy said, spewing some of his carrots onto the table.

"Ick." Michael and Matthew said in unison, making identical faces of disgust.

"Mind your manners," Kate chided gently.

"Darcy was the one who talked with his mouth full," Matthew said, defending himself and his twin.

Though the story of the knockers was one of her favorites, Annie pressed back her chair. "Excuse me."

She picked up her empty plate and silverware and carried them into the kitchen, conscious of the awkward silence left in her wake. Although she had enjoyed the tales her father and Colin related with the lilting accents from their childhood, she couldn't spend another minute in there without exploding. After leaving her dishes in the sink, she stole out the door to the foyer and grabbed her cloak. She tugged it on, pulling the hood over her head, and left the house.

Restlessness made her scurry down the walk to Thomas's home, which was only two blocks away. The two of them had attended school together, and when they had been six years old, they'd promised to marry one another when they were all grown up. Annie smiled in the darkness at the childhood simplicity of the vows. Her smile faded as she tried to determine when things had become so much more complicated and out of control.

Standing on the Moraleses' wide porch, Annie knocked. The door was swung open by a woman as short as she but three times as round.

"Hello, Mrs. Morales," Annie said. "Is Thomas home?"

The woman's thin-lipped expression didn't change. "He is busy."

As a child, Annie had been welcomed into their home, often indulging in sweet Spanish delicacies with Thomas after school. However, in the past two years Mrs. Morales had taken a dislike to her and Annie was unable to determine why. She'd asked Thomas, but he had insisted she was merely imagining the animosity—his mother cared for her as if she were her own daughter. Annie doubted that, but she didn't argue with him.

"Could you tell him I'm here? I just need to speak with him for a minute," Annie pleaded.

The olive-skinned woman frowned. "Does your father know you are visiting at such a late hour?"

"It's only seven o'clock."

"Too late for a respectable *señorita* to be walking alone."

Annie struggled against the rise of impatience. Every time she saw Mrs. Morales, the inquisition intensified. "Please. It'll only take a minute."

Annie kept herself from fidgeting beneath the woman's judgmental gaze. Finally Mrs. Morales stepped back and motioned for her to enter. She closed the door behind Annie. "Stay."

Annie had the sudden urge to bark and she covered her smile with a hand. That would not be the way to endear herself to Thomas's mother—not that Annie had any clue as to how she *could* charm the woman, even if she wanted to. Which she didn't. Mrs. Morales had obviously decided to dislike Annie for whatever reason, and she accepted that.

Footsteps approached and Annie looked up to see Thomas, a smile on his dark-complected face. He held out his hands and she placed hers within them.

"Good evening, Annie," he said with the regal accent of a Spanish nobleman. She wouldn't be surprised if his family had some blue blood running through its veins. "What brings you out this time of night?"

"You sound like your mother—it's not that late." She had to tilt her head back to meet his brown eyes, which were set in an aristocratic face. His jet black hair caught the light and reflected bluish tints. Often she wondered why she didn't feel more than friendship for the handsome man. Maybe because they had grown up more as sister and brother. Much like her and Colin.

Or maybe not.

"I have a favor to ask," she said.

"Come. Let us sit in the parlor," Thomas said, urging her into the house.

Annie dragged her heels and tugged her hands

out of his gentle grasp. "I have to get back before my family starts to worry."

He arched a dark eyebrow in disapproval. "You did not tell them you were coming here?"

"You know how they are. Besides, what I have to ask you will only take a minute. Would you like to attend the theater with me tomorrow evening?"

After a moment's hesitation, he asked, "What of your friend, the other man who is visiting?"

How did he know about Colin? "He's a friend of Papa's and Kate's from years ago."

"Then he will be our chaperone, yes?"

Sometimes Thomas was as old-fashioned as her father. "Yes. He's also escorting a woman friend."

"Then I would be honored."

Annie laughed. "You don't have to be so formal, Thomas. We've known each other for most of our lives."

"I remember our childhood well. You were always leading me into trouble." He smiled, revealing even white teeth.

"And you didn't mind in the least." She leaned closer and whispered, "I think you liked annoying your parents."

Thomas stiffened. "We were children, and oftentimes children like to rebel against their parents' rules."

"And sometimes as adults, too," Annie said, remembering her own predicament. "I'd better go. Come to the house at seven tomorrow evening and we'll walk from there."

"All right, but I shall escort you home now. You

should not be out by yourself this late. It's not safe for a woman."

"God save me from knights in shining armor," Annie murmured. "Lead on, Sir Lancelot."

Thomas walked her to her door, then returned home.

Sometimes he acted more like a father than a friend, and Lord knew she didn't need another papa. She opened the door a crack and peeked inside. The area was clear and she quickly entered, removing her cape as she did. Listening to the voices, she figured Colin and her father were visiting in the front room. Kate was probably upstairs getting little Kathryn and the twins settled in for the night.

Annie usually helped her stepmother with the younger children, who were a handful in the evenings. After she left for San Francisco, Kate would have to do it herself or convince the self-centered Lucy to help her. Shaking her head, Annie wondered if she had been as selfish as her half sister at that age. With more than a twinge of guilt, Annie realized she had probably been more so.

Ascending the stairs, she heard the shriek of Kathryn, and Michael and Matthew arguing. She couldn't let Kate handle the little savages by herself. She went directly to the twins' bedroom, fixing her schoolteacher mask firmly in place.

An hour later the house was relatively quiet as Annie sorted through her clothes, trying to decide what to take with her to San Francisco and what to leave behind. Knowing she wouldn't be returning made the decisions that much more difficult. Although no one but herself knew, she was saying good-bye to her old life.

A knock at the door startled her, but then she remembered Kate had said she would help her pack.

"Come in," she called out, not even turning around.

"Funny. I didn't see a tornado go through here," a male voice said.

Annie spun around to find Colin standing in the doorway, amusement lighting his expression. His gaze flickered to what she held in her hands and his smile grew. She glanced down at her fanciest, frilliest camisole, and quickly shoved it behind her back.

"Don't worry. All my mistresses"—he paused, mischief appearing in his eyes—"excuse me, *courtesans*, wear similar undergarments."

Her cheeks burning, Annie couldn't be certain whether he was teasing her or not. She regained her aplomb and withdrew the camisole from its hiding place. She held it up, pretending to examine it closely. "So lace and diaphanous material are standard for courtesans?"

As Colin tried to maintain his composure, Annie attempted to restrain her grin, but her mouth refused to obey.

Colin's smoky eyes froze her smile and she was intimately aware of his presence in her room, dwarfing herself and everything else within the four walls.

He reached toward the undergarment and he caressed the material. His breath hitched, and Annie saw the same heart-stopping expression Colin had immediately before the wagon had nearly run them over.

"It's silky." His low timbre felt like a cloudless winter day—the sun's rays warm on her skin, but cool air giving rise to gooseflesh. Then he traced his forefinger lightly down her cheek. "Nearly as soft as you, lass."

Her knees trembled and she shifted almost unconsciously so the tips of her breasts grazed his chest. Her nipples puckered, causing her to gasp in surprise. She wanted—needed—him to touch her. The camisole was forgotten as it fluttered to the floor between them and Annie wrapped her fingers around Colin's hand. She raised it, but found she wasn't brazen enough to place it where she wanted him to touch her.

She lifted her gaze to find Colin staring down at her with a hunger so deep it nearly paralyzed her. She had seen that look directed at her before, but never by someone she *wanted* it from.

"Please," she whispered hoarsely, hoping Colin understood. He had always understood her before.

For a moment that seemed both to last forever and to be over in the blink of an eye, Colin and Annie remained frozen. Then Colin slowly skimmed his fingertips along the outer edge of her breast. Annie gasped, shocked by the intense pleasure of the feather-light contact.

His breathing thundered in her ears and she was aware of Colin's arousal. Her head was telling her to push him away, but her body wanted more . . . so much more.

Colin took a step back. Cool air rushed between their bodies, returning a measure of sanity. He dropped his hands to his sides, but not before she noticed his trembling.

"That wasn't what I planned to do when I came in here."

Annie licked her dry lips, hoping she appeared as coolly composed as Colin. "I did say you needed to be more spontaneous."

"Any more spontaneous and we would have combusted," Colin said, dragging a hand through his hair.

She laughed, feeling some of the tension ease, though her belly remained knotted and expectant, but for what she was uncertain. "Is that how the courtesans do it?"

He eyed her warily. "Why?"

Annie didn't understand or like the suspicion in his voice. She tossed her hair over her shoulder. "I might have to play a courtesan some day."

"Acting the role or becoming the role?"

"Either. Both," she replied with a sassy shrug.

"I hope you're joking, Annie." His tone was deadly serious.

"What if I'm not?" She knew she shouldn't

push him, but something made her see how far she could stretch his patience.

"I'll lock you in your room until you come to your senses."

She took a step back instinctively, then realized it might be construed as fear. Straightening her back, she faced him with false bravado. "If you think you can treat me like a child, you don't know me very well."

He smiled coolly. "If you're going to act like a child, I'll treat you like one."

His eyes glittered and Annie realized she didn't recognize the stranger in front of her. Surely Laddie wouldn't have touched her breast.

But then, his "little lass" wouldn't have asked him to, either.

She swallowed. "You made your point. I'll behave myself as long as you don't think of me as a child."

His gaze raked her from head to toe, leaving her feeling as if he had bared her with his perusal. "Only a blind man would mistake you for a child."

His tone sent a shiver down her spine. "And you're not blind," Annie dared.

"Not nearly as blind as I should be. You're a handful, lass, and I'm only a man." He inhaled then exhaled slowly. "How is the packing coming?"

Deciding Colin had the right idea about lightening the mood, Annie glanced around at the disaster. "What do you think?"

"Do you need some help?"

"And what do you know about what a woman needs?"

His heavy-lidded eyes gleamed and made her bite her tongue. Why had she chosen those words?

He shrugged with one shoulder. "I've lived out of a bag most of my life and I figure men and women aren't that different in what they need. Women just need more of it."

Annie laughed, letting the facade of normalcy arise between them. "That's only because men want us to dress up so they can be the envy of their friends."

"Something like a prize?"

"Exactly. If I were your prize, what would you have me take?"

Again there was a flicker of heat and promise in his hazel eyes, then Colin asked, "How many trunks do you have?"

Two hours later, Annie plopped down on her bed. Two trunks had been filled, leaving one bag to pack the night before she left. Kate had come in to help, but had left when she'd seen her step-daughter in Colin's capable hands.

Annie blushed, thinking how she could have ended up in those capable hands if they had continued with their little game earlier.

Colin lowered himself to the chair across the room. "Did you remember to keep some clothing out to wear to the theater tomorrow?"

Annie nodded.

"Who's escorting you?" Colin asked curiously.

"Thomas Morales. We attended school together. His parents are from Mexico. I think they were fairly wealthy," Annie said.

"Why did they move up here?"

She shrugged. "I never thought to ask."

Colin shifted in his chair. "Is he a beau?"

"No, we've been best friends for years."

"You used to tell me *I* was your best friend," Colin joshed.

Annie plucked at a knotted yarn on her quilted comforter, ignoring the humor in his voice. "You were, until you disappeared for nearly ten years." Surprisingly, saying the words aloud hurt.

"I told you I didn't have a choice. I had a job to do."

"And you could never take two or three days off?" Annie rose and came to stand before him, her arms crossed beneath her breasts. "I remember Papa wondering why you didn't stop by since you weren't that far away. He said you could ride the railroad free and that you could come into Denver if you wanted to." Her voice quivered with the lonely hurt that she had kept bottled up within her for years. "You must not have wanted to."

Colin's jaw muscle flexed. "That's not true. I just didn't have the time. I figured I could always come to visit next year, but next year never came."

"If you hadn't been injured, you still wouldn't be here, would you?" Annie accused.

She saw an array of emotions cross his face until he shook his head wearily. "No. You're right, Annie. It took almost getting killed for me to realize what I'd been missing." He laughed bitterly. "My da always said I had a hard head. I guess he was right."

The effort for Colin to rise seemed herculean and Annie had to fist her hands to stop herself from helping him.

"Goodnight," Colin said wearily.

She pressed her lips together, confused and angry, though uncertain why.

He left, closing the door behind him.

Annie dropped onto her bed and lay on her back, staring at the ceiling. Should she cry? No, she didn't feel like it. Maybe she should hit the wall as Brynn had done two years ago when he had lost his temper. He had put a hole in the wall and Papa had made him fix it himself. Although that idea had merit, she would probably just break her hand.

The following evening Colin tugged at his starched collar and fumbled with his tie. It had been a long time since he had escorted a proper woman out and doubts made him clumsy. Rolling on the ground and cushioning Annie with his body yesterday had brought new aches and pains this morning that had eased only slightly throughout the day. For two bits he was tempted to cancel his date with Margaret, but that would mean Annie would be alone with her Thomas.

Colin scowled at his reflection in the mirror. Why did it bother him that Annie would be escorted by a young man he didn't know? It wasn't any of his business whom she saw, except from a brotherly standpoint. He snorted, unable to lie to the face staring back at him.

"I'm jealous," he said aloud to the image. "Are you satisfied?"

He dragged a hand through his hair, mussing it but not giving a damn. Margaret was the type of woman he was interested in having as a wife, and with her as Annie's escort all the way to California, he had time to court her and decide if she was *the* one. Hell, it would save him a lot of time if he settled for her instead of continuing the search in California.

Settled for her.

Annie was right. I'm a damned pig.

No, you're practical, he argued with himself. He closed his eyes and pictured Margaret's thick dark hair and doelike eyes. He imagined kissing her and touching her . . . but now the woman had blond hair and sparkling blue eyes and looked a hell of a lot like Annie.

His eyes flashed open. All right, so he wanted Annie.

You can't have her.

That was clear enough. Tonight he would be attentive to Margaret and ignore Annie. He could do that . . . he *would* do that. Besides, Annie would be busy with Thomas.

Not too busy, though, or Colin would have to

step in and take action. He owed it to Trev and Kate to watch out for their daughter.

Even if it was to protect her from himself.

Colin went down the stairs deliberately, taking care not to put too much strain on the leg that had been broken so badly.

Hearing Trev's voice in the parlor, Colin joined the family. He paused in the doorway, noticing Kate as she sat on the floor, engrossed in stacking blocks with Kathryn. Michael, Matthew, and Darcy were rearranging a town they had built from wood blocks and empty thread spools, complete with horses, buggies, and people. Trev and Brynn were seated on either side of a small table, a chess board set up between them. Only Lucy and Annie were absent.

It was a gentle homey scene that was unfamiliar to Colin.

"My, don't you look handsome," Kate exclaimed, rising to her feet and brushing her skirt folds.

Colin's face heated. "Thanks, Kate, but I feel like an overstuffed politician."

"Now *there's* a picture I can't imagine," Trev said, joining them. "Colin stumping for office."

"You and me both," Colin said. Inserting a finger between his collar and neck, he tugged again at the stiff material. "I can hardly breathe."

"I'll take care of that," Kate said, reaching for his tie.

Colin stood patiently while she loosened the

collar. "Thanks, Kate. You saved my life," he teased.

She smoothed his lapels and plucked a thread from his shoulder. "It's the least I could do considering that without you, Trev and I wouldn't be here surrounded by our family. You saved his life that day the mine burned, Laddie."

Her use of his long-ago nickname told him how deeply affected she was.

"You and Trev have repaid me ten times over with your friendship," Colin replied. "I'm only sorry it took this long for me to realize how much it means to me."

Kate leaned forward and kissed his cheek. "You'll always have a home here. I hope you know that."

She looked past him and Colin knew that Annie stood behind him. He could feel her presence—a contradictory bundle of simmering passion and naïve innocence.

He turned and was stunned at the vision before him. Wearing an off-the-shoulder gown of emerald green that hugged her full bosom and small waist, Annie bore no resemblance to the imp Colin knew so well. Instead, there was only Annie the woman . . . a woman who could destroy Colin's heart if he foolishly let down his guard.

Chapter 6

Before Colin could say anything, Trev crossed his arms and angled Annie a disapproving look. "That dress is a little daring, isn't it?"

The last thing she wanted was another confrontation with her father, but she *was* twenty years old. Some people would even call her an old maid. She released a long-suffering sigh. "Rachel Thompson, who's younger than I am, wore one that dipped even lower than this."

"Rachel Thompson is a married woman," Trev said.

"You're wearing a shawl, aren't you, Annie?" Kate broke in.

Annie glowered at her papa another moment, then switched her attention to Kate, her eyes softening. "Yes, I am." She aimed a glare back at her father. "At least, I *was* planning on wearing one."

"Go get it, lass," Colin broke in gently. "You'll be glad to have it later."

Colin's friendly voice and the wink that accompanied it reined in Annie's temper. She took a moment to study him, noting the paisley waistcoat and dark brown frock coat that stretched across his broad shoulders. The light spun his burnished brown hair into golden red. A tendril dipped across his forehead and she reached up to sweep the silky strand back from his brow. Her gaze caught his and a spark of desire flared momentarily in his eyes. She shivered and drew away.

The presence of her father and stepmother extinguished the slow burn in her belly.

"I'll go get my shawl. There's no reason to catch a cold." She spun around and hurried up to her room, suddenly embarrassed by the display of one of her less-than-admirable traits—the stubbornness she shared with her father.

Sometimes she almost wished she could be the demure daughter her father wanted her to be, but that wasn't who she was and he couldn't expect her to pretend to be someone else . . . unless of course, she was on stage.

Smiling, she glided back down the stairs, shawl in hand. A precise knock sounded on the door. She knew it would be Thomas, since it was exactly seven according to the Regulator clock chiming in the parlor. Hurrying down the remaining steps, Annie swept open the door.

"Good evening, Thomas," she said, regarding

his pitch black suit with an approving eye. His high collar was impeccable, but the deep red ascot around his neck gave the black and white attire a somewhat less formal appearance, as well as emphasizing his dark Spanish features. Her childhood friend had matured into a very handsome man—a man most women would swoon over.

Thomas's gaze settled below her neck and the odd light in his eyes made the hairs at her nape stand up. Then the look was gone and he was smiling affably. She puzzled over his strange reaction, then dismissed it. She had always had an overactive imagination.

Footsteps behind her alerted her to the arrival of her family. When she turned, she noticed her father's displeasure at her still-bare shoulders. Giving in for the sake of Kate, Annie tossed on the shawl, covering herself.

Kate nodded slightly at Annie, both in relief and amusement, then greeted the young man with a fond smile while her father shook his hand.

"Thomas, I'd like you to meet a dear friend of the family, Colin McBride," Annie introduced.

She immediately noticed the cool measuring looks exchanged between the two men. They reminded her of two tomcats getting ready to mark the same territory. The analogy almost made her laugh, except that the idea that *she* was the "territory" dispelled her humor.

"Hello, Thomas," Colin said with little inflection. "Annie has told me about you."

She couldn't tell whether the latter was a warning or a cordial comment. By the narrowing of Thomas's eyes, he'd interpreted it as the former.

This is not starting out well.

"We should be going. Margaret is expecting us at seven-fifteen," Annie said. She threaded one arm through Thomas's and the other through Colin's.

"Have a nice evening, sweetheart," Kate said, exchanging a womanly sympathetic look with her.

"We will. Good-bye, Kate." She purposely forgot to say farewell to her father. By the thunderclouds in his expression, she regretted that Kate would have to put up with his ill temper. Though she knew her stepmother loved her father, Annie couldn't help but wonder how she tolerated his narrow-mindedness. Hades would freeze over before Annie would answer to a man.

Walking between the two tense men down the street, Annie wondered if all males were so exasperating. She had been the recipient of Colin's overprotectiveness on more than one occasion, and Thomas had his moments of treating her like a child, though they were only three months apart in age.

"So you have known the Trevelyans for many years?" Thomas asked politely, though with a distinct wariness in his tone.

"Over fifteen. I met Annie when she was just a wee lass," Colin replied, equally as stiff. Then he laughed. "One minute she was as sweet as pie, the next a little devil strainin' the patience of the saints."

"I wasn't that bad," Annie said, miffed that they were talking about her as if she wasn't there.

"*Sí*, I believe it," Thomas said. "Many times she would have to stay after school because of some mischief."

"It's nice to know she didn't change too much," Colin said.

They made her sound like a spoiled brat. Granted, she had pulled a few stunts, like tying the schoolmaster's shoelaces together as he'd sat behind his desk, then having Thomas yell, "fire." Releasing the snake near Miss Leonard had been another of her memorable deeds. The teacher had swooned as the class had erupted into chaos.

But to sit without fidgeting all day had been nearly impossible and her mind often wandered, cooking up all sorts of mischief. Why couldn't she have been more like Brynn—quiet and studious?

But why would I want to be?

Annie's musings faded as they stopped in front of Margaret's small, cozy house. "We'll wait here while you gather your paramour," she said to Colin.

He cast Annie a scolding glare, but didn't say anything in front of Thomas, just as she knew he wouldn't.

As she stood beside Thomas, his arm slid around her waist and drew her close to his side.

"Are you cold, Annie?" he asked softly.

She shook her head, deciding how to extricate herself from his grasp politely. "No. It's a nice evening." When his grip tightened, the same shiver she'd experienced earlier returned. She began to pull away from him. For a moment she thought he wasn't going to release her, then his arm loosened and she stepped away. What in the world had come over him? His hold had been almost proprietary.

Puzzled and not sure what to do, Annie chose to ignore the episode. Certainly Thomas didn't harbor feelings like *that* toward her.

She focused on Colin, who stood in the shaft of light streaming from Margaret's door. He appeared at ease, but Annie recognized the subtle shift of his weight from one foot to the other and the clenching of his hands behind his back. Who would have believed Colin would be nervous about escorting a woman to the theater?

Margaret stepped onto the porch and Annie's eyes widened. The widow wore a short rust-colored velvet cape over a rich brown dress that glinted as it caught the light of the growing dusk. Her dark hair had been piled on her head, revealing a long pale neck. Margaret was the epitome of elegance and understatement. Annie glanced down at her own daring dress, suddenly finding it too flashy. Almost tawdry.

Colin and Margaret made a handsome couple, Annie noted reluctantly, and complemented one another well, dressed in varying shades of brown.

"You look lovely, Margaret," Annie said sincerely.

"Thank you, my dear. I bought the gown after my year of mourning, but never had reason to wear it until now." Margaret's cheeks bloomed with color as she looked up at Colin.

If Colin's behavior was any indication, he liked Margaret's transformation. Too much, to Annie's way of thinking. But wasn't that her plan—to have Margaret occupy Colin's time so completely that he forgot about her? If the widow dressed this way all the way to San Francisco, Annie's scheme would be successful.

Why didn't that make her feel better?

Thomas cleared his throat and Annie returned to earth. "Oh, I'm sorry. Margaret, I'd like you to meet Thomas Morales. Thomas, this is Mrs. Margaret Mopplewhite."

Comical confusion flashed across Thomas's face, but he took Margaret's hand in his and kissed the back of it gallantly. "It is a pleasure to make your acquaintance, Señora Mopplewhite."

Annie almost dissolved into a fit of giggles at the sound of the woman's name spoken with a Spanish accent. When she had first met Margaret, she had been unable to restrain her laughter at the odd last name. Kate had made up some excuse for her hilarity, then had proceeded to lecture her about it all the way home that evening.

"As it is mine, Mr. Morales," Margaret said in a cultured voice.

Annie and Thomas led the way, and Colin and Margaret strolled behind them. Ten minutes later they arrived at the theater, where four tickets were waiting, as promised. The seats were in the middle, giving them an unhindered view of the stage.

The playhouse was filling quickly and the two hundred seats would soon be occupied. Although she wasn't performing, Annie still felt a ripple of nervous excitement. She knew how actors thrived on an audience's rapt attention and their reactions to the unfolding of the story. The more the audience was pulled into the play, the more the actors would sink into their characters, and vice versa. It was an odd symbiotic relationship, the actors' performances being sustained by the audience's emotions. It was a feeling Annie yearned to experience again and again.

She glanced at Colin and Margaret, who were talking with their heads close together so they could hear one another above the buzz of conversation. Colin's brow brushed Margaret's head as he leaned even closer to listen to her.

Annie quickly turned away. Maybe Margaret was the woman for him—the woman he would marry, bed, and raise his children with. Annie's stomach knotted painfully. Why did the thought of them making a home together bother her so much?

It's not as if I'm the kind of woman Colin's looking

for. A rancher's wife? She snorted at the image of her mucking out a horse stall.

"Not likely," she muttered.

"The play will begin soon." Thomas spoke, his lips close to Annie's ear.

She glanced up at his patrician face and realized this might be the last time she would see him. Tonight would be filled with a lot of "last times." Looking around, she tried to memorize the place where she'd first set foot on stage in front of an audience. It had been a heady feeling, one she had embraced for days afterward.

The lights dimmed and Annie settled back in her seat. She wouldn't let her confusion about her feelings for Colin intrude upon this evening. Tonight she would simply enjoy the play and the company.

When Thomas reached for her hand, she willingly clasped it.

The curtain fell and applause filled the theater. Startled, Colin clapped politely, though he couldn't remember exactly how the play had ended. He had been watching Annie's expressive face instead of the stage. She had mouthed many lines of dialogue, telling Colin that yesterday hadn't been the first time she'd gone against her father's edict. The fact that she knew all of the actors personally was also a dead giveaway. He should have told Trev of his daughter's transgression, but didn't have the heart to do so. Like Kate, he hoped this was merely a phase Annie was going through.

During the play, he'd also remained vigilant while Thomas had held Annie's hand. If the younger man tried to do more than that, Colin would have had to take steps to protect Annie's virtue. Fortunately Thomas had been content with Annie's hand and nothing more.

He tried to stifle a yawn as the players took their final bow, but Margaret didn't notice. She had been enthralled by the play and was whispering in his ear that she had never seen anything like it. After hearing about her dearly departed husband before the show began, Colin was sure she *hadn't* seen anything like it. The man sounded like a tyrant, issuing Margaret only a pittance of an allowance and never letting her out of the house unless he accompanied her.

If Annie wanted to rant about men being autocratic, Margaret's husband definitely deserved some of her wrath. It explained why the widow was so reticent, though tonight she seemed to bloom before his eyes.

The lights came up in the playhouse and Colin blinked in their brightness. He glanced over at Annie, who had a dreamy look upon her face as she rested her head against Thomas's shoulder. His stomach clutched at the possessive arm the Spanish man had around her. When had the hand-holding graduated to a full-arm embrace? How had he missed it?

As if reading his mind, Thomas removed his arm and Annie sat up.

"Essie and Percival did a wonderful job, didn't they?" Annie commented.

Margaret blinked in surprise. "You know the actors?"

The way Margaret said "actors" implied that she disapproved of associating with them socially.

"They're friends," Annie said, lifting her chin in challenge.

"We should probably go—" Colin began, trying to smooth the awkwardness.

Annie stood abruptly. "I want to say good-bye to them."

Before anyone could protest, she was descending the stairs against the flow of exiting people.

Margaret sniffed. "I can understand why Kate and Mr. Trevelyan wanted a chaperone to accompany her. She is a headstrong young lady."

"You haven't seen anything yet," Colin muttered under his breath.

"She has always been this way," Thomas said, spreading his hands in apology. "I had hoped she would grow out of it and be ready to settle down."

With you? Only in your dreams.

Shoving the unbidden thought from his mind, Colin stood. "I'll go retrieve her." He turned to Thomas. "Could you stay with Margaret? I'll be back in a minute."

Before Thomas could argue, Colin descended

the now-empty stairs and stepped onto the stage. He found the curtain's slitted opening and slipped behind it, not surprised to see Annie talking animatedly with her friends.

"Why, hello, good-looking," Essie said, still dressed in her costume.

Colin kept his gaze aimed above the low décolletage, meeting her heavily made-up eyes. "I enjoyed your performance," he said, for want of anything better.

Essie sidled up to him, swinging her generous hips, and pressed her full breasts against his arm. "That was nothing. You should see my private performance."

"I don't think the lady friend who's waiting for me would appreciate that," he said dryly.

"And here I thought I was your only lady friend," Essie said, feigning a pout.

Annie left Toby and joined them, an innocent smile on her face—the kind of smile that alarmed Colin. "Didn't you know, Essie? Colin likes variety in his women, isn't that right?" She batted her baby blue eyes.

"If he wants variety, I can do that, too." Essie waggled her eyebrows suggestively.

Percival clapped his hands once. "Essie, my dear, we may be accustomed to your wit, but I'm afraid you're embarrassing Annie's Colin."

"I'm not *her* Colin," Colin said.

"He's not *my* Colin," Annie said at the same time.

"There, you see, Percival, he's free for the taking," Essie said triumphantly, grabbing Colin's arm and giving him full frontal body contact.

Annie laughed. Essie grinned. Percival snorted. Toby and Alexander merely shook their heads.

"What is the meaning of this?"

Colin jerked around, dragging Essie with him, and spotted Margaret regarding the scene distastefully. Thomas stood behind her, his own eyes wide with disbelief.

"It's not what you're thinking, Margaret," Colin said.

"How could it not be?" the widow demanded, staring at him . . . at them.

Essie stuck to him like moss on a tree and was creating some pleasant but untimely reactions in certain parts of his body. He looked to Annie for support.

"You're on your own with this one, Colin." Annie was clearly enjoying the show.

Percival glided over to Margaret's side. "And who are you, lovely lady?"

Margaret blushed behind her stern expression. "I am Mrs. Margaret Mopplewhite."

"Such a unique name for a woman of such unrivaled beauty. I am Percival Fortunatas and I am your servant." He bowed deeply.

Margaret's flush deepened and her censure faded. "I am pleased to meet you, Mr. Fortunatas. I, uh, I enjoyed your acting immensely."

He ducked his head as if embarrassed. "I am

not worthy of such acclaim. But you, Mrs. Mop-plewhite—Margaret—are a bouquet of roses in a colorless room. A shaft of sunlight and beauty in the drabness of a cloudy day."

Margaret giggled.

Colin's stomach rolled. He couldn't take much more of Percival's outlandish compliments.

"Annie, perhaps we should leave," Thomas spoke up, his face ruddy with anger or embarrassment, or both.

"No!" Colin cleared his throat and spoke in a quieter, more controlled voice. "Margaret and I are your chaperones. We will accompany you."

Annie snorted. "I think the chaperone needs a chaperone. What do you think, Margaret?"

The question brought Margaret back to reality with a thump. "Yes, of course. I think this evening, as pleasant as it has been, should end."

"I'm just getting started, honey." Essie gazed up at Colin with inviting—and lust-filled—eyes.

He grasped her forearms firmly and removed her plastered-on body from his. "Behave yourself, Miss Essie," he murmured. "I think you've gotten me into enough trouble already this evening."

She smiled crookedly and winked. "You haven't even gotten close to trouble yet."

Colin fought laughter and glanced at Margaret's thinned lips. Now *there* was trouble, and not the kind Essie was talking about.

He stepped away from Essie and joined Margaret, who seemed determined to keep a good three feet between them as if he had the plague.

"Come, Annie. We must leave," Thomas said.

Essie found herself another target and homed in on the younger man. "Hello there, handsome. My name is Essie Charbonneau."

"I am Thomas Morales," he said with a slight bow at the waist.

Colin noticed he didn't kiss the back of her hand as he had done with Margaret.

"Thomas is a friend," Annie said, still smiling like a cat with a mouse.

Essie's lips turned downward in a pout. "Why do you get all the good-looking friends?"

"A clean and pure heart," Annie shot back with a saucy grin. Her smile faded as she looked at the four members of the small traveling troupe. "I guess this is good-bye."

Colin watched as all pretenses disappeared from Percival and Essie and they hugged Annie in turn. Toby and Alexander, who had been hanging back to stay out of the line of adult fire, came forward to say their farewells. In spite of their eccentricities, the actors cared for Annie and she for them.

After they'd said their good-byes, Colin found himself once again engulfed in Essie's soft arms, then he was shaking Percival's hand. After saying good-bye to Annie, Toby had stepped into the background once more, his arms crossed as he eyed Colin suspiciously. Alexander stood to the left and behind Toby, his pose a mirror of the boy's.

"Do you think we should rescue them?" Annie whispered in Colin's ear.

Colin hadn't even heard her approach, but now with her so close he couldn't help but notice her. Especially the creamy skin revealed by the low-cut dress. Trev was right—the damned thing was too daring. "Uh, who?"

"Margaret and Thomas."

Colin followed her pointing finger and didn't try to stifle his laughter. Percival appeared to be regaling Margaret with more nonsensical flattery and Essie had wrapped herself around Thomas like a snug glove.

"Or maybe we should leave them, and you and I can go together," Colin suggested, with more frankness than was safe.

Annie leaned close. "Are you sure you can handle me?"

"Without a doubt, imp." Colin kept his voice light and teasing.

Annie tipped her head back to meet his gaze and the smoldering heat in her eyes nearly scorched him. "Promises, promises," she whispered throatily.

Colin's brain dropped a couple feet. This girl-woman was treacherous, waiting for the right moment to strike below the belt.

Definitely below the belt.

Why couldn't Annie have grown up into someone like Margaret—safe and staid? A woman a man could feel comfortable with, who didn't hold any surprises, and never made comments like *that* in public.

Annie was completely unpredictable. She didn't give a flying fig what other people thought.

In short, she was everything a man was looking for in a . . . courtesan.

Damn.

Chapter 7

While Annie rescued Thomas, Colin managed to pry the flushed Margaret away from Percival. He guided her up the stairs to the exit and heard Annie's gay laughter as she and Thomas followed outside. The temptation to see her expression overcame his prudence and he turned only to catch his breath at the pale vision of Annie in the moonlight. Her silver-gilded hair and pale skin made her appear ephemeral—a stunning wraith against the evening's backdrop. It wasn't surprising to see Thomas close beside her, as if proclaiming to the world she was his and no one else's. Annie, however, didn't seem to notice his possessive touch as she chatted about the theater and those involved with it.

"Is something wrong, Colin?" Margaret asked, drawing his attention away from Annie.

"No, nothing at all, Margaret," he reassured her, patting her hand. "I was just making sure Annie and Thomas hadn't gone off by themselves."

The widow tsk-tsked. "Young people these days are so forward. Back when we were their age, we would never have attempted to escape our chaperones for a tryst."

Speak for yourself.

Colin dashed away his rude thought. If Margaret's husband had been half as brutish as she claimed, he could understand her righteous comment. But Colin had sown some wild oats back in his day, including a few trysts. Which was why he knew what to watch for with Thomas and Annie.

"Why, I never would have considered attending the theater when I was Annie's age," Margaret remarked.

"Why's that?" Colin asked curiously.

She leaned close, shielded her mouth with her hand, and whispered, "We all know what kind of people actors and actresses are."

She was only echoing Colin's previous thoughts, but her prejudice suddenly made him feel uncomfortable. He didn't have anything against Percival and his troupe. In fact, he found their earthy candor a welcome change from the politics he'd experienced while he'd been with the railroad.

"Oh? Just what kind of people are those?" Colin asked, relishing the devil's advocate role.

"Surely you understand that actors do not belong in polite society," Margaret began. "As a rule their behavior is amoral and licentious. A young woman like Annie would do well to stay away from people like them, lest her reputation be tarnished simply by association."

"Then I suppose it's good the Trevelyans are sending Annie away so she can't be corrupted any further."

"Exactly, Colin. It is most reassuring to know you and I are of similar minds." Margaret sighed. "I have a feeling Annie will be a handful on the trip to San Francisco."

Colin pictured Annie's lush curves. "Definitely a handful."

He ignored Margaret's quizzical expression. "Here we are already," he announced as they paused in front of her home. "I had an enjoyable evening, Margaret." He raised her hand to his lips and pressed a kiss to the back of it. "Thank you for accompanying me."

"The pleasure was all mine, Colin." She looked past him to Annie and Thomas. "It was nice to meet you, Thomas. And Annie, I shall see you the day after tomorrow at the train station." She raised herself on her tiptoes and said close to Colin's ear, "I shall look forward to seeing you, too."

"Same here, Margaret." He squeezed her hands companionably, then released her.

Colin waited until Margaret had entered her home and light spilled out of a window, then he turned to the two younger people. "Now it's time for us to return home."

"It's early," Annie said, her lower lip curled in a pout.

Colin tugged on the silver chain across his waistcoat and withdrew his pocket watch. "It's after ten o'clock." He tucked it away. "Late enough."

"*If* you're an old man. Thomas and I would like to go to the Brown Palace."

"That's on the other side of town. How will you get there?"

"Have you heard of a streetcar?" she asked with feigned gravity.

Margaret was right—young people *were* much too forward these days. "I am tired, which means we are going home." Colin glanced at Thomas, who had remained silent throughout the exchange. "Is that all right with you, Thomas?"

He bowed slightly. "*Sí.* When a man gets to be your age he is more easily fatigued, and I would not disgrace Annie by appearing without a chaperone."

The younger man's acquiescence gratified Colin, though the part about age and fatigue certainly didn't. "Let's return to the Trevelyans, then," he said stiffly.

Colin began walking, but the absence of footsteps and Annie's hushed whisperings told him he wasn't being followed. He stopped. "Is there a problem?"

"No problem, *Señor* McBride," Thomas reassured.

"Yes, there's a problem," Annie countered. "I don't want to go home yet and I'm old enough to make my own decisions, thank you very much."

"You're unmarried," Colin said flatly. "That means you cannot make your own decisions."

Annie's mouth dropped open, then closed. Dangerous sparks lit her eyes. "Are you saying that because I am not a married woman, I'm not allowed to make decisions on my own?"

Colin had no patience for a temper tantrum. "That's right." He stepped back and took hold of her arm. "Come along, lass."

She dug her heels in. "You're worse than my father."

Colin flinched—that one stung. "If I was worse than your father—who, by the way, is a saint for puttin' up with your tantrums—I wouldn't be lettin' you out of the house at all until you were wedded."

Her eyes widened impossibly further. "You wouldn't!"

Colin leaned close, his nose two inches from hers. "I would."

She held his stare for a long minute. The fearlessness in her face brought a certain amount of pride to Colin, but it was overshadowed by frustration. He easily recalled the too-quiet little girl she had been fifteen years ago and was grateful she was no longer so introverted. But who would have believed she would grow up to possess so much audacity?

"Annie, *Señor* McBride," Thomas said. "You are both behaving like children."

Colin snapped back, his gaze flying to the younger man and a sharp rebuke on his lips, but then embarrassment heated his cheeks. "You're right, Thomas." He stiffened his spine and tugged down his waistcoat, ignoring Annie's glare. "It's time to return home. Now."

This time he didn't stop, but assumed they were following him. If they didn't, he knew where to find them. But Thomas seemed to have a sensible head on his shoulders.

It was a good thing Margaret was accompanying them to San Francisco—he and Annie would probably need a mediator. Or a referee.

Ten minutes later, Colin and Annie stepped into the Trevelyan home. Thomas had continued on to his own house after saying goodnight. The moment Colin closed the door behind him, Annie jerked her shawl off and tossed it across the banister, then stomped into the parlor.

Sighing, Colin followed, though he would have preferred to stick his hand in a lion's cage. It would have been safer and less painful.

"I can't believe you treated me like a child in front of Thomas," she said the moment he joined her.

"I didn't treat you like a child. I treated you with the respect you deserve as an unmarried young lady," Colin said. He loosened his tie and undid the top two buttons of his shirt. He let out a sigh, able to breathe again without his neck being pinched. He had a feeling he'd need all the breath he could get in the next few minutes.

Annie whirled around and stabbed her forefinger into his chest. "I thought you were my friend. I thought I could trust you."

"Trust? You're talkin' about trust, lass?" Colin's Irish accent crept into his exasperated voice. "I trusted you to ask your father about goin' to the theater yesterday. You lied to me, Annie. I've never known you to do that before. And how do I know you won't be doin' it *again* to get what you want?"

Annie's face flushed red. "He wouldn't have given me permission. He doesn't trust me, either."

"Maybe you haven't given him reason to."

She balled her hands into fists at her sides. "I'm a grown woman, Colin. I know what I want in my life."

He stared into her glistening eyes, feeling himself weaken at the abject misery in them. He held her bare shoulders and ignored his immediate male reaction to the feel of her velvety skin. "He's protected you since the moment you were born, lass. Yes, you're a woman to anyone with eyes, but to your father you'll always be his little girl and he'll always want to take care of you.

"He also wants you to be happy, and we all know how theater people are looked upon. He wants to protect you from the terrible things people will say about you if you become one. You

know as well as I do how men view actresses."
Colin sighed. "And as much as I like your friend
Essie, she does nothing to change that impres-
sion."

"But I'm not like her," Annie argued. "I would
never want to be with men like she does."

Colin smiled gently. "Ah, lass, you say that
now, but a woman has needs just like a man. One
day you'd realize that and not concern yourself
with your reputation. It only takes one indiscre-
tion to ruin you."

"Why?" she demanded.

"What do you mean?"

"Why can a woman be ruined by an indiscre-
tion, while a man is expected to have a lot of dal-
liances before he settles down to marriage?"

Even as a young girl, Annie had never asked
the easy questions. Colin released her and moved
to the love seat. "Sit down, lass."

She joined him, leaned back and crossed her
arms. With her low-cut dress, the position gave
her a cleavage that rivaled the Grand Canyon.

Colin cleared his throat and forced his gaze to
her face. "A man should enter marriage knowing
how to satisfy his wife."

"But a woman shouldn't know how to satisfy
her husband?"

He held up a hand. "I'm saying that a man
wants to marry a woman who has never been, uh,
possessed by a man before. He wants to be her
first and teach her how it's done."

"So what you're saying is a man wants to train

his wife in the ways *he* likes to be pleasured, so she can please him whenever he has an itch?" She snorted. "Figures."

Colin fought back his exasperation, and his gaze settled on her bountiful bosom. Cursing his straying eyes, he brought his attention back to her face. "That's not what I said."

Annie scowled. "That's what it sounded like to me." She jumped to her feet and paced in front of him. "Thomas and I are friends. We grew up together. I wanted to spend some time alone with him to talk, since I may never see him again."

"You'll be back here in six months."

She halted to look down at him. "Maybe. Maybe not. What if some handsome stranger sweeps me off my feet and we get married and move to Europe?"

"I thought you weren't going to get married?"

She shrugged. "I don't plan to, but we're talking about falling head over heels in love. Nobody intends to do that."

"No, and it rarely ever happens. Your father and Kate are the only two people I know who fell in love like that, and they didn't even know it."

"See what I mean?"

Colin reached up and snagged her slender wrist, tugging her down onto the love seat. "I know you think all this is unfair for a woman, but it's only that men have a need to protect and care for the weaker sex."

Annie jerked out of his hold and sprang to her feet like a jack-in-the-box. "The 'weaker sex'? I'll have you know that if men had to have babies, the human race would die out!"

Colin clamped down on his urge to laugh. "Why do you say that, lass?"

"I've done volunteer work at the hospital. I've seen men and women with similar injuries, and the man is always the one crying that he's going to die from the pain."

He thought he knew her, but found himself learning something new about her every day.

"Maybe some men can't tolerate pain as well as some women, but that doesn't mean a man isn't stronger than a woman." She opened her mouth, but he held up his hand to halt her rebuttal. "Would you sit down before I crick my neck and cry like a baby?"

Annie's lips twitched with a grin and she lowered herself back onto the love seat.

"When you were a wee lass, I knew the answers to all your questions, or at least, enough to bluff my way through them." He was gratified to see a smile steal across her face. "Now I don't seem to have any answers, and you're too smart to try to bluff. All I can tell you, Annie, is that if something should happen to you, your father, Kate, and I would be heartbroken. That's the reason we're so strict with you. Maybe you feel like you're being suffocated, but it's the only way we can feel that you'll be safe."

"So Papa is only sending me to that stupid finishing school to protect me?" She harrumphed. "It'll be like a jail, where everything I do and say is regulated." Annie sagged in the cushions, her shoulder pressing against Colin's, and he lifted his arm so she could snuggle closer. "I understand why Papa feels that way in here"—she pointed to her head—"but I get so angry when no one will take me seriously."

"I take you seriously."

She tilted her head back to gaze at him. "Do you, Colin? Or do you still see me as a little girl?"

Colin looked down at the obvious womanly body; at the brilliant blue eyes sparking with spirit; at her Cupid's bow lips which were parted slightly. Her essence—a mix of sweet honey, flowery powder, and her own uniqueness—swirled through him.

Woman and girl.

Knowledge and naïveté.

Worldliness and innocence.

He drew a fingertip down her cheek. "I don't see a child when I look at you."

"What do you see, Colin?"

He cupped her cheek in his palm, brushing her velvety skin with his thumb. "I see a beautiful woman who can do anything she puts her mind to."

She took hold of his hand and studied his fingers, running her fingertips up and down each one. "Why did you stay away for so long, Colin? I missed you so badly."

Her feathery touches brought his senses into sharper focus, like a spring day after a rainstorm. "I can't give you an easy answer, lass. I can only tell you I missed you, too. I'm sorry I didn't see you grow into a woman."

"Will you kiss me, Colin?"

His heart skipped a beat at the unexpected request. He searched her pleading expression, the fear and attraction that vied in her expressive eyes. "Why?"

"I want to kiss you."

The simple reply made his decision. "All right."

Before his mind could come up with ten reasons why this was a bad idea, he tilted her chin upward as he lowered his mouth to hers. The kiss was gentle, like the barest hint of a breeze over warm lips. She tasted perilously sweet. Though he wanted to deepen the kiss, to open her mouth to his, he drew away.

"Thank you," Annie whispered. "It's getting late. I should go to bed."

Colin's mind envisioned his own bed . . . with Annie in it. He blinked the uninvited image away. "Goodnight, lass."

"Goodnight, Colin." She stood and walked to the door, then paused and said in a voice so low it was almost inaudible, "I liked it." Then she was gone.

Colin touched his lips, which still tingled from her taste. "I did, too. More than I should have," he said softly to the empty room.

"How was the play, Colin?" Trev asked the next morning.

Colin reached for his coffee cup. He was glad he'd awakened early enough to have breakfast with Trev; it gave them time to talk without anyone else around. "It was interesting," he replied. "Annie said it was the troupe's last performance."

"Oh? How did Annie know?"

"They're her friends," Colin said casually, though he wondered if he was doing the right thing.

Trev propped his elbows on the edge of the table and clasped his hands. "What the hell am I going to do with her, Laddie? She goes against me at every turn. No matter what I say, she always says or does the opposite."

"She's not the same little mute girl you were so protective of in Orion. I know you don't want to see it, but she *is* a woman—a lovely, intelligent woman with a mind of her own."

"It sounds to me like she got you wrapped tight around her little finger. Didn't I warn you?"

Colin leaned back, resting his laced hands above his belt. "You warned me, all right, but it's not that, Trev. We talked in the parlor last night after we got back." *I kissed her, too.* He banished the thought. "She thinks the finishing school is just like being sent to prison."

"She gave me the same argument, but young ladies are sent there to better themselves. That's what I'm hoping will happen with Annie."

Colin studied his longtime friend. "You don't think Annie is good enough the way she is?"

Trev glared at him. "You're twisting my words around. I don't want her throwing her life away on stage. She'd be no better than a . . . than a whore."

"Do you honestly believe that?"

"She's going to the damned finishing school if I have to hog-tie her and take her myself." He paused. "If you're so much against this, maybe you shouldn't accompany her and Margaret to San Francisco."

Colin thought about it a moment, then shook his head. "I want to make sure she arrives safely and has someone other than Margaret watching out for her. Besides, I love Annie, too. She's like a little sister."

Liar.

He ignored his conscience and last night's kiss, which taunted him.

Trev sighed in relief and raked a hand through his snow white hair. "Thanks, Laddie. As much as I want her to go, I'm just as afraid to let her go. Knowing you'll be with her will ease my mind."

"That's what friends are for."

"And Margaret going along won't hurt either, will it?" Trev teased.

Colin's face warmed. "She's a nice woman, just the kind a man could settle down with."

"We've known her for many years. We knew her husband, too." Trev grimaced. "He was a vicious bastard. I always felt sorry for Margaret, but she'd made her bed and was determined to lie in it. Kate tried to get her to leave him, but Margaret wouldn't. I could never understand that."

"Maybe she settled for second best when she couldn't have her first choice," Colin said. He blinked the image of Annie from his thoughts.

"Is that what you're doing?"

"Maybe."

"Who is she?"

The younger man glanced up to find his friend's sympathetic eyes aimed at him. "Nobody you know," he replied softly.

Trev studied Colin for a long moment, then changed the subject. "I have to get to work. Will you be down later?"

"I planned on picking up my train ticket and was going to stop by if you weren't too busy."

Trev pushed his chair back and stood. "This is the last day you'll be around and it feels like you just got here. Come around lunch time and we'll eat in the school's cafeteria."

"That sounds good."

Trev went up the stairs and returned two minutes later, a smile on his face.

"Only Kate can make you grin like that," Colin teased.

"I'm a helluva lucky man."

Yes, you are.

"I'll see you around noon, then," Colin said.

Trev lifted a hand in farewell.

Colin sipped his coffee. He would escort Annie to the finishing school as promised and hope that some fellow didn't sweep her off her feet. In fact, he would have to guard his own heart carefully.

As Annie had said, nobody ever planned to fall head over heels in love.

Chapter 8

Colin left the house before Annie came downstairs for breakfast, uncertain what he would say to her. Why had she asked him to kiss her? Was he the first man she had ever kissed? No, he didn't believe that—not impetuous Annie. If nothing else, she might have kissed a man merely for the experience in case a theater role called for it.

That didn't make him feel any better than if she had kissed a young man out of fondness . . . or passion.

On his way to the train depot, he stopped by the butcher shop.

"Good morning, Mr. Heinemeyer," Colin greeted as the bell on the door tinkled to announce his arrival.

"Mr. McBride. Where's your beautiful escort?"

"Still sleeping."

Heinemeyer chuckled. "Young people today." He sobered. "I've watched her grow like she was my own child. The days'll be a little less bright without her."

Colin slid his hands into his trouser pockets, thinking how his own life would be duller without her in it. "Aye, she has a way about her. I'm here to pay the Trevelyans' bill."

Heinemeyer canted an eyebrow. "Does Trev know what you're up to?"

Colin smiled smoothly. "It's a gift."

"He's a proud man."

"I'm a stubborn man."

The butcher told him the amount and Colin paid it.

"I expect *you* to tell him. I value my life too much to do it," Heinemeyer joked.

"I will," Colin reassured him. He extended his hand to Heinemeyer and the men shook. "I'll be traveling with Annie to San Francisco to ensure that she arrives safely."

"I'm certain you will, McBride." Heinemeyer winked. "Good luck to you."

As Colin left the shop, he wondered if his attraction to Annie was that obvious. He would have to keep his thoughts hidden better.

Colin strolled to the nearby department store to buy presents for Trev, Kate, and their children. After spending two hours picking out just the right items, he had the clerk wrap his purchases and put them in a box, then gave him the address. The man told Colin the gifts would be delivered by six o'clock that evening.

Colin's next order of business was to send wires to the broker he'd employed to search for a ranch in California and to the Spanish gentleman from whom he had bought his Andalusians. He told the clerk to send the replies by messenger to the Trevelyan home. Leaving the telegram office, he paused on the walkway and glanced up and down the street. People flowed in both directions, and the clop of horses' hooves, the occasional neigh of an animal, and the squeak of wagon wheels added to the city's din. For a man accustomed to the barren silence of the mountains, the noise was enough to make his temples throb. A buxom woman bumped him and caused him to put most of his weight on his sore leg. The matron glared at him and Colin was tempted to scowl back, but gentlemanly courtesy prevailed and he tipped his hat in apology.

His temper growing shorter with every passing minute, Colin waved down a hansom cab rather than take the cablecar.

"Union Station," he said as he painstakingly stepped up into the cab.

Settling back with a heartfelt sigh, he stared unseeing out the window. Why had he agreed to accompany Annie to San Francisco? It would add at least three more days to his journey.

Because Trev and Kate are my friends.

And what's Annie?

The kiss they had shared was anything but sisterly. Even thinking about it now made him yearn for another taste—a more thorough sample of the honey and fire that was Annie.

The cab rolled to a stop and Colin alit. "Wait for me here," he ordered the hackney driver.

"Aye, sir," the man replied.

Colin limped into the bustling depot, trying to avoid the jab of elbows and flurry of passengers boarding and disembarking. The lines for the ticket counters were long and Colin inwardly groaned. Finally, after a ten-minute wait, his turn came.

"A ticket to San Francisco on tomorrow's train, please," he said.

"I'm sorry, sir, but there are no seats left," the harried ticket agent said with a shake of his head. He looked to the customer behind Colin. "Next!"

Gritting his teeth, Colin remained in place and leaned against the counter, his face mere inches from the clerk's. "That's the nine-twenty to San Francisco?"

"Yep. She's booked solid. You could come by tomorrow and wait to see if someone doesn't show up," the agent said impatiently. "Nothing else I can do for you."

"There aren't even any places left in the club car?" Colin continued in a dangerously calm voice.

"I told you—booked solid. Nothing left anywhere. If you want a seat on the day after train, get it now. If you don't, please move on." He motioned to the line of people behind Colin. "I got other customers to take care of."

Colin's temper rose a few notches. "I have to go tomorrow. I'm to escort two women to San Francisco and they have tickets for that train." He ran a hand over his windblown hair and glared at the man. "What about a parlor car?"

The clerk's gaze raked across him skeptically. "How do you expect to pay for it?"

He wasn't the first person to judge Colin incorrectly. If a man didn't wear an expensive suit or use important-sounding words, he couldn't possibly have any money.

"Is there one or not?" Colin asked curtly.

The agent nodded reluctantly. "Some big shot from the railroad is coming in tomorrow from Kansas City. He'll be staying here for a week and no one's using the parlor car after him."

"I'll take it."

Still incredulous, the man told him the amount and Colin wrote out a draft without blinking an eye.

"The bank is here in Denver so you can get confirmation today that there's money to cover this." Colin handed him the check. "Who's the official coming in?"

The agent glanced down at a paper on another pile. "Rudolph James."

Colin smiled, the name eliciting pleasant memories. "I haven't seen Rudy in over two years. Maybe I'll run into him tomorrow."

"Uh, you might at that." The nonplussed ticket

agent handed him a paper to sign. After Colin had done so, the man filled in a form and gave it to him. "If you need anything, the porter will be happy to assist you, Mr. McBride."

"I'm sure he will," Colin said dryly, amused at the agent's abrupt change of attitude. He had ridden in parlor cars a number of times and wondered what Annie would think of the experience. Smiling to himself, he knew she would treat it much like she approached life—like an adventure.

He returned to his hansom cab and gave the driver his next destination—Trev's office. Though the past had been filled with difficult years, Colin had learned much from Trev, and not only about mining. In some ways, Trev had become a second father, and after tomorrow, Colin didn't know when he would see him again.

Determined to enjoy the beautiful early fall day, he turned his attention to the mothers and children strolling through the park. Tomorrow was soon enough to start missing his friends.

Whirlwind Annie abruptly dropped onto her bed and groaned aloud. Though it was only mid-morning, she was already exhausted.

"What's wrong?" Kate asked, pausing in her doorway.

"Nothing. Everything." Annie raised her arms above her head. "I want to go, but I don't want to." She lowered her arms and rolled onto her belly, propping her elbows on the mattress and resting her chin in her palms. "Does that make sense?"

Kate entered the room, perched on the bed, and laid her hand on her back. "Perfectly. It was the same way I felt when I left Kansas as a mail-order bride."

"You never told me you were a mail-order bride."

Kate smoothed the bedspread. "I had little choice. My father died, leaving me penniless and without any relatives. I had no beau and there was no man who wanted anything to do with me."

"Why?"

Kate smiled, humor reflecting in her eyes. "I think most of them were intimidated by my height. But that wasn't the main reason." Her amusement faded. "My father used to drink a lot, and when he did he became mean. Everybody learned to steer clear of him then, and it wasn't long before he was drunk all the time. By the time he died, he'd used every penny and more for liquor. Our home was so heavily mortgaged, there was no way I could possibly continue to live there. There were only two options for me: get a job in one of the saloons, or become a mail-order bride."

"Then how did you end up taking care of Brynn and me?"

"The man I came to Orion to marry died in a cave-in the same day I arrived. If your father hadn't offered me a job, I don't know what I would've done."

"So if the man hadn't died, you would have married him, not knowing anything about him?"

"I didn't believe I had any choice." Kate smoothed a strand of hair back from her step-daughter's forehead and smiled gently. "The unknown frightened me even more than the humiliation and loneliness of staying but I had to go. So you see, I understand what you're feeling."

Annie turned onto her back and stared at the ceiling. "The unknown doesn't scare me, Kate. I'm excited about seeing new places and meeting different people."

"Then what's wrong, sweetheart?"

She thought for a moment, hoping she could explain what frightened her so much about leaving her family and home. "I don't want anything to change while I'm gone. When I come back, I want everyone to be just like they are now."

"We all grow and change, Annie. That's life. And when you come back, you'll look at us through changed eyes—your experiences can't help but make you see things differently. It's all part of growing up."

"I guess maybe that's what I'm scared of—I don't want to become stodgy and ordinary, just like everyone else."

Kate's eyes danced. "Why do I get the feeling I've just been insulted?"

Annie sat up quickly, laying a hand on Kate's arm. "No, that wasn't what I meant."

"I know what you meant," Kate said with a little smile. "However, maybe what you're seeing as stodgy and ordinary is actually contentment."

"Is that what it is, Kate? I truly don't know. All I know for certain is that I want to see and do things that other people only imagine. I want to sail across the ocean and see the Royal Court in England and kangaroos in Australia and bushmen in Africa."

"And act on stages around the world," Kate added.

Annie nodded, not surprised her stepmother had guessed her fondest dream. "Yes."

"Your path won't be an easy one, sweetheart."

"You aren't going to try to talk me out of it?"

"Could I?"

Annie plucked at a loose thread on the coverlet. "No. Nobody could."

Kate studied her, her steadfast love as reassuring now as it had been when Annie was five years old. "Then all I can say is, be careful. There are people out there who will try to use your dream against you. Remember this, sweetheart—nothing in this world is free, and if it sounds too good to be true, it probably is."

Annie smiled. "Pearls of wisdom?"

"Stones of experience. You'll be running into all kinds of men. Some will be rocks and some will be gems—make sure you can tell the difference between the two."

"I can't imagine my father as a gem."

"He did have to be polished up a bit, but beneath it all, he's the kindest and most honest man I've ever met." Kate blushed. "And the handsomest."

Annie smiled absently. "What if you had never met him?"

"I can't imagine what my life would've been like without your father." She cupped Annie's cheek. "Or you and Brynn."

Annie's throat thickened and she wrapped her arms around her stepmother. "I can't imagine what our lives would've been like without you, either." She swallowed the lump in her throat. "I'm going to miss you so much."

"There's a part of me that wants to hold onto you and never let you go, but I know you would wither away if we didn't let you fly." Kate hugged her closer. "Just don't fly too close to the sun, sweetheart."

"I'll try not to." Annie's throat tightened. "But if I do, will you and Papa be there to catch me?"

"Always, Annie. Always," Kate promised her.

Annie roamed around the too-quiet house. The afternoon sun hung midway to the earth, casting long shadows both inside and out. Her father was still at work and Kate had taken the younger children to the park. Brynn and Lucy were off with some of their friends until suppertime. She had no idea where Colin was, which was a bone of contention at the moment.

Annie crossed to one of the windows and pushed aside the sheer curtain to peek outside.

Had Colin gone to see Margaret? The thought of the two of them together all day made her gnash her teeth. The least he could have done was greet her this morning before racing off to spend the day with *her*. After all, they had shared a kiss last night.

Annie traced her lips with her fingertip. If she closed her eyes, she could almost imagine the light touch was Colin. Almost.

A knock at the door surprised her and she rushed to answer it. Half expecting the caller to be Colin, she was startled by a burly man bearing a large box.

"This the Trevelyan residence?"

"Yes," Annie replied.

"I was told to deliver this here. Where can I put it?"

Annie pointed to a corner. "That would be fine."

The man carried it in and deposited it on the floor, then drew a piece of paper out of his pocket. "Just need you to sign here." He handed her a stubby pencil.

Frowning in confusion, Annie signed on the line. With a nod, the deliveryman left. She closed the door after him and turned to stare at the box. Never one to leave a mystery alone, Annie knelt down and opened it. Inside were various sized packages, wrapped in different colored paper. If it wasn't September, she would have thought they were Christmas presents. Peering down at them, she could make out a name on each. She picked them up one by one. By the time she was done, she'd found a package for everyone in the Trevelyan family but herself.

Annie replaced them carefully and closed the box. The only person she could think of who would do something like this was Colin. But if it was him, why hadn't he gotten something for her?

The exclusion stung. Maybe he was upset with her for asking him to kiss her. Men liked to be in charge and she doubted Colin was any different. He had probably been angry with her this morning and that was why he had left the house so early.

Another knock sounded. She rose to her feet, again expecting Colin. Pasting on a smile, she promised herself to remain calm and poised. She opened the door only to find Thomas standing on the other side.

"Thomas. What are you doing here?" she blurted.

"Is this a bad time?" he asked formally.

"Oh, no, I just wasn't expecting you."

"Who were you expecting? *Señor* McBride, perhaps?"

Annie shrugged. "Actually, yes." She drew him into the house. "Would you like some lemonade?"

"That would be very good, thank you."

Annie led him into the kitchen and pointed to a chair at the small table. "Have a seat." She opened a cupboard and pulled out two glasses.

"I'm glad you stopped by. We never really got the chance to say a decent good-bye last night."

"*Señor* McBride is a suspicious man."

Annie bit her tongue to halt her comment. She filled the two glasses with the pitcher from the icebox. "He thinks of me as a little girl still." She handed Thomas his lemonade and set her own on the table.

"He is only concerned for you. A woman of your age is usually married, giving her husband fine children."

"You make it sound like being a brood mare." Annie finished arranging molasses cookies on a plate and placed it on the table between her and Thomas. She lowered herself to her chair and dipped a cookie in her lemonade, then took a generous bite of it. "You know how I feel about that. I don't ever plan to marry."

"My mother says you are too spoiled and headstrong to be a good wife." Thomas stared at her intently, his dark eyes drilling into her. "I do not agree with her. I think you would be a very good wife."

The back of her neck tingled but she pushed aside the strange sensation. "As flattered as I am by your confidence, you should listen to your mother; she's a smart woman. I'd make a terrible wife. I'd never do what you told me and I don't like cooking."

Thomas shook his head. "No. When I was sixteen, I knew that someday you would be mine. I have waited four years, and tomorrow you are leaving. You cannot go, Annie."

She smiled nervously. "You know I've always thought of you as one of my dearest friends, but I don't love you that way. It's nothing against you, Thomas. It's just that I can't make myself fall in love."

"You care for me?"

"Of course. Like I said, you're my friend." She picked up another cookie. "And a friend is better than a husband."

"Why is it so impossible to think you could fall in love with me?"

"It just is, Thomas," she said flatly.

He unfolded his lean body and stood over her. A shiver swept through her, though she had never felt threatened by him before.

"You're scaring me, Thomas," she said, hoping her tremulous smile gave her words a teasing note.

He gripped her arms and tugged her to her feet, holding her firmly. The cookie fell from her hand, rolling across the floor and leaving crumbs in its wake.

"My family is wealthy, Annie. We owned a hacienda in Mexico. Soon it will be ours again and when it is, I want you by my side to rule it," Thomas said.

Annie wanted to pinch herself to see if she was awake or trapped in a nightmare. "I don't want to live on a hacienda in Mexico. I'm going to San

Francisco tomorrow." His fingers tightened and she clenched her teeth to keep from crying out against the pain. "You're hurting me, Thomas."

He ignored her plea. "You are mine."

Anger roiled through her, replacing the fear. "The hell I am. I don't belong to you or anyone else!" She struggled to escape his imprisoning grip, but only succeeded in driving his fingers deeper into her skin. "Let me go!"

"Not until you agree to stay here and allow me to court you in a fitting manner."

Shock stopped her efforts. "Are you crazy? Even if I stayed, I wouldn't let you court me. What is wrong with you, Thomas?"

His eyes smoldered with possessiveness. "Why do you fight me? I am still your friend. I only wish to be more now. Let me show you how good it can be."

He pulled her toward him, nearly lifting her off her feet, and lowered his head to hers.

He's going to kiss me.

Remembering what her father had taught her, Annie moved closer, pretending to acquiesce. Then she brought her knee up sharply, catching him in the crotch.

Thomas immediately released her as he groaned and grabbed at his privates.

"Keep away from me," Annie ordered, "or I'll cut it off next time."

Raising his head, Thomas glared at her. "You must learn your place, Annie."

"My place is where I want to be, not where you put me." Certain he would surrender, Annie planted her hands on her hips. "Get out of here, Thomas. You're not welcome anymore."

Still bowed over, he took a step toward her. "Please, Annie, you cannot mean this."

"Haven't you been listening to me? I don't plan to marry. And if I did, it most certainly would not be to you." Annie shook her head. "Especially now."

Thomas suddenly grabbed her arm and yanked her against him. Before Annie could blink, she found her head pressed into his chest. She managed to turn enough to draw some air in through her nose. "Let go!" she shouted. Thomas's arms were like steel vises around her.

"Please, Annie, marry me like you promised," Thomas whispered.

Suddenly she was stumbling backward as Thomas's grip disappeared. She clutched at a chair, preventing a fall, and stared at the two men who scuffled in the middle of the kitchen. She hadn't heard Colin return, but thank God he had.

Colin was the more experienced fighter and soon had Thomas on the floor, wiping at the blood on his chin.

"Get the hell out of here," Colin ordered in a low, venomous voice. "And if I ever see you again, you better damn well pray I don't have a gun on me."

Thomas glared at Colin. "Annie promised to marry me."

Colin snapped his head around to look at Annie. "Is that true?"

She brushed her hair back with a trembling hand. "When we were six years old, we made a silly promise to get married." She turned to look at Thomas. "We were only children. It didn't mean anything."

"But you said you loved me," Thomas said, his voice low and raspy.

She moved past Colin, ignoring his silent warning, and stood in front of Thomas. "I do, as a friend. Please, don't let our parting words be painful ones."

He stared at her, his eyes hard, but slowly he relented and reached out to take her hands in his. She nearly jerked out of his hold, but knew Colin wouldn't let him hurt her. "I'm sorry, Annie. I—I have loved you for years, but I will not force you." He took a deep breath and gazed down at their joined hands. "You are right. Our final words should not be of anger. Forgive me, Annie."

Her throat tightened. "I forgive you." She leaned forward and kissed his cheek. "Good-bye, Thomas."

He released her and gazed at her, his dark eyes filled with sadness. "If you change your mind, Annie, I will be waiting for you."

She shook her head, her throat tight. "I'm sorry, Thomas."

He sighed and with one final look at Colin, left.

Colin turned and laid his hands gently on Annie's shoulders. "Did he hurt you, lass?"

She shook her head, her emotions tangled into a knot. "No, but I don't think he's going to enjoy using the latrine for a few days," she said quietly.

"Did you—?" The corners of his lips quirked upward.

She nodded. "Papa will be happy I paid attention to his lesson."

Colin winced slightly with masculine empathy.

As Annie cleaned up the floor and table, Colin leaned against a kitchen counter and watched her, his expression somber. She hoped he would just let it lie and not question her anymore. At the moment, she was still trying to figure out what had happened.

"He didn't want you to go to San Francisco?" Colin asked.

Annie nearly dropped the glass she held in a shaking hand. "That's right. He said he wanted to marry me and take me to live in his family's hacienda in Mexico." She shuddered. "He's known for years what my dream has been."

She placed the glasses in the sink, along with the cookie plate, then turned to face Colin. "I can't imagine him believing a promise made when we were six." Her laughter caught in her throat and changed to a strangled sob. "What if I did something to make him think I cared for him that way?"

Colin's arms enfolded her and she leaned into his welcome embrace. Her sobs shook her body and he spoke soothing words close to her ear.

"Hush, lass. It wasn't your fault. Thomas only saw what he wanted to see," he crooned.

As they stood with arms wrapped around one another in the middle of the bright kitchen, Annie was content to let Colin's strength support her.

Finally, she raised her head and drew her hand across her damp eyes. "I got your nice vest all wet," she said with a quivering smile.

"It's had worse, lass." He thumbed away her tears.

His gentleness nearly undid her shaky control, but she managed to restrain any more tears. "I never knew, Colin. He never said a word."

"He was probably afraid."

Puzzled, she tilted back her head to gaze at him. "Afraid of what?"

"Afraid you didn't feel the same way."

"He had reason to be. He must have decided he had to make his move since I'm leaving tomorrow."

Colin nodded, brushing back the damp hair from her forehead. "Love is a tricky thing, lass. It strikes in the oddest places."

"He was one of my best friends."

"It wasn't enough for him." Colin's expression hardened. "But that's no excuse for him to be forcin' himself on you." He peered at her intently. "Are you sure you're all right?"

She grasped one of his hands and squeezed it gently. "He didn't hurt me." She paused for an awkward moment, then smiled gamely. "It reminds me a little of an act in a play."

Colin chuckled. "It would, imp." He stared down at her, his hazel eyes darkening. "I'm glad I'll be traveling with you tomorrow. I'm half-hoping Thomas will try something."

Annie shook her head. "He won't."

"If he does, it would give me a reason to shoot him."

Annie's mouth dropped open at his savage tone. "You wouldn't."

"How about if I just hit the knee?"

"Colin," she warned.

"A flesh wound?"

She fought down her laughter but her lips twitched. "Maybe a little one."

"That's my lass."

And Annie had to resist the urge to throw herself into his arms again.

Chapter 9

As Kate, Annie, and the children cleared the supper dishes, Trev caught Colin's attention and motioned to the front door. The younger man nodded and followed. Once outside, Trev withdrew two cigars from his breast pocket and handed one to Colin.

"This seems fitting. The first and last nights of my visit," Colin said with a touch of sadness.

Trev lit Colin's cigar, then his own. They puffed on them in companionable silence, watching the light breeze carry the smoke away.

"I stopped by the butcher's on the way home. He said you'd paid my bill," Trev said with a note of defensiveness.

Colin grinned. "I was under orders to tell you first so he wouldn't be the recipient of your wrath."

Trev snorted. "Like Heinemeyer couldn't take care of himself. You shouldn't have, Colin."

"I wanted to."

Another long moment of listening to the unceasing sounds of the city and the closer rustlings from the small night creatures.

"You're doing all right, then?" Trev asked hesitantly.

"I'm doing fine," Colin replied with tolerant amusement. It was strange to have Trev worry about him after all these years of living on his own.

His thoughts, which had not strayed far from Thomas's attack on Annie since it had occurred, returned again to the young man. Annie had asked him not to tell anyone, but Colin hadn't promised. He thought Trev should know in the event Thomas tried something tonight or tomorrow morning.

"What's bothering you?" Trev asked astutely.

Colin smiled crookedly. "I never could get anything past you, Trev."

"You never tried too hard."

"Aye, that's true. I've always valued your friendship and advice, Trev. You were always straight with me, even when I was a green kid." He tapped the ash from his cigar, his throat suspiciously tight. "What do you know about Thomas Morales?"

"We've known the Moraleses since we moved here. He and Annie have been friends for almost as long. Why?"

"Has he ever given you the impression he might be dangerous?"

He heard Trev's sharp inhalation. "No. Why?"

Colin took a deep breath and told him what had happened earlier in the kitchen.

"That son-of-a—" Trev marched toward the porch steps.

Colin grabbed his arm. "Where are you going?"

"To teach him a lesson. No one touches my children."

"Let it go, Trev. Between Annie and me, we got the point across." Colin paused and added reluctantly, "Before he left, he apologized to her. He seemed sincere."

The tense muscles beneath Colin's hand jumped, then relaxed. Trev's shoulders slumped and he leaned against the porch rail. "I had no idea."

"Neither did Annie, and she knew him better than you," Colin said. "I didn't tell you so you would beat him up. I just wanted you to know in case he tried anything again."

Trev jerked his head up. "Do you think he will?"

"It depends on how badly he wants Annie."

"What if he boards the train tomorrow?"

"The ticket clerk told me they were all sold out."

"Then how did you—?"

"I have my ways." Colin removed his cigar and stared at the glowing embers at the end. "If he tries to get close to Annie again, I'll take care of him."

"Only if you beat me to it," Trev said without hesitation.

Colin grinned savagely. "I'm glad we agree."

"He didn't hurt her, did he?" Trev asked quietly a few moments later.

"No. He scared her, though."

"You said Annie got her point across?"

"I believe you taught her the finer points of defendin' her virtue against a man's unwelcome advances," Colin said, amused.

Comprehension struck a moment later and Trev's eyes widened. "So my little girl got him where it hurt."

"Aye. Right in the balls."

Colin and Trev eyed one another a moment, then broke into laughter.

The two men finished their cigars in comfortable camaraderie, discussing their future. As the quarter moon rose, Colin and Trev snuffed out their stubs and returned to the house. The sound of children's voices and giggles came from the parlor. Trev started down the hall to join his family.

"I'll be there in a minute. There's somethin' I have to get from my room," Colin said.

Retrieving the box that had been delivered that afternoon, Colin carried it into the large room. He was gratified to see everyone was there, including Annie. His gaze caught hers and she smiled, sending a wave of heat through his belly. He quickly turned away.

"Could I have your attention?" he called out.

Everyone, even little Kathryn, paused to look at him.

"I'd like to celebrate Christmas three months early," Colin said.

"You didn't," Kate said softly, looking at the box.

"I did." Colin shrugged unrepentantly. "You can't deny an old bachelor like me a little fun, can you?"

Matthew and Michael pawed at the box, trying to see what was in it.

"No, you don't," Colin said with a grin, batting their hands away playfully. "You'll have to wait your turn like everyone else."

The twins, Darcy, Lucy, and Brynn gathered around on the floor, while Kate held Kathryn in her lap as she sat beside Trev on the sofa. Annie tucked her legs beneath her on the love seat and made no attempt to draw closer to the group. Though she wore a smile, it didn't touch her eyes. Colin assumed she was still upset about Thomas.

He reached into the box and pulled out the first gift. "This is for Darcy."

The boy who had been named after Colin's brother reached for it with two hands. "Thank you."

"You're welcome. It's a bit heavy there, lad."

Darcy opened it carefully, as if afraid to rip the paper. He lifted out a cast-iron figure of a brightly painted clown sitting on a sphere. Smiling, Darcy traced the clown's face with a fingertip.

Colin reached into his pocket and pulled out five pennies. He handed them to Darcy. "Put a penny on his head, then press the switch."

Puzzled, Darcy did as Colin said. After pushing the lever, the clown began to move, shifting until it stood on its hands and the coin fell into a hole the clown had been sitting on. Darcy clapped his hands and everyone laughed and marveled at the mechanical bank.

Colin passed out the presents one by one, delighted to see everyone liked theirs. He'd gotten Kathryn a jack-in-the-box and each of the twins received a wind-up train. Brynn's ivory jackknife and Lucy's beautiful china doll were oohed and aahed over. The deep green silk scarf for Kate complemented her golden glow and Trev accepted the box of expensive cigars with an appreciative grin.

As everyone admired each other's gifts, Colin walked over to sit by Annie. He lowered himself with a slight hiss at the sharp ache that ran up his leg.

Annie glanced at him in concern, but seemed to understand he didn't want her sympathy. She motioned toward the children. "Uncle Colin has now taken on legendary proportions."

"That wasn't my intent. I just wanted to get everyone a little something."

Annie rested her palm on his forearm. "I know. That's why it's so special."

Michael and Matthew had set up their trains on a collision course in the center of the room, but fortunately the toys were made of tin and survived the crash.

Suddenly Michael glanced up at them. "Hey, what about Annie?"

"Yeah, where's her present?" Matthew added.

Colin smiled and reached into his breast pocket to withdraw a small box. "You didn't think I forgot about your sister, did you?"

"Open it, Annie!" the boys said together.

Her eyes glistened as she took the present and opened it with trembling fingers. Inside, on a bed of velvet, sat a gold necklace. Her mouth made an "O" as she picked it up to see the charm on the chain. "It's an angel."

"With a crooked halo," Colin added, pointing to the ring set at an angle on the cherub's head.

Annie grinned. "Why doesn't that surprise me?" She threw her arms around Colin's neck. "Thank you. It's perfect."

"I thought so," Colin said smugly.

Annie withdrew and punched him in the arm. Her eyes danced with mischief. "You would." She held the necklace up to Colin. "Put it on me, please."

He took it from her and she turned. Gathering her long hair, Annie piled it on top of her head so he could fasten the chain at the back of her neck. Colin took his time, allowing his fingers to brush the fine hairs on her nape. He longed to press his lips to the satiny skin above the necklace's clasp.

"There," he said huskily.

She allowed the blond tresses to tumble down

her back and without thought, Colin skimmed his hand along her silky hair. Desire shot a path straight to his masculinity, taking the blood from his brain with it.

Annie turned and her flushed face told Colin he wasn't the only one affected.

"That's a lovely necklace," Kate said, halting Colin's desire in its tracks.

"Isn't it?" Annie asked breathlessly. "Colin says I'm an angel with a crooked halo."

Trev chuckled. "Sometimes yours fell off, but you always picked it up, shined it, and put it back on your head."

Colin and Kate laughed at Annie's feigned outrage.

Then Annie leaned her head against Colin's shoulder, bringing a rush of awareness to his blood. It spread through his limbs, sparking his nerves and making him conscious of every breath she drew and the gentle thrumming of her heart. He raised his arm to rest it on the back of the couch and she snuggled closer. She shuddered slightly and Colin suspected she was thinking of the incident with Thomas.

"How are you doin', lass?" he asked softly.

He felt her shrug. "I'm still confused and wondering if I gave Thomas the wrong impression at some time."

"It wasn't you, lass. It was him," he reassured, wrapping his arm around her shoulders.

"I suppose you're right." Annie rested her neck

against Colin's arm as she watched her family. "I'm going to miss this the most."

"What?"

"For as long as I can remember, everyone gathered in the parlor after supper unless Papa and Kate had to attend some social. When I was Lucy's age I hated it, but now it'll be what I miss most of all."

"You'll be back."

"It won't be the same."

Colin wished he had some reassuring words for her, but he couldn't even claim understanding. Everyone in his family had started working at the age of six and it was rare when they all sat down together. Looking around the room at the healthy, happy children, Colin knew this was what he wanted for his own family—and with his wise investments, he could afford it.

Now all he had to do was find a wife.

Trev spoke up again. "I know you aren't happy about leaving tomorrow, Annie, but I want you to know I wouldn't be doing this if I didn't think it was for the best." He paused, his eyes glistening suspiciously. "After you've been there for two weeks, if you still think it's so terrible, I'll buy you a train ticket to come home. I wouldn't want you to be miserable for six months."

"I'm sure it'll be fine once I get used to it, Papa," she reassured him, though she still looked melancholy.

"Is everything all right, angel?" Trev asked.

She smiled. "Everything is just fine." She glanced around the room one last time and wistfulness replaced her grin. "I think I'll go to bed. It'll be a long day tomorrow. Goodnight."

She stood, then paused as her fingers wrapped around the cherub at her neck. "Thank you, Colin."

"You're welcome, lass."

Annie called out her goodnights to her brothers and sisters as she wove her way through them and their new toys.

"What was that about?" Trev asked.

"She's nervous," Kate replied. "It's her first time so far away from home and for such a long time."

Colin wasn't so certain, but he remained silent. Something was bothering Annie, something beyond Thomas and leaving home.

"She'll be all right," Kate reiterated, trying to reassure her husband.

With more than a touch of envy, Colin watched Kate and Trev hold hands. The simple gesture spoke eloquently of their love and taunted Colin with the absence of something so precious in his own life.

Suddenly restless, Colin pushed himself to his feet. "Annie's right. It'll be a long day tomorrow. I'll see you in the morning."

"Goodnight, Colin," Kate said. "And thank you again for volunteering to take care of our Annie."

"My pleasure."

Colin hoped she and Trev couldn't read the wealth of truth in those two words.

Although Annie had been awake since four o'clock, she forced herself to remain in bed until six. What little sleep she had gotten had been fraught with snippets of nightmares starring Thomas in the leading role. One time she thought she had yelled out loud, awakening herself, but nobody had come to check on her. She was glad. She didn't want to have to confess to Kate or her father what had happened with Thomas. It was humiliating enough that Colin knew.

With the sun beginning to break the horizon, the nightmares faded. Her stomach fluttered with apprehension and excitement, and she doubted she would be able to eat anything for breakfast.

She made her bed like she did every morning, but spent more time at her toilette than usual. Looking her best would make her feel more confident and she would need all the self-assurance she could muster today.

She finished dressing by six forty-five and headed downstairs. Familiar breakfast smells enveloped her in tranquillity, followed closely by a pang of loneliness. She paused on one of the lower stairs, imprinting the sights, scents, and sounds of her home on her memory to recall whenever she felt homesick. She knew there would be many days filled with loneliness in the weeks ahead.

"Morning, Annie."

She spun around and nearly lost her balance on the step. "What're you doing sneaking up on a person like that?"

"I wasn't sneaking. Your mind was miles away," Colin said.

"You still shouldn't scare a person to death."

He grinned. "You look pretty alive to me, lass." His gaze flickered down to her neck. "You're wearing it."

She tossed her long braid over her shoulder and came down the remaining stairs. "It looked nice with this dress."

"Of course it does."

She stopped so fast, Colin bumped into her back. "Is that another comment on your wonderful taste?"

"Why, thank you. I do have extraordinary good taste, don't I?"

She tried to hold her glare, but the smile tugging at her lips wouldn't be dissuaded. "You got lucky this time."

Colin cleared his throat and his eyes twinkled. The implication of her words struck her and her face warmed with embarrassment.

"Let's go have breakfast before Brynn comes down and devours everything in sight," Annie said, determined to ignore the innuendo. She grabbed his arm and tugged him along into the kitchen.

"Morning, Kate," Annie and Colin said together.

Kate smiled and wiped her hands on her apron. "Good morning. You two look like you've been up to mischief."

"Don't blame it on me. It was Colin's fault," Annie said.

"*Now* what did I do?" Colin asked innocently.

She merely smirked in reply.

Kate wisely ignored the interplay. "Get a plate and dish up whatever you'd like. Eggs will be ready in another minute, and there's flapjacks and biscuits warming in the oven."

"Oooh," Annie groaned as she opened the oven. "You even made cinnamon rolls."

"Your favorite." Kate stirred the scrambled eggs. "Your father should be down in another minute. He was dressing Kathryn."

"Why isn't he at work?"

"Did you actually think he wouldn't see you off at the train depot?"

Annie shrugged, though inwardly a weight lifted from her chest. "I didn't know."

She hadn't wanted to say good-bye to him last night—she wasn't certain she could do it without breaking into tears. But she didn't want to leave without seeing him one last time.

Colin urged her along and once they had their plates filled, moved into the dining room to sit by the table. Annie picked at her roll halfheartedly.

"If you're going to torture the poor thing, give it to me. I'll take care of it," Colin said.

"Would you like some?" She held a bite-sized piece out to him.

Colin narrowed his eyes and leaned forward. He took the piece from her, his lips touching her fingers. She kept her gaze locked with his and licked the fingertips which had just been so near to his mouth. "Mmmmmm," she murmured.

"Imp," Colin growled.

"Knave," she shot back.

"Guilty." His eyes darkened. "I'll take some more, if you're not going to eat it."

Annie recognized the challenge.

Two can play this game.

She twisted off another piece of the sweet bread, noticing in satisfaction that it was an especially gooey part. Annie leaned forward, tempting him with it. She moved it closer and Colin stared into her eyes as he bent forward to take it from her fingertips again.

Suddenly she smushed it against his nose and the piece of roll stuck to the tip of it. Annie burst into laughter as Colin removed the bread, but left a syrupy ring behind.

"So you thought that was funny, did you?" Colin asked calmly—too calmly.

"It was . . . p-pretty funny," Annie admitted in between giggles.

Still unruffled, Colin used his napkin to wipe the end of his nose. He picked up a muffin slathered with strawberry jam and took a deliberate bite out of it. Chewing unhurriedly, Colin watched Annie.

"Uh, what are you thinking, Colin?" Annie asked nervously.

"What do you *think* I'm thinkin', lass?"

"That you're mad at me?"

He shook his head and narrowed his eyes. "I never get mad, lass, I get even."

Suddenly a muffin, complete with jam, was pressed to her mouth. It fell to her plate when Colin let go of it.

She licked her lips. "Not bad, but I prefer my jam with more strawberries in it."

"Really?" Colin said thoughtfully.

"Good mor—" Trev's greeting was interrupted by a puzzled, "What's going on?"

Annie was barely able to contain her mirth. "Colin wanted to taste my cinnamon roll in exchange for a piece of his muffin with strawberry jam."

Trev dropped down into a chair with Kathryn in his lap. "I see."

"Dada, dada," Kathryn said excitedly, pointing to Annie's red-smeared face. "Messy."

"Yep, messy, all right." Trev angled a look at Colin, who was casually eating his eggs. "What have you got to say for yourself?"

Colin glanced up with feigned confusion. "Kate makes great cinnamon rolls?"

"Uh-huh." Trev stood Kathryn on his thighs so that she was at eye level with him. "I think your big sister and Uncle Colin are not setting a very good example. In fact, I would say that you and I are the most mature people in this room."

Kathryn giggled and leaned over to swipe some jam from Annie's face. She put her finger in her mouth and smiled in delight.

Annie and Colin gave up the battle and laughter filled the room.

Chapter 10

~~~~~~

Annie clung to the wagon's wooden seat as
her father steered around the crowds at the
train depot. Colin sat beside him in the front
while Annie, Kate, and Margaret Mopplewhite
were squished together like sardines on the seat
behind them. Glad she was on an end rather than
in the middle where Kate sat, Annie could absorb
the bustling chaos of the station.

Her two trunks and suitcases were stowed in
the back, taking up most of the room. Fortunately,
Margaret had brought only one large suitcase, but
then, she was spending a mere three weeks in
California—unless she and Colin came to an
agreement. Annie still had difficulty imagining
them romantically involved. Although Colin was
three years senior to Margaret, Annie couldn't

help thinking she was too old for him. It didn't stand to reason, but when it came to her feelings for Colin, nothing seemed to make sense.

She had never gotten around to asking him if he had spent yesterday with Margaret, but the more she thought about it, the more she didn't think he had. Buying all the presents as well as purchasing his train ticket had probably taken most of the day. Besides, neither he nor Margaret had mentioned seeing one another since the evening they had attended the theater.

Annie couldn't help but be perversely pleased with that conclusion.

"Is your young man seeing you off?" Margaret asked, as the wagon slowed in the traffic around the depot.

"My young ma—oh, you mean Thomas?" Annie used her acting skills to hide her queasiness and smiled a little too brightly. "No, he was only a friend."

She glanced at Kate and the compassion in her stepmother's eyes told Annie she knew about Thomas's attack. Colin must have told her and Papa. She should be angry, but she was surprisingly relieved her parents knew.

"Such a handsome, polite young man. Those are quite rare these days," Margaret continued.

Annie shuddered inwardly. "Yes, he *was* rare, wasn't he?"

"Perhaps you should have attempted to gain his favor."

Annie bit the inside of her cheek to keep from

snapping a sharp rebuttal. It wasn't Margaret's fault that she didn't know Annie's feelings toward marriage or Thomas's unwelcome proposal. For old times' sake, Annie would keep quiet about his behavior—she owed him that much.

"Thomas and I had been friends since we were six years old. Since my feelings have been nothing more than brotherly toward him, I couldn't lead him on that way," she said.

Margaret smiled. "He's much like Colin is, then."

Nothing like Colin. "Why's that?"

"You are like his little sister."

The vivid memory of the kiss she and Colin shared in the parlor two nights ago returned. What she had felt had been nothing like sibling love. Oh, no, definitely not. She had finally learned firsthand what lust could do to a body, and it was a heady feeling. She understood a little better why a woman might imprison herself in a marriage. Glancing at her stepmother, Annie knew she was being unfair. Marriage wasn't a prison to couples who loved one another.

"Colin and Annie have known each other for years," Kate said, filling the silence. "He used to carry her around on his shoulders and try to keep her out of trouble."

"Not much has changed," Colin said, turning around in the seat ahead of them. He smiled and winked at Annie. "Right, lass?"

Annie wrinkled her nose. "Have you ever

thought of going into vaudeville with that sense of humor?"

"And here I thought you didn't believe I had one." Colin placed his hand on his heart. "You wound me, lass."

"Yes, you're soooo sensitive."

Margaret's mouth gaped slightly as Kate covered her own smile with her palm. Annie was hard-pressed to keep her face straight as she bantered with Colin.

"Wouldn't you be knowin' how sensitive Irishmen are?" Colin said with an exaggerated brogue. "Why, a pretty love poem can bring a tear to the most hardened Irish heart."

"Would it bring a tear to your heart?" Annie asked, canting an eyebrow.

"Love would, lass."

Colin's steady gaze unsettled Annie, making her wonder if he could see more than she wanted him to see . . . more than she wanted to see within herself.

The wagon came to a halt and the conversation ceased. Annie's heart thumped in rhythmic harmony with the brisk activity surrounding them and the excitement of what was to come.

"I'll go find a porter to take care of our luggage." Colin hopped down from the wagon and Annie heard his slight hiss and saw him limp as he moved into the crowd. She wished she could kiss it and make it all better, just as he had done for her as a child when she had skinned an elbow or knee. Back then his kisses had made her laugh;

now they made her insides warm and mushy. Sighing, she allowed her father to help her down from the wagon.

She shaded her eyes against the early morning sun as she absorbed the sights, sounds, and smells. Denver was large, with well over a hundred thousand people, but San Francisco was supposed to be even bigger. She had spent hours reading about it—Nob Hill, the opera house, Fisherman's Wharf, the Chinese and their section of the city, and the overabundance of theaters. She smiled. Deep in her heart, she knew one of those theaters would have a place for her.

"Woolgathering, angel?" her father asked.

Annie turned to see him standing directly behind her, his expression teasing. A wave of love washed through her and she fought back the tears that sprang to her eyes. The years disappeared and she could clearly recall his rich laughter as he'd twirled her around and around when she was a girl. The recent quarrels faded away under the wonderful memories she held close to her heart.

"Just thinking," she replied huskily.

Trev wrapped an arm around her shoulders, his size dwarfing her, but it didn't anger her like it usually did. She only felt loved and secure, just as she had as a child. "I'm going to miss you, Annie," he said quietly. "You've always been my little angel." He lifted the tiny cherub on her necklace and smiled tenderly. "Laddie picked your gift well."

Annie's throat tightened and she swallowed convulsively.

"I trust him with you, which means I trust him with my life." Her father took a deep breath and looked up. "He's coming back with a porter."

Annie turned to see Colin stopping to shake hands with a man in an expensive suit. The porter halted, too, but Colin sent him on. She watched curiously as Colin and the stranger visited as if they were old friends.

"Who is he, Papa?" she asked curiously.

"I don't know. Maybe someone Colin worked with on the railroad."

Colin wasn't surprised to see Rudy James—he had half-expected to cross his path this morning. The hand he shook was still strong, not weakened by the past three years Rudy had spent working behind a desk.

"It's good to see you, Rudy," Colin said with genuine fondness. "I was hoping to run into you; I heard you were coming in this morning. You didn't leave the parlor car a mess, did you?"

Rudy ignored the good-natured gibe. "I was told somebody had leased the car to San Francisco. You were the last person I expected it to be." Rudy was ten years older than Colin, with thinning hair and weathered skin that had grown paler but no less leathery since he had worked the line with Colin. The long, lonely hours of their job had turned the two men into good friends.

Colin shrugged. "Did you know I'd resigned?"

Rudy nodded somberly. "Your paper came across my desk, but I wasn't surprised. After those days trapped in the tunnel, I probably would have made the same decision."

Black fear clenched Colin's gut and he had to force a smile. "It's over and I'm alive."

"With all the railroad shares you own, I'm surprised you didn't just demand a place in management. There were those who thought you would."

"My heart wasn't in it anymore."

Rudy's perceptive gaze searched his face. "So why are you headed to San Francisco?"

"I'm going to buy a ranch, and raise horses and a family."

Rudy's eyes widened in shock. "That doesn't sound like the footloose man I used to know."

"Things change," Colin said quietly.

The older man studied him for a moment. "Have you married?"

"Not yet. But I'm working on it." Colin glanced toward the Trevelyans and waved at them. Annie lifted her hand in reply.

Rudy whistled low, his gaze on Annie. "With a woman like that, a man could go far."

Jealousy and anger surged through Colin. "She's not the one," he managed to say evenly. "I've known her father for fifteen years."

"So she's like a sister?"

"I suppose you could say that," Colin said reluctantly. "I'm traveling with her and her chaperone to San Francisco so she can attend a finishing school." He paused. "Margaret, her chaperone, is a widow. She's the woman I'm considering to be my wife. She's healthy and has a sensible head on her shoulders."

Rudy dragged his gaze away from Annie and shook his head. "Sounds like you're looking to buy breeding stock."

Shocked, Colin took a step back. At that exact moment, a gunshot sounded and Rudy was thrown back as if an invisible hand had shoved him. He slumped onto the wooden platform. Instinct made Colin drop to the ground as another shot rang out. The bullet lodged in the boardwalk by Colin's leg and wood splinters exploded.

An unnatural silence filled the air. Half-expecting a bullet in the back, Colin crawled closer to Rudy and spotted a line of blood on his left temple.

"What the hell happened?" Rudy demanded hoarsely.

"Somebody shot you." Colin clenched his teeth.

Colin heard footsteps and jerked his head up. Trev, keeping low, scurried toward them. Annie followed three paces behind, her face pale but determined and Colin's heart tightened with his fear that the shooter was still out there.

"Keep down," he shouted.

Trev and Annie hunched over as they crossed the remaining distance.

Trev knelt beside him. "What happened?"

"It was an ambush. Annie, you should've stayed with Kate and Margaret!"

She lifted her chin in familiar stubbornness. "Whoever it was is gone."

Colin gritted his teeth, and turned back to Rudy. "How're you feeling?"

The vice president of the railroad swore under his breath. "Other than a headache the size of the Rockies, I'm all right. Help me up, Colin."

With Trev on one side and Colin on the other, they aided the injured man to a sitting position. Rudy placed his hands against his head and groaned.

Colin looked up to see an overweight man dressed in a railroad uniform waddling over to join them. "What . . . happened here?" he demanded between puffs. He glanced down at Rudy and his eyes widened. "God almighty. Are you . . . all right, Mr. James?"

"No, but at least I'm not dead," he replied wryly.

Colin chuckled. "Still the same bad sense of humor."

"Aren't you going to introduce me to your friends, Colin?" Rudy asked.

"Rudy, this is Trev Trevelyan and his daughter Annie. Trev, Annie, this is Rudy James," Colin said.

Rudy shook Trev's, then Annie's hand, lingering longer than necessary with the young woman's. "Tell me you aren't married, my dear."

"No, and I have no plans to ever be tied down, Mr. James," Annie said with an amused smile.

Colin separated Rudy's hand from Annie's and said dryly, "That's a good thing, since your wife might not approve of your interest Rudy."

He tilted Rudy's head back and examined the gash on his forehead. "You should get to a doctor and have that cleaned out. It's going to need some stitches, too."

Colin heard more thundering feet and spotted two officious-looking men running over to join them. Recognizing one of them, he knew immediately they were part of Rudy's entourage.

"What the hell happened?" the one Colin didn't know demanded.

"Somebody tried to kill him," Colin replied.

"McBride?" The other man, Leonard Jenkins, asked as he stared at Colin.

Smiling, Colin extended his hand to one of the men who'd been working on his crew when the tunnel had collapsed. Leonard's brother had died in that same cave-in Colin had hurt his leg in so badly. "How've you been, Jenkins?"

"Better, now that I'm out of the tunnel business. Looks like you finally got smart, too."

"It took a few tons of rock to convince me, but yeah, I got out of the business, too."

"I hate to interrupt this little reunion, but Mr. James should be taken to a doctor," Annie broke in.

"Such an intelligent young woman, too,"

Rudy commented, his admiring gaze wandering over her.

"Don't even think about it," Annie warned. "I just don't want to see you bleed all over the depot."

Colin fought a grin at her feisty reply. "She's right. We'll have to catch up some other time."

Rudy's two business associates helped him to his feet.

"I'll have someone look into this," Rudy said, his expression now somber. "I've made a few enemies in my line of work." He paused, searching Colin's face. "You have, too."

"None that would want to kill me."

"I wouldn't bet on that," Rudy said.

Colin glanced at Jenkins, who was also nodding in agreement. "I'll be careful." He shook hands with Rudy, then Jenkins. "Good luck."

"You, too," Rudy said.

They walked away with Rudy supported between his two assistants, and with them went the gawking crowd. Colin had been so intent on making sure his friend wasn't badly hurt he hadn't even noticed the people who had gathered around.

"Are you all right?" Trev asked Colin.

"Fine. The first bullet got Rudy. The second missed us both."

"Who is he?"

"Rudy? One of the three vice presidents of the railroad line."

"The vice president is a friend of yours?" Annie asked with wide eyes.

He smiled crookedly. "We met about nine years ago. We were both working on the line—he was my supervisor. He moved up in management but I stayed in the blasting business until the, uh, accident."

Trev frowned but didn't comment. Annie, with her inexhaustible curiosity, looked like she could make the Inquisition seem like a cakewalk with the questions flitting in her eyes.

"The train will be leaving in fifteen minutes. We'd better make sure our things get aboard," Colin said, hoping Annie would at least postpone her curiosity.

As he walked back to the wagon where the porter was piling their luggage on a conveyance, Colin considered Rudy's words. What if he *had* been the target and not Rudy?

What if the traffic incident when he and Annie had been walking home from the butcher's shop hadn't been an accident? Could that have been the first attempt to kill him and this the second?

But it made no sense. Who would hate him so much? Colin kept his face expressionless, though fearful rage surged through him. Annie could have been killed by the wagon three days ago, and Rudy was fortunate he'd suffered only a flesh wound. How much longer could luck intervene if someone truly was after him?

He glanced at Annie, then at Margaret. What if

something happened to either of them when they were under his protection?

Damn. It was too late to change their plans. Besides, the train had been booked solid and Colin doubted if the killer—if he was indeed after him—had bought a ticket before they were sold out. The attacker wouldn't have known Colin was going to California.

Colin surreptitiously searched the faces in the crowd. He didn't recognize anyone, but then he didn't expect to. For all he knew, he was being paranoid, but with Annie's life in his hands, he couldn't afford to ignore the possibility. He would remain vigilant throughout the entire trip.

Annie's life depended on it.

All the trunks and suitcases were loaded and the passengers began to board. Because of the shooting, the train was running thirty minutes late.

Annie stood off to the side while her father and Kate thanked Margaret again for chaperoning her to California. Annie brushed at her eyes when her parents said good-bye to Colin—Kate giving him a hug and kiss, while her papa shook his hand, then gave in to his emotions and pulled him into a back-slapping embrace.

Colin helped Margaret up the three steps into the train car. He remained standing there, giving Annie privacy to say her farewells.

A tear rolled down her stepmother's cheek and

Annie forced herself to take quick, short breaths. She had no intention of breaking into a feminine show of tears.

"Write as often as you can, sweetheart," Kate whispered, holding her close.

"I will," Annie promised, a hitch in her voice.

Kate stepped back and Annie found her father directly in front of her. She tipped her head back to meet his eyes and was shocked to find them glistening with moisture. Her throat ached with a damning fullness and she couldn't speak to save her life. Her big, strong father seemed to have the same problem, and he suddenly drew her into the shelter of his arms.

"I love you, Annie." She could barely hear his husky voice as he spoke against her hair.

"I love you, too, Papa," she managed to sneak out past the lump.

Before she lost her courage, she drew away from him and dashed into the train car, barely noticing Colin's helping hand.

"I'll take care of her," she heard Colin say solemnly to her parents. "I promise."

Then Colin was beside her, his firm hand on her waist as he guided her into a spacious car. She glanced around through tear-blurred eyes and noted no rows of uncomfortable seats. Instead, a plush sofa was anchored against the center of one wall. A love seat and two chairs were connected to the wall across from it, with Margaret sitting primly in one chair. In a corner sat a table with two benches braced against the walls. There was a discreet curtained-off area which Annie assumed contained a chamber pot. An Oriental carpet covered the floor and fancy shades were rolled up to allow the sun's light and warmth into the car.

Before she could ask any questions, the train's whistle blew three short bursts.

"We'd better sit down. The train is getting ready to pull out," Colin said.

He escorted her to the sofa and she lowered herself to it gratefully. He sat at the other end, giving her time to regain her composure.

The clang of the metal couplings warned them a second before the train lurched ahead. They were leaving. Annie frantically twisted around and peered out the window behind her. Kate and her father stood on the platform, her papa's arm around her stepmother's shoulders and hers around his waist. Annie waved and they spotted her, waving as furiously as she. The sad smiles on their faces tore at Annie's control. Would this be the last time she saw them?

"Are you all right, lass?" Colin asked gently.

She nodded, uncertain whether her voice would cooperate.

"It's perfectly natural," Margaret said, her eyes damp as she dabbed them with a dainty white handkerchief. She sent Annie an understanding smile. "Go ahead and let it out, dear."

Though Margaret was sincere, her words made Annie steel her backbone. She had never been one to share her sadness; it seemed wrong to have others see her weakness. Tonight when the darkness hid her tears, she would give in to the loneliness.

"I'm fine. It was just a momentary lapse," Annie said firmly, stuffing her hanky back in her reticule.

A smile teased Colin's lips. "Somehow, that doesn't surprise me."

She sniffed and chose to ignore his comment. "So what are we doing in here? I thought we had seats in one of the passenger cars."

Colin shrugged. "You do, but I don't. When I went to buy my ticket yesterday, they were sold out. I had to settle for this."

"You mean since they didn't have a seat for you, they gave you this car?" Annie asked incredulously.

"In a manner of speaking."

Annie considered this new piece of information along with Colin's friendship with the important railroad official. There was something Colin was hiding from her. "Why?"

He let out a little sigh of impatience. "I used to work for the railroad, Annie. Because of that, I get some special considerations."

"Like this car?"

"Like this car," he confirmed.

She eyed him closely. "What other kind of considerations do you get?"

"I can tell them to throw certain passengers off the train if they get too nosy."

Annie scowled. "Ha ha. Very funny."

Colin waved an admonishing finger at her. "Do you want to walk all the way to San Francisco?"

"The company would probably be better." Annie glanced at Margaret. "Present female company excepted, of course."

The older woman's lips twitched. "I can see this trip won't be boring with you two along to amuse me."

Surprised but pleased by Margaret's sly humor, Annie shook her head in mock horror. "How did I ever end up with the two of you?"

Colin canted an eyebrow. "Lucky?"

Annie groaned. "It had to have been that mirror I broke last year—seven years of bad luck, you know."

"Think on the bright side, Annie: only six years left," Margaret said.

Colin laughed and Annie couldn't help but join in. The joking had gotten her past the first wave of sadness and she suspected Colin and Margaret had known it would.

She realized she could come to like the older woman, which would make it even more difficult if Colin courted her all the way to California. How could Annie just sit by and watch Colin whisper sweet nothings in Margaret's ear?

However, the image amused her. He didn't seem the type to court a woman with flowery words and Shakespearean quotes. Colin would be blunt, to the point. If he wanted to kiss a woman, he wouldn't ask permission, but merely do it.

Unless the woman asked him. She still found it hard to believe she had actually had the courage to ask him, but she was glad she had.

The only problem was she wanted to ask him again . . . and again . . . and again . . .

Chapter 11

Colin was amused by Annie's ceaseless energy. Margaret had fallen asleep after only an hour of the train wheels' steady clacking rhythm. He had dug a book out of his suitcase and settled in to read, but Annie's constant motion kept drawing his attention.

She would sit for two minutes, squirming in her seat and twisting around to look out the windows on both sides of the car. Then she would stand up and walk around, keeping her balance with a delicate hand poised on a piece of furniture or the paneled wall. She examined everything—from the plush maroon material of the sofas and chairs to the gold gaslight fixtures on the wall to the icebox which held cool drinks and food the railroad provided for their special guests who rode in the Pullmans.

"This is how rich people travel, isn't it?" she asked as she leaned over to peer into the roomy sleeping compartment with one berth over another.

Guiltily, Colin shifted his gaze from her backside. "It's how people who can afford it travel."

Annie dropped the curtain back in place across the sleeping area and crossed over to sit on the sofa beside Colin. "I'm bored."

"We've been traveling less than two hours."

She crossed her arms and bounced a heel on the floor. "How long does it take to get there?"

"Three days with all the stops."

Her foot halted six inches above the floor. "Three days? I'll go stir crazy."

"Find something to read. I know you brought some books with you."

"I'm too excited."

The bright flush of her cheeks confirmed her words and Colin couldn't help but pat her peach-velvet skin. The pink deepened to scarlet and her lips parted slightly. She closed her eyes and leaned her head back against the couch.

"Do you know what would be nice?" she asked in a voice so soft Colin almost missed the question.

"What's that, lass?"

She rolled her head toward him and opened her eyes. "Another kiss."

Lightning arced through Colin, causing his heart to miss a beat and heat to rush to his groin. He asked the first question that came to his blood-depleted brain. "Why?"

"Because I liked it the first time. I want to see if the second time would be just as good, or if it was only because it was new."

Annie spoke so matter-of-factly Colin was annoyed by his body's response to her request. She obviously felt he was safe to experiment with.

He looked over at Margaret, who seemed to be sleeping soundly. Good God, he was actually considering her request. Again. But then, what harm was there? It wasn't like he would ravish her.

Unless she wanted him, too.

He thrust the uninvited thought aside, but Pandora's box had been cracked open. Images of Annie—in his bed, beneath him, above him— ambushed him.

"I don't think that's such a good idea, lass," he finally said, feigning interest in his book.

Out of the corner of his eye, he watched her reach out and rest her hand on his leg, above the knee. His semi-erect manhood twitched.

Down, boy. This is Annie, the little girl who used to tug on your leg and beg to ride on your shoulders.

The image didn't help, especially when he envisioned the grown-up Annie tugging and begging.

He cleared his throat and shifted carefully, hoping she wouldn't notice anything . . . like trousers that were a little snugger than they were five minutes ago. Her roving hand had moved another inch or two upward; she was getting into dangerous territory. "What are ye doin', lass?"

"Kiss me, Colin. Please."

If only she hadn't said please. To kiss her again would be a mistake—a *big* mistake. But it wasn't his brain that had taken control of his body.

Annie's blue eyes glowed, like a summer sky unbroken by clouds. Blond wisps of hair framed her still-flushed face. Colin cupped her chin, and inch-by-inch lowered his mouth onto hers.

Her sweet breath cascaded across his lips a second before he met her in an intimate caress. Holding himself back, Colin ghosted his lips over hers, touching their silky softness with his tongue. He kept his gaze focused on her eyes, which widened, then closed when their mouths met.

Desire poured into Colin's veins like vintage wine, rich and mellow . . . and intoxicating. Annie's untutored tongue swept out to meet his, taking her cue from him. Colin stifled his groan. His lass was a quick study—too damned quick.

A sane piece of Colin's brain reminded him this was merely an experiment for Annie, not a sensual feast for his hedonistic pleasure. But how could a red-blooded man ignore the banquet she offered?

A little moan arose from Annie's throat as she pressed her lips firmly against his. Colin's answering moan shocked him back to reality and he valiantly drew away. His heart pounded and he forced himself to breathe normally. "What was the result of your experiment?"

Feathery lashes swept across her cheeks, but Colin saw passion's glaze before she could mask it. He should have been alarmed that she had been as enthralled as him by the simple kiss, but instead he was . . . satisfied.

"The results were inconclusive," she replied. "I need more rehearsal time."

Any further rehearsals and Colin would have to order blocks of ice from the porter.

"Rehearsal is over," he said firmly.

Mischief lit her features. "For today." She glanced at Margaret, who had thankfully slept through Annie's study. "I suppose she has the right idea."

"It wouldn't hurt for you to get some rest, too. I doubt if you slept very well last night."

"How did you know?"

"I know you were nervous about the trip, so it makes sense that you were too anxious to sleep much."

Annie sighed. "It wasn't nervousness—it was excitement." Her eyes sparkled, her tiredness evaporating. "I've dreamed of traveling to far-away places for so long, Colin. San Francisco will just be the first of a hundred more places. London and Paris and Rome—all of the great European cities—and each and every one of them with grand theaters."

Colin's chest tightened as her voice rose and fell with passion. Had he ever felt anything so passionately? His life had been filled with work for so long—work which had been a necessity, not a goal. The days seeped into one another, obliterating the boundaries between one year and the next. Always one more job, one more silver mine, one more tunnel . . .

Even now, with his pursuit of a horse ranch and a family, he didn't feel the burning desire that flared in Annie's expressive eyes and reddened her cheeks. She was like the northern lights in the night sky—a kaleidoscope of energy and color set against an infinite backdrop.

A knock sounded and Annie jumped up to open the door. The cool air eddied across the car as the porter entered, shutting the cold out behind him.

"Is everything to your liking, sir?" the man asked Colin in a respectful voice.

Glad for the respite from his melancholy thoughts, Colin said, "Everything's fine. How's the route looking?"

"There's some snow and I 'spect we'll be running into more as we go higher into the mountains. If the winds kick up, we might have some problems with drifts."

Colin nodded. He understood all too well the hazards of traveling this high in the mountains in September. It wasn't uncommon for work crews to get stranded by an early snowstorm.

"If there's anything you're needing, just find me. My name's Paul." The porter gave them a wide, practiced smile.

"We'll do that," Colin said.

Paul ducked out of the parlor car, his shoulders hunched against the wind made brisker by the movement of the train.

"We could get trapped up here?" Annie asked softly.

Colin glanced at Annie, surprised to see her face had paled. "Don't worry, lass. If we're able to keep a good speed, the cowcatcher will make short work of the drifts."

"And if it doesn't?"

"Don't go borrowin' trouble, Annie," he said. "I've been riding trains for over ten years and there's nothin' safer."

She plopped onto the sofa. "I suppose. It's just that I don't want this trip to take any longer than it has to."

Colin smiled gently. "Don't forget to enjoy the journey on the way to your dreams, lass, or you may miss out on some adventures along the way."

Annie studied him a long moment, her expression pensive. "I didn't realize you were a philosopher."

"I didn't either, until my journey almost ended unexpectedly." He pressed his lips together. "Now, why don't you either take a nap or find something to read?"

Colin steered his attention to the words on the page in front of him, but was unable to concentrate enough to make sense of them. Annie's lilac scent kept luring him.

Annie sighed heavily and stood. "I'm going to walk around."

Colin kept his gaze firmly on his book and nodded. If she took a few turns around the car, maybe she could settle down. Though he was determined not to watch her, his hearing was attuned to her every movement. He could distinguish the rustling of her petticoats beneath her dress and the quiet thud of her heels on the floor. Then there was the sound of a door opening and the train's clacking noise increased tenfold.

Colin jerked his head up to see Annie step out of the Pullman. "Annie!"

She either didn't hear him or chose to ignore him because the door closed behind her. Swearing, Colin pushed himself upright and crossed the car to follow her. He opened the door, only to have the wind steal his breath away. Why the hell had Annie tempted fate? Though it was only five feet between the train cars, the connecting platform was narrow. Colin had visions of Annie slipping under the train's steel wheels.

Thrusting the horrific image aside, he took two long strides and entered the passenger car. Heads turned in his direction, but he ignored the curious looks. He searched for Annie, expecting to see her in the aisle ahead. She wasn't there.

Had she fallen between the cars? Colin's chest constricted as he tried to breathe. She had been under his protection for less than three hours and he had already failed to keep her from harm.

Familiar laughter floated over to him and he focused on the sound. There. He spotted a blond head in a seat toward the front of the car and rushed down the aisle. The sight of Annie sitting there made him close his eyes momentarily in relief, which was shunted aside by anger a split second later.

"What in hell do you think you're doin'?" he asked in a demanding tone.

She turned her head, startled to see him, then smiled. "Colin, you didn't have to follow me. I'm perfectly safe." She pointed to her companions. "You remember the acting troupe, don't you?"

He'd been so thankful to find her safe that he hadn't even noticed her companions. There sat Percival Fortunatas, Miss Essie Charbonneau, Toby, and Alexander.

"Good day, Mr. McBride," Percival said graciously. "I hope you don't mind our stealing the lovely Annie for a little while."

"Of course he doesn't mind," Essie said. "And if he does, I'll make it my sole responsibility to ensure he doesn't become lonely." She moved her hot gaze up and down his body and Colin had the irrational urge to cross his hands in front of his privates.

"No, that's quite all right, Essie," Colin said quickly. "When Annie said she was going for a walk, I didn't expect her to stroll out of our parlor car." He eyed Annie steadily.

"It was boring and Margaret was snoring," Annie said in a sing-song voice to her friends.

"She doesn't snore," Colin fired back. It was hard to believe this brat was the same young woman he had been kissing only minutes earlier. "Time to go back, young lady."

"I'm going to stay here and visit for a little while. I'll go crazy if I stay back there," she said stubbornly.

Colin barely hung onto his temper. He didn't want to create a scene. Of course, Annie and her group of actor friends would probably relish it. "Your parents entrusted your safety to me and I can't watch you if you're here and I'm back there."

"Then join us."

"There's no room."

Essie stood. "You can have my seat." She batted her heavily made-up eyes at him. "But only if I can sit on your lap." She leaned close and said in a stage whisper, "Believe me, it'll be well worth your while, handsome."

Colin's mouth dropped open but he quickly caught himself. "As much as your offer tempts me, Essie, I'm afraid I couldn't take a woman's seat."

"You must be losing your touch, Ess," Toby spoke up from his place beside the hulking Alexander.

She tossed a half-serious scowl at the boy. "No comments from the peanut gallery, young man."

"Yes, ma'am." Toby's eyes twinkled mischievously.

"And what did I tell you about calling me ma'am? You call me that, and I have to check over my shoulder to make sure my grandmama isn't standing behind me."

"You said I should respect my elders." The boy's feigned innocence brought laughter from everyone but Essie, though her eyes filled with fond humor.

Suddenly Annie sat upright. "I have an idea. Why don't you all come back to the private car? We have more than enough room, don't we, Colin?"

Damn—Annie knew he couldn't very well say no without appearing to be an ogre. He glanced around at the expectant faces that peered back at him. Well, what harm could it do? They would visit for an hour or two, then return to their seats. Colin could keep close tabs on Annie and she would be satisfied with her friends' company.

"If you all would like to join us—" Colin began.

The four troupe members immediately rose, and Annie led the way to the Pullman, leaving Colin to follow in their noisy wake. He met the glares of the jostled passengers with a fierce scowl and finally stepped across the platform into the warmth and spaciousness of the private car.

"What is the meaning of this?" Margaret demanded, her hat askew from her having slept on the sofa.

"I brought my friends over to visit," Annie replied. "I didn't think you'd mind, since you understand how lonely I am, leaving behind my family." Her lower lip quivered and her eyes filled with moisture.

She appeared so lost and alone that Colin had the almost overwhelming urge to take her into his arms.

Margaret immediately rushed to Annie's side and patted her back. "I'm sorry, my dear. I've forgotten what it's like to leave your family for the first time."

A tear rolled down Annie's cheek. "Then it's all right if they stay here?"

"Of course it is."

As Margaret hugged her, Annie winked at Essie. Colin drew back, startled. The imp had been acting and he had fallen for it, as had Margaret. What else had been an act—her reaction to their kiss? His masculine pride stung at that possibility.

Colin narrowed his eyes. Now that he was aware of her abilities, he wouldn't be taken in so readily next time.

Annie shifted her wide baby blue eyes to him. "It's all right with you, too, Colin, isn't it?"

Two could play this game. He smiled and said in a benevolent voice, "Of course, Annie. Whatever makes you feel better."

"Thank you, Colin."

He suspected she had known her acting friends would be aboard this train. She'd spent too much time with them not to know their plans.

Annie motioned for her visitors to seat themselves and invited Margaret and Colin to join them. Keeping her back straight, Margaret lowered herself to the couch beside Percival.

Colin shook his head. "I'm going to sit over by the table and read." He walked across the plush carpet, and a moment later, Toby and Alexander slid onto the wood bench on the opposite side of the table.

"You must be rich," Toby said without preamble.

"Why do you say that?" Colin asked.

Toby deliberately looked around the fancy interior—from the heavy curtains to the cabinets built into the walls to the thick, exotic carpet. "Because I ain't never known anybody to travel in one of these things unless they had themselves a lot of money."

"I do okay." Colin studied the boy, noting his defensive posture and wariness. It was as if he was constantly looking for someone . . . or keeping watch for an enemy.

"How'd you end up with Percival?" Colin asked curiously.

Toby studied him a moment with eyes that held too much wisdom for one so young. "Got lucky, though I didn't think it was so lucky then."

He shrugged. "Me and Alexander was in this home for folks who didn't have nobody. We didn't like it there, so we ran away. Percival found us hiding in his theater one night. Asked us if we needed a job. We been with him ever since."

"How long ago was that?"

"Two years."

"How old are you, Toby?"

"Don't rightly know. Folks at the home said I was seven or eight back then, so I figure I'm nine or ten now."

"What happened to your parents?"

"I guess they died," Toby replied matter-of-factly. "I don't remember them."

"What about Alexander?"

Toby's expression hardened, making him appear far older than his tender years. "Nobody wanted him. Said he was a dummy 'cause he can't talk and he's a little slow, but he ain't a dummy. He's smarter than a lot of folks I know. He can make animals and stuff out of paper, and he can build just about anything a body could want."

Colin's attention went to Alexander's monster-size hands. His sausage fingers were folding and creasing a piece of paper that appeared too small for him to handle. The tip of the big man's tongue peeked out of a corner of his mouth as he concentrated on what his hands were doing. After another minute, he set a tiny paper figure on the table.

"What is it?" Colin asked Alexander.

"It's a cat," Toby replied with a tone that clearly implied Colin was blind.

"May I look at it?"

Alexander nodded.

Colin picked it up and studied the small object. He could make out little ears and a tail. He smiled. "This is very good, Alexander. How did you learn how to do this?"

The big man shrugged and lowered his gaze to the table.

"He just knows," Toby said. "The way he knows a lot of things other people don't."

Colin set the paper cat back on the table and smiled at the gentle giant. "You have a gift, Alexander."

The big man shifted on the bench, clearly embarrassed by the attention.

"You got any cards?" Toby suddenly asked.

"I think there might be a deck around here," Colin answered. "Why?"

"Thought we could play us some blackjack."

Startled, Colin stared at the boy. "Blackjack?"

Toby frowned. "You don't know how to play?"

"I'm surprised *you* do."

"Not much else to do. You wanna play or not?"

"I don't want to take your money," Colin said.

"Don't worry. You won't."

"You're not one of those cardsharps, are you?"

"Who? Me? I'm just a little boy."

Toby reminded Colin of himself at that age. "All right. Blackjack it is." He found a deck of cards and poker chips in a built-in credenza and shuffled them. "Does Alexander play?"

Toby shook his head. "Nope. He don't like cards. But if you got some paper, he'll make more of them animals."

Colin had discovered some sheets of paper in the same place he'd found the cards and retrieved them for Alexander. The big man stared at him, as if he waited for an answer.

"What?" Colin asked.

"He wants to know what you want him to make," Toby said.

Colin's gaze moved from Toby to Alexander and back. Their silent communication fascinated him. "How about a horse?"

Alexander's face lit up and he began folding a piece of paper.

"He likes horses," Toby said, watching his friend. "When we were at the home, they used to let him take care of the two old mares that pulled the wagon. I used to go with him, but I'd mostly let him do the work. He liked it."

"I'm starting a horse ranch," Colin said.

Toby eyed him and snorted. "You don't look like no rancher to me. Probably don't know a horse's hind end from a hole in the ground."

In his suit and the gold watch fob, Colin had to admit he did look like a tenderfoot. "Clothes don't make the man," he said calmly.

"You don't know anything 'bout horses, do you?"

He shrugged. "I'll hire someone who does."

Toby shuffled the deck of cards and dealt one face down to Colin, then one to himself. "Ante up."

Using poker chips, each tossed a blue one into the middle of the table. Colin checked at his face-down card—queen of spades. Toby did the same, not even a flicker of emotion on his young face.

The boy tossed a card face-up in front of Colin—seven of diamonds—then did the same for himself. Toby had a two of clubs. Stifling a smile, Colin added another chip. "I'll hold."

Toby matched the chip thrown into the pot. He turned over another card for himself. Five of hearts.

"What do you have?" Toby asked.

Colin turned over his queen. "Seventeen."

The boy lifted his hidden card, revealing an ace, and he grinned. "Eighteen."

Intrigued by Toby's poker face, Colin dealt the next hand. They continued playing until Annie sat down beside Colin, her presence a welcome interruption.

She propped her chin in her palm. "How much has Toby taken you for?"

Colin glanced at the pile of chips in front of the boy. "Don't ask."

Annie laughed. "I should've warned you, but I hated to take away Toby's fun." She glanced at Alexander, who seemed to be hiding something in his lap. "What do you have?"

He blinked owlishly. Scooping up something in his palms, he raised his hands. Cupped within them were more than half a dozen paper horses.

"Oh, they're wonderful. May I see one?" Annie asked.

He nodded shyly and Annie picked out one of the little horses. She set it on the table and studied it. "I can see the ears and the mane and the tail. It's beautiful, Alexander."

He set the other horses around the one Annie had stood up.

"You made a herd of horses," Colin said in surprise.

Alexander nodded enthusiastically.

At Annie's questioning look, Colin said, "I told him I was going to raise horses."

"Looks like you have a start on your herd," Annie said.

Alexander plucked a horse from the herd and pressed it toward Annie.

"You want me to have this?" she asked gently.

He bobbed his head up and down.

Annie gripped his big hand and gifted him with a beautiful smile. "I'll always treasure it."

Colin couldn't help but smile. Though she could be impossible at times, Annie's heart was definitely in the right place.

Chapter 12

Annie touched the small horse figure Alexander had given her. He had also given Colin one, but had kept the remainder for himself. She knew he had a collection of paper animals he kept hidden away and only pulled out when he was alone. Every so often he would give one of his creations to someone, but Annie had never been able to figure out why. Toby had a bear standing on its hind legs; Percival some kind of bird with a long tail; and Essie carried her paper cat in her reticule.

"You've wiped me out, Toby," Colin said, throwing his cards into the middle of the table.

The boy grinned as he raked in his winning chips. "I'd say you owe me about three dollars and twenty-five cents."

Annie pressed her lips together, squelching a smile at Colin's dark mutterings.

Colin reached into his pocket and dug out the exact amount. "Here you go, but don't expect me to fall for your innocent act again."

Annie noticed the barest twinkle in his eyes, and suspected he might have lost on purpose. Colin's generosity was something she had always taken for granted, not seeing it because she'd become so accustomed to it.

Although Annie had led a sheltered life, she had met some unsavory men while working at the theater. Those men had propositioned her with crude words, teased Alexander mercilessly, and eyed Toby with perverted gazes which she hadn't understood until Essie had explained some of the harsher facts of life. Because of those experiences, she could truly appreciate Colin's kindness and decency.

His eyes caught hers and held. Annie gazed into their depths, seeing affection and something more, something that smoldered just beneath the surface and made her feel warm and safe. And a little lightheaded.

She turned to look out the window and reminded herself Colin wasn't interested in her *that* way. But the memory of the electricity that sizzled when he had touched her contradicted that. Even now she could feel his barest touch on her breast, sending a shiver of desire through her.

It made no difference. She was bound and determined to remain independent, and Colin was just as adamant about finding a wife.

Dusk had fallen and snow continued to swirl past the train at a dizzying rate. She listened to the train's wheels for a moment, not surprised to hear them clacking at a slower cadence than when they had left Denver.

Although troubled by the prospect of being trapped in the mountains by snow—she had read about the Donner wagon party—Annie was comforted by Colin's presence. She knew he would do everything in his power to keep her safe. That knowledge soothed her fear . . . and made her heart skip.

She glanced over at Percival and Margaret, who were talking animatedly. If Colin wasn't careful, he would lose her to the actor. Annie pushed aside the satisfaction that possibility brought.

"Looks like Margaret isn't quite the prude I thought she was," she said to Colin.

He cast her a disapproving glance. "Watch your tongue, lass. You'd do well to take some instructions in refined behavior from her."

"There's nothin' wrong with Annie," Toby said in her defense.

Colin's eyebrows arched upward in surprise. "Looks like you have a loyal defender."

Sitting next to Toby, Annie put her arm around his thin shoulders and drew him against her side in a fond hug. "A woman couldn't want a better champion."

The boy's face flushed as he ducked his head. Annie knew she embarrassed him, but Toby needed to be hugged now and again. Both he and Alexander had lived lives nobody should have to endure, much less a nine-year-old boy and a simple man.

Essie came out from behind the curtain hiding the necessary and joined them. She lowered herself to the bench beside Colin, nearly sitting in his lap. When she wiggled her backside against Colin's thigh, Annie had to clench her hands into fists to keep from bodily removing the woman from his side.

"The last time I was in a car this fancy, I was a special guest of the governor of Wyoming," Essie said dreamily. "I was young and foolish and too full of myself to realize a good thing when I had it." She sighed. "I often wonder what would have happened if I hadn't turned down his offer."

"He asked you to marry him?" Annie asked.

Essie laughed, a husky-throated sound that Annie envied. "Heavens, no. I would never have been foolish enough to accept a marriage proposal. No, he wanted to put me up in style and visit me whenever he could get away from his wife."

Colin frowned, disapproval written in his features. "I don't think this is a topic you should be discussing in front of a child."

The boy snorted. "Watch who you're calling a child."

"You *are* a child, Toby."

Knowing Toby's temper, Annie placed a hand on his shoulder. "He's been on his own for a long time, Colin. He's probably seen and done things you can't imagine."

Colin thought of the year after he'd lost his family, when he had seen and done things he didn't want to remember. "That still doesn't make it right. He should be with a family who'll care for him."

"And what are we?" Essie asked, an edge of steel in her voice.

Colin's face reddened. "You're an acting troupe that's always traveling. Toby and Alexander need a stable home and people they can count on to be there from day to day."

"We had that at the home." Toby's young face darkened. "The headmaster there thought he was helping Alexander by beating the devil out of him."

Annie felt sick to her stomach. How could anyone hurt another human being, especially one as gentle as Alexander?

"What did he do?" Colin asked quietly—too quietly.

Toby leaned close to Alexander and said something in his ear. The big man nodded reluctantly and turned, raising his shirt so they could see his back.

Annie inhaled sharply. Vicious pale scars the width of a belt marred Alexander's flesh. She drew her horrified gaze away and looked at Colin. His jaw muscle clenched tightly and fury sparked in his eyes.

"So you see why living with us is more like family than that damned home could ever be?" Essie asked, her voice vibrating with intensity.

His jaw still locked, Colin nodded. "I'm sorry."

Toby smoothed Alexander's shirt down over his scarred back. "Yeah, well, me and Alexander ain't. Percival and Essie and Annie is our family now."

Tears burned in Annie's eyes. If only she could stay with them . . . a realization dawned on her—Percival had told her he wanted to quit traveling and buy a theater in San Francisco when he had enough money. Maybe she could join them instead of looking for another theater company! She had been so single-minded, she had failed to see what was right in front of her.

Annie's stomach took that moment to growl, and everyone's attention shifted to her. She shrugged. "I was too nervous to eat breakfast."

Colin glanced into the darkness outside, then at his pocket watch. "It's nearly six-thirty. We should have some dinner."

"Yeah, me and Alexander are hungry, too," Toby said.

"Did you bring any food with you?"

"I brought a basket," Essie said. "I left it under our seats in the other car."

"We'll go get it," Toby volunteered.

Annie stood and let the boy and Alexander slide off the bench. "Be careful," she said to them.

"What could happen?" Toby asked in exasperation.

"Don't play dumb, Toby. You're not that good an actor," Essie said sternly.

"Not yet," Toby added with a cheeky grin. "Give me a few more years and I'll be running circles around you and Percival."

Essie cast him a feigned glare. "You two watch yourselves."

"Yes, ma'am."

After Toby and Alexander left the car, Essie shook her head. "I never had any children—didn't want to ruin my girlish figure—and after being around those two, I see I made the right decision. No respect for their eld—for adults."

Annie smiled, seeing through her thinly veiled affection and said in a teasing tone, "That's right. Everyone can see how much you despise Toby and Alexander."

Essie's eyes danced though her expression remained firm. "I wouldn't want folks to be thinking I'm soft on them or something."

"I'm sure nobody would ever think that," Colin said, a smile twitching his lips. He glanced over at Margaret, who was still enthralled by Percival. "I'm going to rescue Margaret."

Essie didn't budge, effectively keeping Colin prisoner on the bench behind the table. "She doesn't need any rescuing. I, on the other hand, could use a strong, handsome hero."

"Unfortunately, I don't slay dragons," Colin quipped.

Essie's hand strayed down his shirt front, stopping at his waist. "I do."

Annie's mouth grew dry at the double meaning of Essie's husky words and she felt an overwhelming tide of possessive jealousy sweep through her. She had seen too many men fall prey to Essie's charms and it had never bothered her before. But then, none of them had been Colin.

He grasped Essie's wrist and lifted her hand away from him. "My dragon doesn't need slaying."

Undaunted, she pressed a full breast against his arm. "All dragons need slaying at one time or another. It's a fact of life."

Annie leaned across the table. "His dragon *doesn't* belong to you."

Essie arched her eyebrows. "Is there something I should know about you two?"

"No," both Colin and Annie replied in unison, then frowned at one another.

"If there isn't something going on, there ought to be," Essie said as she sat up.

Before Annie or Colin could come up with a retort, the train braked abruptly. Essie slipped off the edge of the bench and cried out as she hit the floor.

"What the hell," Colin cursed, hanging on to Annie's hands across the table.

The train lurched to a stop and Annie released Colin's strong hands to drop down beside Essie.

"Are you hurt?" Annie asked anxiously, touching her friend's shoulder.

She groaned. "My ankle . . . I think it's broken."

Colin knelt beside the two women, guilt warring with concern. "Can I examine it, Essie?" he asked gently.

Wicked humor flashed in Essie's eyes. "You can examine whatever you want, handsome."

Colin smiled, relieved that she could still joke. Maybe the injury wasn't as bad as she claimed.

"Essie, are you all right, my dear?" Percival asked.

Colin glanced up to see the actor and Margaret standing behind them, gazing down at Essie with worry.

"I'll be fine, Percival. I'm not going to let you get rid of me that easily," Essie said.

Colin admired the actress's spunk. She probably needed that mettle to live the life she led.

The door opened and cold air eddied across the floor as Toby and Alexander returned. The chill made Essie shiver.

"What happened?" Toby asked, sounding like a scared child.

"When the train braked, Essie fell and hurt her ankle," Annie replied. "Are you two all right?"

"Yeah, but lots of folks was yelling about being

hurt, though. The train must've run into a snow-bank," the boy said, gesturing excitedly.

Annie bit her lower lip. She didn't want to think about being stranded, surrounded by nothing but snow and rugged mountains.

"Toby, I have a mission for you and Alexander," Colin said. "See if there's a doctor aboard the train. If there is, bring him back here."

The boy nodded and turned to Alexander. "Come on."

After the two left again, Colin turned to Annie. "Lass, I want you to hold Essie's hand while I check her ankle. It may hurt and I want her to have somebody to hang onto, all right?"

Slightly pale, Annie grasped one of Essie's hands between hers and said, "You just go ahead and squeeze as hard as you want."

Essie chuckled. "Reminds me of this man I once—" she broke off and cleared her throat. "I'll tell you that story some other day."

"Good idea," Colin murmured with a trace of humor.

Annie watched as Colin gently examined Essie's ankle, his expression concentrated as he glided his fingers over her stockings. He paused, wrapped his capable fingers around her ankle and shifted it slightly.

Essie increased her pressure on Annie's hand and closed her eyes tightly. Annie tried not to flinch at the steely grip, surprised since Essie usually appeared deceptively weak. But then, she was an actress.

"How're you doing, Essie?" Colin asked gently.

"It isn't exactly how I pictured you touching me the first time, but I'm doing all right," Essie replied, keeping her eyes closed.

Annie glanced at Colin, and caught his self-conscious gaze on her. She couldn't blame Essie for wanting Colin; any red-blooded woman would be a fool to turn him away.

"I don't think it's broken," Colin finally said.

"Thank heavens," Percival said in relief.

"But I do think it's a bad sprain." Colin stood. "Let's get Essie up onto the couch. She'll be more comfortable there."

"Hallelujah," Essie muttered. "This floor is damned cold."

Annie caught the fond exasperation in Colin's eyes, and her lips tilted upward. Colin's answering grin made her giddy, like she was a girl again who was discovering boys for the first time.

Annie moved out of the way as Percival and Colin helped Essie to the overstuffed sofa. The actress tried to rest some weight on the ankle and groaned.

"Are you sure it's not broken? It feels like it," Essie complained.

"I'm sure," Colin replied patiently. "I've set enough broken bones to know the difference."

He and the actor settled Essie on the couch and she leaned her head back. Her face was so pale it frightened Annie.

"A sprain shouldn't hurt so bad, should it?" Annie asked anxiously.

"Oftentimes they're worse than a break, lass," Colin said.

"We're to stop over in Reno and perform one night," Percival said, his eyes darting between Essie and Colin.

"You'll have to cancel it," Colin said flatly. "Essie's going to have to stay off that ankle for at least a week. After that, she'll be limping for another two or three weeks."

Percival twisted his hands together. "I can't just cancel our engagement."

"Why not?"

The actor squirmed like a little kid caught stealing a peppermint from the store. "I used the advance money to buy our train tickets."

"Oh, Percival. I thought you learned your lesson years ago," Essie said with a sigh.

Percival's face reddened.

"What will happen if you can't perform and you can't pay back their money?" Colin asked.

"We would be tarred and feathered and our good names would be ruined." Percival's theatrics made Colin shake his head.

"What if I lend you the money to pay them back?"

Percival's expression changed like quicksilver. "Would you?"

Annie stepped forward and spoke up before her brain caught up to her mouth. "No, I won't allow it."

Colin cast her a confused look. "I thought these people were your friends."

"They are, but I can't let you use your money. You'll need it to start your ranch."

Annie didn't expect the tender look in his eyes or the gentle curve of his lips. "It's my money, lass. I can do with it what I wish."

But he had worked so hard for his dream. "I know, but Percival won't pay you back."

"My dear—" Percival huffed.

"She's right, Percy, and you know it," Essie said sternly. "Lending money to you would be like spitting in the wind."

Margaret stepped up to Colin and laid her hand on his arm. "They're right, Colin. You have to save your money for your ranch." She paused. "And your family."

Annie's breath caught in her throat. It looked like Percival hadn't made her forget about Colin, and the way Colin was gazing at Margaret told Annie he was definitely considering her as a potential wife.

Annie had to stop caring what they did. She had her own dream to follow and Essie's accident suddenly seemed a fortuitous boon for her. Taking a deep breath, she asked, "How about if I take Essie's part?"

Four gazes landed on her and silence filled the Pullman, broken only by the whistling of the wind and the rattle of snow against the car. Percival looked at her like she was the pot of gold at the end of the rainbow; Essie nodded in approval; Margaret stared, her mouth hanging open like that of a largemouth bass; and Colin looked like he was about to explode.

"It's 'The Taming of the Shrew,' right?" Annie asked.

"Yes. You would have to learn all your lines in three days," Percival cautioned, though there was an undercurrent of satisfaction.

"I can do it." Annie wasn't certain whether she could, but she had to try.

"The costumes will have to be altered," Essie spoke up.

Percival moved to Margaret's side. "Do you sew, my dear?"

The widow appeared torn. "Yes, but I don't believe Annie should be allowed to act upon the stage. She is a young lady of good breeding and upright morals, and as her chaperone I feel I must do what is in her best interests."

"Are you saying I don't have any good breeding or any of those upright morals?" Essie demanded.

Margaret flushed. "Of course not, Miss Charbonneau, but this is *your* job. It is not Annie's."

"Not yet," Annie said, trying to rein in her temper. "But someday I want to be just like Essie." Her cheeks grew warm at the added implication of her words, but she didn't lower her stubborn chin.

"That's not what your parents want for you. They want you to learn how to be a lady," Margaret said.

"Maybe we should let her try it," Colin said,

surprising Annie. "Besides, she probably won't be able to learn her lines, in which case they'll have to cancel anyhow."

Annie's first reaction was anger, but there was a niggling suspicion in the back of her mind that Colin had issued her a dare—and he, more than anybody, knew how she had never been able to ignore a dare.

She met Margaret's narrowed gaze with defiance, then changed her approach. "Please, Margaret. It's just for one performance. Please let me try." She forced a smile. "Maybe I'll find out being an actress is too difficult and forget about wanting to be one."

After an expectant silence, Margaret nodded. "All right, but I insist on helping with the costumes so I can be assured Annie will maintain her modesty."

Annie swallowed her sigh of relief. Although she had acted before, Margaret didn't know that and what the woman didn't know wouldn't hurt her—or Annie.

"We would be forever in your debt," Percival said with a smile that nearly split his face in two. He paced with nervous little steps. "First I must find your costumes and bring them in here so Margaret can work on them. Essie, where's your playbook?"

She pointed to a bag lying in a corner. "There." She looked at Annie. "You'd better start studying right away, sweetie. Though the play isn't nearly as long as the original, you have the most lines."

Annie's heart kicked against her ribs. There would be so much to memorize and learn in the next three days! Could she do it?

Annie retrieved the book while Percival continued to tick off the details that needed to be ironed out before they arrived in Reno.

"And where are Toby and Alexander? I need them," Percival asked impatiently.

"They went to find a doctor for Miss Charbonneau," Margaret replied softly.

Percival stopped his ranting and gave Margaret's arm a pat. "Thank you, my dear. I had forgotten."

"Margaret, could you give me a hand wrapping Essie's ankle?" Colin asked, his irritation at Percival's familiarity obvious.

"Of course."

Annie sat in a chair with the playbook while she watched Colin and Margaret. They worked so closely that Annie suspected Margaret could feel Colin's warm breath against her cheek. Annie shivered—she wanted to be beside him, feeling his lean body against hers and his breath against her face.

I'm jealous. The admission brought only a moment of shock. She had no right being envious of Margaret—Colin wanted a wife; Annie wanted to be an actress. No middle ground existed there.

The door flew open and Toby and Alexander stumbled in along with a cold blast of arctic air. Though they had been outside only long enough to cross between cars, the two of them were covered with snowflakes.

"It's snowing like a son-of-a-bitch out there," Toby commented, stamping his feet and blowing into his cupped hands.

"Well-bred young men don't use such language," Margaret scolded from beside Colin.

Toby wrinkled his nose. "I guess I ain't no well-bred dandy."

Margaret merely pressed her lips together.

"Did you find a doctor?" Colin asked.

"Nope. A few other folks were hurt, too, but nobody was real bad." Toby shook his head as he crossed the car with Alexander as his ever-present shadow. "How's Essie doing?"

"Essie is doing just fine," the actress answered. "Colin says I have a sprained ankle."

"That don't sound so bad."

"She'll be back to normal in a few weeks," Colin said.

"Good." The relief in the boy's face revealed his concern.

Annie knew Toby had been troubled by Essie's injury; in spite of all their tough talk they were more like mother and son than either would admit.

"You gonna be better by the time we get to Reno?" Toby asked.

Colin shook his head. "She won't be able to perform for at least a week or two, and even then she'll limp."

"Then who's gonna—"

"I am." Annie was amazed at how calm she sounded, when inside she felt like she was ready to fly apart like a clock that had been wound too tight.

"Does that mean you're going to stay with us and not go to that stupid finishing school?" Toby asked, his eyes glowing.

Annie bit her tongue before she answered that truthfully. "I'm going on to that 'stupid' school after the performance in Reno."

Then I'll be joining you.

Chapter 13

Colin listened to the silence that was broken only by the hushed sounds of slumber within the Pullman. Percival muttered in his sleep from the sofa and Alexander's soft snores were punctuated by Toby's whistling breaths beside him on the floor. Rustlings from the berth told Colin one of the three women was also having trouble sleeping. Probably Essie, who had one of the beds to herself because of her ankle. Margaret and Annie shared the one above her.

Colin shifted, stifling a grimace when his knee protested the discomfort of sleeping in a chair. He had looked forward to getting a good night's sleep in the private car while they traveled, but fate had thrown him a curve. He could have insisted that Percival, Toby, and Alexander sleep in their own seats in the passenger car, but one look at Annie's puppy dog eyes and he'd surrendered without a battle.

He had known her display was an act, but it hadn't made any difference. Trev had been right—Annie could wrap a man around her finger without his being the wiser. The sad part was that Colin knew he'd been a slave to her whims ever since he'd set eyes on the four-year-old imp.

He sighed and focused his hearing on the wind, which hadn't lessened since they'd been halted abruptly by a ten-foot snow drift hours ago. Once the wind and snow let up, the porters and engineers would be out shoveling to free the train. Unfortunately, they'd probably run into more snow walls as they went deeper into the mountains. He only hoped they wouldn't become completely covered by snow—it would remind him too much of what had happened three months ago.

Trapped.

Blackness.

Hurting.

Alone . . . except for the lifeless body of one of his crew.

Colin shuddered and cold sweat dotted his forehead. Restlessness made him throw off his blanket and he laid his palms on the chair arms, intending to stand. A movement from near the compartments made him freeze. The person was too short to be Margaret, and as the apparition approached, he noticed she wasn't limping. It had to be Annie.

"What're you doing up?" Colin asked quietly, grateful for the reprieve from the distressing memories.

Annie halted. "Colin?"

"Aye."

"I'm sorry. I didn't mean to wake you."

"You didn't. My leg's botherin' me some." His Irish brogue slipped into his speech.

Annie glided across the floor, coming to stand before him. After a moment's hesitation, she knelt on the carpet and laid a hand lightly on his bad knee. "When Papa hurt his back, I used to rub it for him. Do you think that might help your leg?"

Colin's heart missed a beat, then stumbled to catch up. *It might not help, but it would make me forget about the knee, as well as the memories.*

"I'd like that, lass," he said huskily.

She brought her other hand onto his leg and kneaded the flesh around his knee. He stared at the pale oval surrounded by a halo of hair that shone silvery white in the moonlight. He narrowed his eyes, her head and shoulders blurring until he could imagine her as an angel.

Without thought, he reached out to lay his palm against her slender neck. She faltered, but continued the massage. Colin felt the chain around her throat and followed it until he found the angel charm.

An emotion somewhere between awe and happiness filled him. "Do you wear it to bed?" he asked.

"Yes."

Her heartbeat fluttered like a cherub's wings beneath his fingertips. "Why?"

"It reminds me that you're never far away," she said in a barely audible voice.

Colin's throat tightened, stealing his voice. He leaned back, closed his eyes, and concentrated on the feel of her fingers. She somehow knew how much pressure to exert against his muscles to work out the soreness.

He imagined Annie's sensual touch moving upward, across his thigh . . . stroking and caressing even higher. Passion moved through him like a wide, lazy river meandering through his veins.

Annie stopped and reality chased away the sultry heat. He opened his eyes and found her standing over him.

"I can't go to sleep yet. Would you mind if I sat with you for a little while?"

He should refuse her, but he couldn't. He never could.

Shifting in the chair, he patted the cushion beside him. "Sit down, lass."

Dressed only in a gown and a light robe, Annie settled in the open space between him and the chair arm. Although the chair was oversized, it wasn't intended for two people. Annie curled up against Colin's side and rested her head in the curve of his neck and shoulder.

Colin wrapped his arm around her shoulders. He concentrated on breathing deeply rather than on the sear of her womanly curves that pressed so intimately against him. As if of their own volition, his fingers feathered up and down her silky sleeve.

"Do you remember the time when you were taking care of me because Papa and Kate were gone?" Annie asked quietly. "We were still in Orion. I'd had a bad dream—I don't remember what it was about—and you rocked me in your arms until I fell asleep?"

Colin nodded, recalling it easily. "At first you only wanted your father, but finally you let me hold you. It was the first time I'd seen you so still, so quiet. I wanted to shelter you in my arms so nothing could ever hurt you." As he spoke, Colin wrapped his other arm around Annie, holding her in an embrace close to his chest like he'd done to the young girl so many years ago when he had been little more than a boy himself.

Annie shifted, bringing her legs over Colin's thighs so that she was sitting in his lap. "I never forgot how safe I felt. You told me a story about an elf and a troll."

"You remembered that?"

"I remember everything—how your shirt smelled; how soft your whiskers were compared to Papa's; how your heartbeat sounded so close to my ear, just like now."

Colin's arms tightened around his precious bundle and he kissed her brow tenderly. "Do you remember when I did that?"

Annie nodded. "Yes. But the kiss doesn't feel the same." She tilted her head back to gaze into his face. "I'm not that same little girl, and I want more than a sisterly kiss, Colin."

He wanted the same—but he couldn't do it. It wasn't fair to either one of them.

"I'm sorry, Annie," he said softly. "It would be wrong."

She leaned back far enough that she could look up into his face. "I know it's not because you think of me as a sister."

The certainty in her voice jolted him. He wanted to refute her words, but he wouldn't lie. "I won't use you."

"I *want* you to use me."

"No, you don't. Kisses lead to other things— things that could hurt you."

"You'd never hurt me."

The absolute trust in her tone made Colin shift uncomfortably. She had no idea what kinds of thoughts ran rampant through his mind with her lush body pressed to his. If she did, she would run back to her sleeper.

"A man can only be trusted so far, Annie. Even me," he said huskily.

"It's not going to work."

"What?"

"Trying to scare me off."

Was that what he was doing? He had thought he was only preserving his self-respect.

She laid her head back down on his chest. "I know you too well."

"You may *think* you do."

Her fingers played with his top shirt button. "If you were the type of man you say you are, you would be doing more than holding me right now."

He could hear the smile in the imp's voice and stifled a sigh of exasperation. It looked like he was going to have his hands full—literally—for a while longer.

He could send her back to bed, but he enjoyed holding her in the cocoon of darkness. Maybe he could steer the conversation to a safer topic.

"Did you know about Alexander and Toby?" he asked.

Her fingers stilled a moment and she shook her head. "No." She continued toying with the button. "Why would anybody want to hurt him like that?"

Colin involuntarily tightened his arms around her. "I don't know, lass. But if I'd been there, I'd have turned the belt on the man who held it."

"Me, too." The ferocity of Annie's voice startled him, though he understood it.

They remained silent for a few minutes, listening to the rustle of dry snow against the windows. A cold draft wafted through the Pullman and Annie shivered. Colin reached for the blanket he'd tossed on the floor earlier and draped it over her, holding their combined body heat under the coverlet.

"Why do you want to act, Annie?" Colin asked, needing to understand the woman he had known so well when she was a girl.

"I told you."

"That may have been part of it, but there's more to wanting to become somebody else or hear the applause of hundreds of people."

She remained quiet, her breathing shallow and more rapid than normal. As Colin decided she wasn't going to answer his question, she finally spoke.

"Did you know my mother?"

Startled by the question, he shook his head. "Not very well. She died not long after I moved to Orion but I never met her."

"Papa said she was beautiful, that I look a lot like her."

Colin thought back to the brief instances when he'd seen Trev's first wife. She had been with child then. The other thing he had noticed about her was her thick blond hair, which had been gathered loosely by a tie at the nape of her neck.

He opened a hand that rested against Annie's back and rolled a strand of her soft tresses between his fingertips. "You do look like her, lass. You have her hair."

"What about her eyes?"

Colin shook his head reflexively. "No. They may be the same color, but hers were cold."

"What do you mean?"

He silently cursed his thoughtless answer, but the damage had been done. "I didn't see her often, only two or three times in town," he began. "I would always tip my hat, knowing she was my boss's wife and I owed her my respect, but she would just ignore me. I remember being embarrassed, and then I would look down at you and try to talk to you." Colin smiled tenderly with the memory. "You were so shy then. It's hard to imagine you're that same bashful little girl."

"I don't remember her," she said after a minute or two. "Kate said I was with her when she gave birth to Brynn. I asked Papa about that day and about her, but he wouldn't talk about either one. He just told me that my mother loved me and gave her life to bring Brynn into the world."

Colin felt her muscles grow taut. "Does that bother you, Annie—that your father doesn't like to talk about her?"

"Yes," she replied without hesitation. "I wanted to know about her. I wanted to know about her family and where they came from. I wanted to know what people had thought of her and how she died. But he wouldn't tell me."

"Did you ask Kate?"

"She said Papa should be the one to tell me about her."

Colin sensed there was more to her idle conversation and he waited patiently.

"I've been having dreams," she said quietly.

Colin understood dreams too well, especially those of the nightmare variety. "What are they about?"

"I see a woman, but her face isn't clear. I have the strangest feeling that she's my mother but she doesn't act like my mother."

"How does she act?"

"Like she's mad," she whispered, her voice trembling. "She's yelling at me—" Her voice broke.

Colin snugged her against him, wishing he could take away the memory of her nightmare. "Shhhh, it's all right, Annie. You don't have to talk about it."

"Yes, I do. I used to have the same dream once every year or two. In the past two months, I've had it twice." She paused, and when she spoke again, her voice held childlike puzzlement. "Is it her, Colin? Is it my mother in my dreams?"

His throat convulsed and he tried to swallow, but failed. The night before Trev married Kate, he had told Colin about his first wife's sickness—the melancholia which had destroyed her and the love between the married couple. However, Trev's greatest fear had been for Annie—he'd been frightened that she would remember the hatred directed at her from her own mother. He never wanted his "little angel" to learn the truth.

Colin had agreed with him at the time; a five-year-old girl wouldn't understand. But now that Annie was a young woman, she deserved to know the truth.

Except that it wasn't Colin's place to tell her.

"I don't know if it was your mother or not, lass, but your father said she loved you," he reminded her gently.

"I don't know . . ." she murmured. "It's not just the dreams. It's the memories, too."

Colin forced himself to relax. He kissed the top of her head lightly and rested his cheek atop the pale crown. "Are you sure they're real?"

Annie's hand slid across his chest to his shirt collar. She brushed her fingers across the material and the vee of skin at his throat. "Sometimes I think so, but other times I can't believe it. Why wouldn't a mother love her own child?" She paused and he felt her warm breath fan across his neck as she whispered, "Unless that child did something really bad."

"Even if a mother hated her child, it wouldn't be the child's fault." Colin eased her up until she was sitting and he could look into her face, dimly lit by the snow's illumination and shadowed by

the night. He framed her face between his palms.
"You were only a little girl, Annie. If some of your
memories are real, then it was your mother's
fault, not yours. A person cannot dictate how another person feels—our feelings are our own,
lass. And we make our own decisions whether to
be happy or sad, pleasant or ill-tempered, mean-
spirited or generous."

Annie remained silent, her searching gaze on
his thoughtful face.

"What is it, lass?"

Annie inhaled sharply. "I don't want to be like
her."

"You're not like her."

"I'm my mother's daughter," she said softly,
but with a ring of steel beneath it.

"Annie—"

She slid from his lap. "I should go back to bed."
She paused and smiled, but it didn't reach her
eyes. "Margaret hogs the bed and she has cold
feet. I thought I should warn you in case you decide to marry her."

The thought of sharing a bed with Margaret
brought an unsavory taste to his mouth. "Thanks
for the warning, imp."

"Goodnight, Colin."

"Goodnight."

When he watched her shimmering shadow
glide across the car's floor, and even after she disappeared into her berth, he continued to stare at
the curtain . . .

And wondered if Annie stayed on her side of the bed and if her feet were warm.

Even after a cup of strong coffee, Annie was still trying to wake up. She propped her elbows on the table, ignoring the conversations around her as the others rose and washed using the pitcher and basin in a corner.

She had lain awake long after she had spoken with Colin and had reviewed their conversation over and over in her mind. Although she had tried to draw some information from him regarding her mother, he had been uncharacteristically closemouthed.

As an actress, Annie studied people: each little nuance of their actions and conversations, the pause between words, eye contact or lack thereof. Even though it had been dark, she had read the hesitation in Colin's speech and the subtle shift of his gaze. He hadn't lied to her, but he hadn't been completely honest, either. He *knew* something about her mother and had withheld that information . . .

It angered her and hurt her. She had a right to know about the woman who'd brought her into this world, the woman who had died giving birth to her brother.

But most of all, Annie had the right to know if her mother had been sane. Only a woman who wasn't could possibly treat her child the way Annie half-remembered being treated. She had read and heard about how mind sicknesses ran in some families. Did it run in her mother's? In a few years, would Annie herself succumb to madness? Or were the hazy memories not memories at all?

She rubbed her brow, willing the headache away. She had lines to memorize, and later there would be rehearsal. Both dreading and anticipating that, Annie picked up the book, determined to bury her unsettled thoughts for a little while.

Just as she opened the book, Margaret slid onto the bench across from her.

"Good morning, Annie."

Annie managed a polite smile to the woman with the polar feet. "Morning, Margaret." She deliberately buried her nose in her book.

"Did you sleep well?" Margaret asked.

So much for being subtle.

"Fine, thank you."

The widow sipped her coffee with a watery slurping sound that made Annie gnash her teeth.

"I slept like a baby myself," Margaret said.

Annie didn't bother to move her gaze from her book. "That's nice."

"I wonder how Essie is feeling this morning."

Annie carefully lowered the book to the tabletop and smiled brittlely. "Why don't you ask her yourself?" she asked, enunciating carefully.

"She hasn't risen yet." Margaret harrumphed. "Theater people and their odd hours. I can't imagine why anyone would *want* to do it."

"It's fascinating, fun, exciting, challenging, interesting, and gratifying." Annie paused, opening her book again. "Not to mention that I won't have to take orders from an oafish husband."

Margaret's face reddened and her gaze dropped to her coffee cup, which she clenched with white-knuckled hands.

Nice job, Annie. Forget that she was married to a man who didn't deserve to live.

She reached across the table and clasped Margaret's hand. "I'm sorry. That was a very thoughtless thing to say."

The older woman smiled tremulously. "That's all right, my dear. To merely say he was oafish would be a compliment. However, while I was married I didn't see an escape from his abuse. When he died—" Margaret worried her lower lip. "When he died, I was glad. I know that's a horrible thing to say and I'll probably go to hell for saying it, but it's true. I can't hide what's in my heart."

Annie's compassion welled up. "I understand. I'm sure God does, too."

The anxious creases in Margaret's face eased. "I pray so." She leaned forward and said in a low voice, "I suppose that's the reason I was so enthralled with Colin. He seemed so different from my husband, so courteous, and I could see in his eyes he was a decent man, just as I had come to see evil in my husband's eyes."

Annie couldn't help but think of her mother. "What do you see in my eyes?"

Margaret seemed startled, but then gazed appraisingly at Annie. "I see a young woman with a little too much independence, but I know your heart is good in spite of your misguided notion to become an actress."

Annie moved her hand away from the other woman's. "It's not misguided. Didn't you have dreams when you were my age?"

Annie watched the play of emotions across her face.

"Doesn't everybody?" Margaret finally said.

"What were yours?"

"Nothing as nefarious as becoming an actress."

"Then what?"

"It's silly."

"Tell me."

"I wanted a man who would give me flowers for no other reason than that he loved me. I wanted someone who treated me as if I were the most important person in the world and who put me ahead of everything else." She ducked her head, her cheeks flushing with embarrassment. "I told you they were silly."

"Those aren't silly. Even though I have no wish to marry, it seems to me you shouldn't settle for anything less than what you truly want."

"Like you will not settle for anything less than being an actress?"

Annie nodded vehemently. "Exactly. If a man makes you feel that way, then you should pursue him until you catch him."

Margaret looked past Annie and her expression softened. "I might just do that."

Annie turned to follow Margaret's line of sight and spotted Colin talking to Percival, who still lay on the sofa. A hand seemed to squeeze her heart in two.

She had just given Margaret her blessing to go after Colin.

Not even nine o'clock, and this was already headed toward being one of the worst days of her life.

Chapter 14

Toby sat on the love seat, swinging his legs back and forth. With each swing, his heels scraped the carpet with a little *shush* sound. From beside him, Alexander glanced down, a question in his face.

"I'm tired of sitting," Toby whispered to his friend.

Alexander nodded in understanding and turned back to the piece of paper he was folding. Watching him for a moment, Toby decided he was probably making another horse. He liked those the best.

He sighed and his friend mimicked him, a habit the younger boy had gotten used to the past three years. The first time Toby had seen Alexander, the big man had been in the barn, sitting on a pile of old straw. Toby had rushed in, searching for a place to hide from the home's headmaster. Toby had tried talking to Alexander, but the slow man would only copy everything he did. It had made Toby angry, thinking Alexander was making fun of him.

But when the barn door had opened and the headmaster stood framed in the doorway, Alexander had motioned for Toby to hide in a pile of straw. With no other alternative, Toby did. The headmaster, a small quirt in his hand, had walked over to Alexander and asked him if he'd seen Toby. Alexander had shaken his head, lying to protect the boy. Even after the headmaster used the small whip on his arm Alexander didn't tell on him.

Ever since that time, Toby and Alexander had been inseparable.

Toby brought his attention back to Annie, who recited her lines one more time. It was a scene they had been rehearsing for the last two hours. He was used to sitting around while Percival and Essie practiced, but today he didn't want to stay in one place. He felt like he had ants crawling inside of him, making him want to jump up and down and run around. It was the same feeling he had when he had been ordered to sit in a corner for hours after he had done something wrong at the home.

He glanced over at Annie's friend, Mr. McBride, who leaned back in a chair, one leg outstretched in front of him. Probably the one he limped on. Toby would have to be stupid not to notice he had a hurt leg, and one thing Toby wasn't was stupid.

No sirree, not Toby Williams. He had managed to trick a lot of grown-ups and continued to practice his wiles on his friends occasionally to keep his wits sharp. But nowadays he never tried anything like stealing or cheating, at least, not around them.

Thinking of the poker game yesterday, he squirmed some more. Okay, so maybe he'd cheated a little then. Mr. McBride had to be pretty rich to ride in this train car, so he figured taking money from him wasn't really cheating.

As if reading his mind, Mr. McBride met his eyes. A moment later, he came over and sat down on the sofa on the other side of Toby.

"It gets kind of boring, doesn't it?" the man asked.

Toby shrugged. "Nothin' else to do."

"Except play blackjack."

The boy whipped his head around to look at him. Did he know? "Blackjack's fun once in a while," he said cautiously.

"Especially when you're winning."

Toby tensed and more ants got under his skin, but he knew how to sit still. He had been taught well at the home. "Yep. Luck's better'n skill anytime," he said with a nonchalant shrug.

"Only if you help luck along."

The game's up. Toby turned his most innocent face to the man. "How do you help luck along?"

Then Annie's friend laughed, surprising him. Toby expected the man to punish him.

"I know grown men who aren't nearly as good as you at palming a card," Mr. McBride said.

Shit. He should have known any friend of Annie's wouldn't be an easy mark.

"What do you mean, 'palming a card'?"

"Don't play innocent with me, Toby. I didn't mind losing to you, but someday someone will, and then you won't be alive to enjoy your ill-gotten gains."

Alexander nudged Toby with an elbow and the boy turned to his friend, reading his mind easily. "It's okay. He won't hurt us." He laid a hand on the giant's arm, reassuring him. The last time someone had hurt Toby, Alexander had beat up the other man real bad. "Mr. McBride is Annie's friend, okay?"

After a moment, Alexander nodded and Toby let out the breath he had been holding. His friend needed him. Toby was the only one who understood Alexander and could figure out what he wanted. If something happened to him, Alexander would be thrown into another bad place.

"So I suppose you want your money back." Toby put as much growl into his voice as he could muster.

Never let them see how scared you are.

McBride shook his head. "I'm not worried

about the money. I'm worried about you and Alexander. I don't want either of you to get into trouble and be put someplace where you can't be together or where they won't treat you well."

Had he heard Mr. McBride right? Naw, Toby didn't believe it. The man was only trying to make Toby lower his guard, then he'd strike when he wasn't expecting it. He had fallen for that trick once; he wouldn't do it again.

"I'm serious, Toby. I know how much Annie cares for you and Alexander, and I don't want her hurt knowing you two were put someplace you didn't want to be," Mr. McBride said.

Toby blinked as dust made his eyes water. "All right. I'll be more careful."

"No. I want you *never* to cheat again. Understood?"

Toby could lie—he had done it often enough. But something told him Annie's friend would know. "I understand."

The boy scrubbed at his eyes with his knuckles, and when the moisture was gone, he tried to concentrate on the rehearsal again.

"When we first met, you asked me if I was a do-gooder," Mr. McBride said. "Have you had trouble with do-gooders?"

Toby shrugged. "Folks think that because I'm a kid and Alexander don't act like a grown-up that we'd be better off in a home or something." He pointed at Margaret, who was busy sewing, but not so busy that she couldn't watch the rehearsal. "Just like her."

"She only thought it would be better than traveling around all the time."

Toby snorted, keeping his eyes on Margaret. "Yeah, a do-gooder who thinks she knows what's best for people she don't even know. People like her do their duty, get me and Alexander in a home, then forget about us. Do-gooders don't care what happen to the kids they think they're helping—they just want to make themselves feel better."

Mr. McBride studied him for a long time.

"What?" Toby demanded, nervous beneath his stare.

"I never thought of it that way. I suppose you're right about some of them being that way, but not everybody is like that."

"You don't know nothin'."

Mr. McBride chuckled. "I know more than you think, and I think as long as you and Alexander are happy working for Percival, then it's okay."

Out of the corner of his eye, Toby saw McBride pull something out of his pocket. After a moment, he could tell it was the horse Alexander had given him.

"How did he learn how to make these?" Mr. McBride asked.

"I dunno. Every since I knew him, he's been making them."

"He's very good."

Toby felt a flush of pride for his friend. "Yeah, he's a lot smarter'n folks think."

"Can he talk?"

Toby shook his head. "I heard someone at the home say that he didn't have no voice box in his throat."

"How do you understand him?"

"I just do."

"He seems pretty protective of you."

"I guess."

"Just as protective as you are of him."

Toby didn't know what to say so he merely shrugged.

"I want you to know that if you and Alexander get tired of staying with Percival, you can stay with me."

Toby shoved down his sudden rise of excitement. Grown-ups, even ones who seemed as nice as Mr. McBride, couldn't be trusted. Maybe he only wanted them to be slaves on his ranch. "Naw, me and Alexander like traveling."

He glanced out the window and noticed that the snow had almost stopped and the sun was trying to peek out. "Me and Alexander are gonna go outside for a while."

He stood and Alexander followed suit.

Before he walked away to don his coat, Toby reached into his trouser pocket and his fingers curled around the money he had won during the poker game. He withdrew his hand and held out some coins and crumpled bills. "Here's your money back, Mr. McBride."

The man shook his head. "No, you keep it. Just remember our deal—no more cheating."

Toby stared at him for a long moment, trying to see if he really meant it or if he was just waiting for a time when he could take it back and hurt him. Not seeing anything but friendliness, Toby shoved the money back into his pocket. Maybe McBride was okay. "Thanks."

Colin noted the reluctance in the boy's tone. "You're welcome."

His gaze followed the two as they pulled on their coats and he wasn't surprised to see Toby check to ensure Alexander had buttoned his jacket correctly. For a moment, Colin wondered if it was all right for the two of them to wander around outside the train.

He directed his attention back to the rehearsal and noticed Annie was watching Toby and Alexander. Consequently she missed her line.

"Annie, Annie—you must concentrate. You must do more than say your lines. You must become Katharina, who wants nothing to do with Petruchio," Percival said in exasperation.

"Take it easy on her, Percy. She's doing you a favor," Essie scolded. "And she's doing damned good, considering she's had less than twelve hours to study the material."

"Can we take a break?" Annie asked. "I need some water."

Percival's shoulders rose and fell on a heavy sigh. "Yes, yes, go ahead."

Annie walked past him and Colin immediately recognized her frustration. He stood and followed her, then watched her slender throat as she finished swallowing the water. She lowered the cup and a drop glistened on her lip. Colin found himself leaning forward, wanting to lick the droplet away with a kiss.

Annie's tongue swept across her lips, brushing the water away, and Colin nearly groaned at the unintentionally erotic sight.

"Percival's tough," Colin commented lightly, hoping his indecent thoughts weren't obvious.

Annie grimaced. "He's also right. My performance has been pretty pitiful."

"Essie says you're doing 'damned good.' " He smiled, trying to lift her spirits, which were usually in no need of lifting.

"Considering," Annie added wryly. "Where did Toby and Alexander go?"

"Outside."

"Is that safe?"

"I figure that together those two can take care of themselves."

"Sometimes I forget Toby is only nine. Most of the time he acts older than me."

"That wouldn't be difficult."

Annie wrinkled her nose. "Too bad nobody else but you thinks you're funny."

"Respect your elders, imp."

"So where's your cane, old man?" she teased. Suddenly her face blanched as her gaze flickered to his knee. "Oh, I'm sorry, Colin. I didn't mean—" She broke off, her face scarlet.

"There's nothin' to be sorry about, lass." Colin gave her fingers a gentle squeeze and motioned to the playbook. "What is this 'Taming of the Shrew' about?"

He could tell Annie was still bothered by her off-the-cuff remark, but she covered it up. "You haven't read it?"

"I tried, but Shakespeare and I don't speak the same language. He was English; I'm a mere Irishman." He winked at her.

"You're not a 'mere' anything," Annie shot back. Then she glanced down at the book, her cheeks reddening. "It's a play about courtship and the games men and women play during it."

Colin leaned back against the wall and crossed his arms. "Sounds interesting. What about your character Katharina?"

Annie grinned. "You'd hate her. She speaks her mind and doesn't care what others think of her."

"You and she must have a lot in common."

"Except her father forces her to marry." Her brow wrinkled. "Just like my father is forcing me to go to this stupid school." Before he could defend Trev, she held up a hand, palm out. "Don't say it. You're not going to change my mind."

Colin liked the way she thrust out her chin, like a little terrier he had seen one time that refused to give up a bone. "It doesn't matter whether you agree or not. You're going to that school if I have to carry you there over my shoulder."

Annie glared at him. "Just like a primitive caveman. And here I thought you said you were progressive in your thinking." She tossed her long hair back and strode with shoulders erect back to Percival.

Colin shook his head in exasperation. He thought about joining Margaret, but she was seated on the overstuffed chair. Although he and Annie had sat together in it last night—albeit with Annie more or less in his lap—he didn't relish the idea of doing the same with Margaret.

He made the mistake of glancing at Essie, who winked as she motioned to the empty place by her feet. Refusing her offer would be rude—although safer—so he wandered over and perched at the end of the couch.

"How's your ankle feeling, Essie?" he asked politely.

"It's hurting some." She gazed at him with an innocent look. "I think you should examine it again, make sure it's nothing worse than a sprain." She tugged the blanket upward, revealing her ankles.

Colin glanced away. "I'm sure it's fine."

The blanket eased up higher, revealing the curve of her calves beneath her sheer black stockings. "Please?"

Essie's wheedling tone grated on his nerves. Still, maybe it *was* injured worse than he'd originally thought. "Will you stop pulling on the blanket if I check it out?"

She batted her eyelashes. If she had been fifteen years younger, the gesture might have tempted Colin. "I was merely showing you my"—she paused deliberately—"injury."

Colin gave a grunt of disbelief, but began unwrapping the binding around the injury. As he carefully examined the ankle, Essie shifted her other foot onto his thigh and stretched out her toes to press against his crotch.

Colin firmly removed the wandering foot. "Behave yourself, Essie."

She wrinkled her nose and scowled. "That's no fun at all."

"Could we have some quiet?" Annie's very irritated voice broke in. "We're trying to rehearse."

Margaret turned so she could see the sofa. "What in the world are you two doing?"

"Not nearly as much as I'd like to," Essie said with a pout.

"Well, I never—" Margaret began.

"Essie, you're supposed to be resting," Annie scolded at the same time.

At the cacophony of female voices, Colin pressed his lips together and rewrapped Essie's swollen ankle. He had spent many hours in train cars with his fellow tunnel workers, but none of them had ever given him a headache.

Percival clapped twice. "Ladies, ladies. We must try to get along."

"He's right," Colin said. "We don't know how long we'll be here."

"But it stopped snowing. We should be moving soon," Annie said.

"Only if they can shovel enough snow away from the tracks," Colin said.

As if in reply to his words, the train gave one long whistle.

Colin smiled in relief. "Looks like it wasn't that bad."

A knock on the door sounded and Paul the porter stepped in. His cheeks were red from the cold and he blew into his cupped hands. "We'll be commencing in five minutes. How is everyone doing in here?"

"We're fine," Colin replied before anyone else. "How do the tracks look up ahead?"

"They're pretty clear. This area is always bad for drifting," he said, shaking his head. "Five minutes, folks." He left.

"Come, Annie, let's finish rehearsing the scene before this abominable creature begins to move again," Percival said.

With a sharp glance at Essie, Annie joined Percival.

Colin put the finishing touches on the dressing and pulled the blanket back over her ankles and feet. "It is still puffy, but that's to be expected." He aimed a forefinger at her. "Now you will act your age and behave yourself, Essie."

The actress sniffed. "Killjoy."

Colin merely arched an eyebrow at her, then gave his attention back to Annie and Percival.

As the rehearsing continued, Colin could see an improvement in Annie's skills from earlier. Although he wasn't sure what all she said meant, he could ascertain the emotion behind it by watching her facial expressions and the way she moved or held her body.

" 'Husband, let's follow, to see the end of this ado,' " Annie said, poised with her arm upraised.

" 'First kiss me, Kate, and we will,' " Percival said.

His sly smile made Colin fist his hands on his thighs. It looked like Annie's kissing lessons were about to be put to use. "Who's Percival supposed to be?" he asked Essie in a low voice.

"Petruchio. Kate's husband," she replied.

Annie's mouth opened in a moue. " 'What, in the midst of the street?' "

As she and Percival's character—Petruchio—argued, Annie brought Katharina alive. The rise of color in her cheeks, the sharp edge of her tongue, and the subtle stiffening of her spine—all were created by Annie to give depth to her role.

" 'What, art thou ashamed of me?' " Percival responded.

Annie leaned closer to him. " 'No, sir, God forbid; but ashamed to kiss.' " Her eyes glittered with mischief.

Colin kept his attention on Annie, not wanting to miss a moment of her performance. The actresses in the few theater plays he had attended seemed lackluster by comparison. He shifted uneasily on the couch. Even his untrained eye could recognize her talent. Did anyone have the right to tell Annie what she could or couldn't do?

" 'Why, then, let's home again. Come, sirrah, let's away.' " Percival took hold of her arm.

" 'Nay, I will give thee a kiss; now pray thee, love, stay.' "

Percival gazed at her lovingly. " 'Is not this well? Come, my sweet Kate: better once than never, for never too late.' "

He swept Annie into his arms and lowered his mouth to hers.

Colin jumped to his feet and took a step toward them, all thoughts of Annie's talent and her right to choose her path in life forgotten. "You can't kiss her."

"Why not?" the actor asked, still holding Annie.

"Well, because"—Colin searched for a reason—"you're old enough to be her father."

Percival released Annie and straightened his backbone, then his lapels. "I most certainly am not," he said, indignation resonating in his voice.

"Who are you trying to kid, Percy?" Essie asked.

Percival's face flushed. His mouth opened, but before he could speak, Margaret broke in.

"Where are Toby and Alexander?"

Annie's eyes widened and filled with concern. "Oh, no. I forgot. They went outside."

"And the train is leaving any minute," Colin said. He hurried to the door, tugging on his warm coat as he went. "Percival, run up to the engine and tell them not to leave yet." The sound of the engines being stoked made his voice sharp. "Now. Hurry."

Percival exited without an argument.

"I'm going with you," Annie said.

She joined him, but Colin grabbed her arms. "No, you stay here with Margaret and Essie. I don't want to be worryin' about you, too."

"Your leg," Annie began.

"It's fine," he said impatiently. "Stay here." He tugged on a wool hat with earflaps and pulled on a pair of heavy gloves, then headed out.

The wind had died down to nothing and the sun shone brightly, casting diamond glitters of light across the fresh-fallen snow. He squinted against the brilliance and wished he had brought his dark-lensed spectacles. Glancing down at the snow-covered ground, he spotted what he hoped was Toby and Alexander's trail heading away from the train.

Why had he let them go out? He should have known they would be leaving soon.

Trudging through the snow that ranged from just inches to three feet, Colin could feel the ache in his leg almost immediately. Maybe he should have allowed Annie to accompany him.

No, he couldn't risk her getting left behind.

He brought his cupped hands to his mouth and hollered, "Toby! Alexander!"

His ears rang from listening so hard. He continued on, lifting one foot then the other, taking it step by step. Colin shouted their names again, but instead of silence, he heard the shrill whistle of the train, followed by the sudden jerk of metal couplings.

"Damn it!"

Percival was supposed to ensure the train didn't leave until Toby and Alexander had been found.

Now it looked like the three of them would be left behind to freeze.

Chapter 15

Annie labored through the snow, cursing her cumbersome skirts and impractical boots in very unladylike terms. With only her thin stockings to keep the snow at bay, the skin above her boots was fast moving from cold to numb. Though there was little wind, the frigid air nipped at her nose and cheeks.

But what was she supposed to do—allow Colin to go after Toby and Alexander by himself? If not for her, the two wouldn't even have been traveling with them.

It was just like her childhood friend to assume responsibility and search for them himself.

She shaded her eyes, but the brilliance didn't fade—it radiated from the snow, making the world a bright white blur. Her eyes watered and her breath misted in the cold air.

Looking back at the train, she was dismayed to see she had managed to walk only about fifty feet. It felt like fifty miles. Suddenly the train whistled and the cars moved, the clanking resounding in the unfamiliar stillness.

The train was leaving without them.

Panic rose in Annie's throat and she shouted, "Colin!"

She took a step and her foot sank through the snow onto uneven ground below. Her body pitched forward and she tried to catch herself with outstretched arms. Her hands sank through the white powder and she fell head first into the crystalline snow.

"Shit." Her unladylike expletive was muffled by the snowbank in her face.

Pressing herself upward, Annie shook her head and scrubbed a hand across her snow-covered face. She gasped and managed to roll onto her back and lie there, staring at the blue sky. If not for the chilly air, she could have enjoyed her soft mattress and the sun's warmth on her now damp face.

Her musings were cut short by the sound of the train's wheels turning on the rails. She sat up and scowled at the train as it pulled away.

"Shit," she swore again with more vehemence.

A shadow on the ground startled her and Colin dropped to his knees beside her. "Are you all right?"

Startled, Annie threw her arms around his neck and he fell against her with an audible *oomph.* He managed to catch himself with a hand braced to the side or he would have ended up on top of her—not a bad position, to Annie's way of thinking.

"I'm glad to see you," she said against his warm neck. "I thought I'd been stranded all alone out here."

Colin awkwardly patted her back with one hand. "It's all right, Annie. I'm here and I'll take care of you."

His patronizing tone struck a discord in her, and she abruptly pushed him away with as much enthusiasm as she had used to hug him. He sprawled back, landing on his backside in the snow.

He glared at her.

She glared back.

"Don't you dare treat me like a child," she said.

After a bit of maneuvering, Annie managed to draw her knees up under her to stand up. Snow clung to her coat, dress, petticoats, and abundance of skirts, thwarting her efforts, and she found herself plopping in the snow once more.

Colin laughed.

"Don't say it!" Annie shook her small fist at him. She knew how she must look—snow-covered with straggling blond hair hanging around her face and her cheeks red from the cool air. Just like a child.

Damn it!

He held up his hands in surrender. "I wasn't goin' to say a word."

Annie snorted.

"The train left without us," Colin said simply.

"I noticed." Annie crossed her arms as if it were the most natural thing in the world to have a conversation sitting in the snow in the middle of nowhere. "Did you find Alexander and Toby?"

"No, but their tracks led back toward the front of the train."

"So they're probably aboard?"

"More than likely."

Relief filtered through Annie, her mood improved by the good news. She wasn't happy about being stranded out here, but she wouldn't have to worry about Toby and Alexander being in the same predicament.

"So here we are," she said.

"Here we are," Colin reiterated.

"We could freeze, and maybe five hundred years from now somebody would find our perfectly preserved bodies and be inspired to write a love story about us. Just think, Colin, we could be immortalized."

Colin's breath misted in the cold air. "First off, we aren't going to freeze because the train will be back for us. Second, this area will warm up and our bodies would thaw out, so we wouldn't remained perfectly preserved." Amusement lit his face. "And last, I'd prefer a good adventure story to be immortalized in."

Shrugging, Annie brushed a stringy strand of hair off her face. "You make up your stories, I'll make up mine. Now what do we do?"

"We either sit here and freeze our ass—our backsides off, or we start following the tracks."

"My ass is already frozen." Mischief sparkled in her eyes.

"Imp."

"Stick-in-the-mud." Her eyes twinkled. "Stick-in-the-snow?"

Colin ignored her comment. "Hopefully, Percival can use his silver tongue to persuade them to come back for us."

"He was *supposed* to keep them from leaving."

"And you were supposed to stay on the train," he said flatly.

"When did I ever do what I was told?" she asked with a saucy grin.

Colin gathered his legs beneath him and stood, then leaned over Annie.

She placed her hand in his and he drew her to her feet with little effort. Annie's body kept going until her chest was flush with his. She wiggled against his solid body. "Thank you."

Colin took hold of her shoulders and pressed her back until there were six inches of breathing room between them. His expression told her he knew exactly what type of game she was playing.

Spoilsport.

"You're welcome." He held up an admonishing finger. "But you're not forgiven for leaving the train."

"What's my punishment?" She backed away and turned in a small circle with her arms outspread. "Banishment?"

Colin heaved a sigh. "You'd try the patience of a saint."

"It's a good thing you're a saint, Colin." She gave him a sincere smile and said quietly, "I'm glad you're with me."

He drew back, startled, then his lips lifted at the corners. "If I'm to be stranded in the wilderness with one person, you'd be my first choice." He grimaced. "Although your father's probably going to have my hide."

"I wouldn't worry about that." She started trudging toward the tracks. "You'll probably die from the cold first."

"Thanks for that bit of optimism."

Once on the tracks, their path was easier to navigate but not completely without a hidden hazard or two. Annie slipped on an ice-covered plank and Colin grabbed her arm, saving her from a nasty fall. His hand moved down to her hand and he threaded his fingers through hers. "Now if you fall, you'll take me with you."

"Or you'll take me with you." Annie curled her fingers snugly around his and wished they weren't wearing gloves. Even though Colin had often held her hand as a child, this was so much different. So much more . . . intimate.

She inhaled deeply and the cold nearly froze the inside of her nose. Silence like Annie had never experienced surrounded her. She was exceedingly aware of their breaths and the crunch of snow and ice beneath their feet. The blue sky was so pure it almost hurt to look at it. The trees to either side of the tracks were a mix of evergreens and hardwoods, which held snow-mantled branches and the occasional gold remnant of a leaf.

"It's beautiful up here," she said, her voice hushed as if she were afraid to shatter the fragile quiet.

"Aye. It's the only thing I miss of my work," Colin said, equally as softly.

Although Annie knew his job had involved working in the mountains, she hadn't really thought about what it entailed. "The only thing?"

Colin glanced at her, then cast his gaze forward again. "I liked the travelin', too. Seein' new places."

"Won't you miss it when you settle down on your ranch?"

"I hadn't thought much about it. The only thing I knew was that I couldn't do my job anymore."

Annie stepped over broken plank. "Why?"

Colin's grip tightened almost imperceptibly and eased again. "It's a long story."

The sadness in his voice echoed the melancholy she had seen in his eyes the first evening after his arrival in Denver. She said lightly, "Something tells me we have the time."

A crooked grin teased his lips and warmth flowed in Annie at the endearing sight.

"Do you know what my job was with the railroad?" he asked.

"You blasted tunnels so the trains could go through mountains instead of all the way around them."

"Exactly. I was the head of a crew of six men. We would check out the stability of the rock, figure out the best spots to place the charges, set the dynamite, and detonate. We'd have to do this many times until we had a tunnel clear through. If we didn't blast in the right places, the whole mountain could've come down on us."

Annie shivered, not from the cold air. "It sounds dangerous."

He nodded somberly. "The most dangerous job of all the railroad crews."

They walked in silence for a time until Colin spoke again. "I had a good reputation. Men wanted to work for me, knowing I was careful and never put my crew in danger. I never gave them a job I wouldn't do myself, like checking the stability of the rock after a blasting.

"We were halfway through a mountain, and after the last blast, I had a strange feeling. Instead of sending someone in to check, I went myself. Two of my men—friends—went with me."

Annie's belly cramped. Something told her this story wouldn't have a happy ending.

"While we were inside, a blast detonated," he said.

"How?"

"It should have blown with the others, but

didn't." The weary tone of Colin's voice told Annie more than his words.

"What happened?"

"My leg was broken and one of the men was killed. The other man, his brother, was far enough behind us that he was thrown back away from the blast." He glanced at her. "You met him at the station yesterday. Leonard Jenkins. He had some cracked ribs, but wasn't trapped inside the tunnel."

"You . . . you were trapped?" Annie couldn't seem to do more than whisper the question.

"Yes."

She tightened her hold on his hand. "For how long?"

Colin stumbled on the rail, but caught himself. "Three days." He paused. "Are you warm enough?"

"Yes," she murmured, her mind trying to wrap around his revelation. "Your leg?"

"A rock fell on it."

Annie's imagination filled in the gaps. She envisioned the darkness, the pain of a broken leg, the helplessness and fear that he might die. Her breathing grew ragged and she pressed a hand to her mouth.

"Did you ever find out why the charge didn't detonate when it was supposed to?" she asked with a husky voice.

"Most everyone figured I'd made the mistake, but it was one of the charges Leonard Jenkins and his brother were supposed to have checked." His gaze turned inward. "The price of the mistake for Leonard was his brother's life. I figured there was no reason to tell anyone."

So Colin had allowed people to think he was to blame, to save Leonard Jenkins from the guilt. Annie's vision grew blurry and she tightened her hold on his hand.

The faint sound of a train spared her from trying to form a proper response.

"It's coming back." Colin smiled. "Percival must finally have done something right."

He led Annie off the tracks to a position about twenty feet away. The clacking of the steel wheels grew louder as the train backed toward them.

Now that they weren't moving, Annie shivered. Colin wrapped an arm around her shoulders and drew her close to share their warmth. She welcomed his secure embrace and melted against him.

She tilted her head back to gaze at his profile—the sweep of his forehead, the strength in his square jaw, and the sensuous lips that she had felt and tasted against her own. At times like this it was impossible to see him merely as a childhood friend. Instinctively, she knew he would always be her friend, but there was more she wanted from him.

Things she had no right asking of him.

Things she couldn't even ask of herself.

The caboose came into view, then the Pullman and the rest of the train backed toward them. As the cars passed them, Annie could see the passengers with their noses pressed against the windows, peering at her and Colin with wide eyes. The brakes squealed as the train stopped.

"Annie."

She glanced up to see Percival hanging off one of the platforms between cars.

"Thank God you're all right," the actor said with a dramatic flourish.

"I'm doing pretty good, too," Colin called out wryly.

"Oh, yes, of course, you too, Mr. McBride," Percival said with somewhat less enthusiasm.

With Colin's hand on her waist, Annie trudged across the short expanse of snow to climb aboard the train. Percival took hold of her arm and helped her aboard, then led her into the nearest train car, leaving Colin to tag along.

Colin scowled and tried to rein in his dislike of the actor. It was damned difficult to do, with Percival's hands all over Annie.

Colin was met by the conductor and the porter, both obviously flustered by their mistake in leaving two passengers behind.

"We had no idea there was anybody outside the train," the conductor said, his brow damp with sweat despite the cool air.

Colin deliberately eyed Percival. "We thought someone was going to tell you."

The actor flushed. "I'm so sorry, but as I was walking through the train, I spotted Toby and Alexander. I gave them a piece of my mind for leaving the train."

"That didn't take ten minutes," Colin said.

Percival's face deepened to scarlet. "Well, I, um, was stopped by a passenger who had seen my performance of 'Hamlet' some years ago."

"And you forgot about us."

The actor shifted uneasily. "Actually, I forgot about *you*. I hadn't realized Annie was also out there until Margaret told me. That's when I hastened to tell them."

At least the man is honest.

"Oh, thank heavens!"

Colin turned only to have his arms filled with Margaret. He awkwardly hugged her back, but her stranglehold threatened to choke him. He disentangled himself from her.

"I was certain you and Annie would be eaten by bears or lions or bitten by a snake." Margaret clutched an abused hanky in her hands.

Colin managed to keep his expression serious as he gave her hands a reassuring squeeze. "There are no snakes this high in the mountains, the bears are hibernating, and mountain lions rarely attack a human being, especially during the day."

Percival pressed past Colin to wrap an arm around Margaret's shoulders. "I told you I would get them back."

The woman narrowed her eyes. "They should not have been left behind in the first place," she scolded.

"You're right, Margaret," the actor said. "It was my fault."

Colin noticed he said it with just the right

amount of contrition and humility. What was it with Percival and women? First Annie, now Margaret.

The widow patted the actor's arm. "Hush now, Percival, everyone makes mistakes."

"Why don't you folks go back to your car so we can get under way?" the conductor suggested.

"That sounds like a wonderful idea to me," Annie said.

Percival guided Margaret through the cars, with Colin and Annie following.

Annie leaned toward Colin as they walked. "You might have some competition for the fair hand of Margaret."

He can have her.

The unbidden thought shocked Colin. Yet it had become painfully clear he preferred someone else—someone who had no intention of settling down soon, if ever.

He had three choices—pursue Margaret; search for another bride; or wait for Annie. Though he preferred the third option, he didn't have the luxury of time. He wanted children before he was too old to enjoy them, and Annie had already made her desire to become an actress clear.

Colin had no wish to start a new search for a wife. That left Margaret. She was attractive, comfortable to be with, and wanted to marry again. He had no doubt she would be a strict but caring mother, too. She was perfect.

She isn't Annie.

Colin shook his head. There was no point wishing for what could never be. He had to be practical.

They arrived at the parlor car and found Essie, Alexander, and Toby sitting quietly inside.

"It's about damn time," Essie said by way of greeting.

"We didn't have a whole lot of say in the matter," Annie said dryly. She crossed over to the sofa where Essie reclined. "How're you feeling?"

"I'm fine, sweetie. I wasn't the one out in the snow for an hour." Essie glared at Percival. "Can you believe him? Allowing the train to leave without you?"

"He didn't know I was out there," Annie said.

Essie harrumphed. "But he knew Colin was. You'd think he was trying to get rid of him or something."

"Essie," Percival said, shocked. "I could never hurt another living thing."

Colin's mind clicked into motion. Percival had been in Denver while he was, and could conceivably have tried to run him down. He also would have had enough time to shoot Rudy at the train station before boarding.

But why? What reason would Percival have for hurting or killing him?

Colin's gaze rested on Annie, who was talking with Essie. Did Percival harbor some twisted affection for her? Right now he appeared to be paying Margaret more attention, but maybe that was merely a ploy.

Colin rubbed his brow, trying to ease the growing headache. He was cold and damp and hungry. It was easy for his mind to come up with conspiracies that didn't exist when he was tired.

"Are you all right, Mr. McBride?"

Colin glanced down to see Toby beside him. He managed a reassuring smile. "I'm fine. I'm glad you and Alexander were back on the train when it left."

Toby studied him, his face too unexpressive for one so young. What kind of life had made him learn to hide his feelings so well?

"Me and Alexander heard the whistle so we figgered we'd better get back on board." He toed the floor. "We didn't know you and Annie went out to look for us. Nobody ever done that before."

Colin squatted down so he was at eye level with the boy. He rested his hands on Toby's shoulders, felt them tense and slowly relax beneath his palms. "What do you mean?"

"Ain't nobody ever cared about us enough to go looking for us. Me and Alexander are used to lookin' out for each other."

"We never would have left you out there by yourselves. I told you, Annie cares a great deal about both of you."

Toby studied him with a measuring look. "Do you?"

Colin blinked, considering the boy's sincere question. True, his first impression of Toby had been that the kid was a cheat and a liar. The blackjack game yesterday had confirmed it. However,

Toby's loyalty to Alexander and his offer to give the ill-gotten money back had changed his opinion considerably. He met Toby's gaze evenly. "Yes, I care what happens to you." He glanced up at Alexander, never far from Toby's side. "You *and* Alexander."

Toby gave him another long gauging look before nodding. "Okay."

"Okay?"

"Okay." Toby slid his hands into his overall pockets. "You want me and Alexander to do anything?"

Colin thought for a moment. "Do you know how to cook?"

"Sure. Me and Alexander cook a lot for Percival and Essie."

"Why don't you throw something together from the food we have?"

Toby headed over to the area that served as a kitchen with Alexander half a step behind him.

Stifling a groan, Colin pushed himself to his feet.

"Do you think they might allow me to help them?" Margaret asked Colin.

He followed her gaze to Toby and Alexander as they sorted through the food. "You can ask them. They're pretty independent, though."

"It's sad, isn't it?"

Colin shook his head slowly. "No, it would be sad if they weren't happy. I'm not sure I can agree that a life on the road with an acting troupe is better than life in a good home, but I think it's up to Toby and Alexander."

"I hadn't thought of it that way."

"Most people don't."

"And I'm 'most' people?"

"You can't tell me you hadn't thought about going to the authorities about them."

Margaret glanced away. "Perhaps I entertained the idea for a day or two." She smiled. "I think I'll see if they would like my help. If not, I shall take the refusal gracefully."

She joined Toby and Alexander, and Colin watched in surprise as the boy gave her a task and Margaret accepted it graciously. Shaking his head, he went in search of dry clothes.

Bone weary, Annie didn't even attempt to join in the conversation that swirled around her that evening. She noticed Colin was uncharacteristically quiet, too. Perhaps he too was exhausted from their little misadventure that afternoon. But at least he hadn't had to rehearse for two hours after it.

She stared down at the open playbook in her hands, knowing she should be going over her lines so she could try rehearsing tomorrow without the book. The day after tomorrow they would be in Reno, and the second evening there they would be performing.

Merely thinking about it set her stomach fluttering like a dozen hummingbirds had taken residence there. However, after her stage debut earlier that summer, she knew the nervousness would disappear a minute after she stepped onto the stage. She would fall into her role and forget about the audience.

Her attention wandered again and she couldn't help but narrow her eyes when Margaret whispered something in Colin's ear and he smiled down at her. Annie's stomach twisted painfully, wishing she could be on the receiving end of his smiles. The two of them perched on the loveseat side by side, while Percival lounged in the chair and Toby and Alexander sat at the table, playing with a pair of dice. Essie lay sprawled across the couch, shooting dagger looks at Colin and Margaret every so often. Annie could definitely relate to her disgust.

Hell's bells.

She had brought this on herself. *She* had been the one who'd initially pushed Colin and Margaret together. *She* had been the one who'd encouraged him to court her. *She* had been the one to point out Percival's interest in the widow.

Of course, *she* hadn't counted on her own possessiveness getting in the way. Just because she and Colin had been the best of friends didn't mean she could dictate whom he could and couldn't be with.

She closed her eyes and leaned her head back against the cushion. The rhythm of the train lulled her and her traveling companions' voices faded away.

Someone shaking her shoulder awakened her. She blinked in the dim light and it took her a few moments to remember where she was.

"You'd best retire for the evening, lass," Colin said quietly.

She glanced around, noticing that Toby and Alexander were already sprawled out on the floor, covered with blankets. Percival lay sprawled across the couch.

"Essie and Margaret have already gone to bed. I thought about letting you sleep here, but you'll be more comfortable in the compartment."

"With Margaret hogging the mattress?" Annie smiled wryly and stood with Colin's assistance.

She glanced up at Colin and caught the glint of something in his eyes. "I'd rather sleep with you," she said softly.

Colin started and retreated a step. "You're not a little girl anymore."

She took a deep breath and let it out slowly. "You're right. I'm behaving like a silly child instead of a grown woman."

"After what happened today, it's understandable."

"I wasn't scared."

Colin smiled. "I know. But even I was a little worried."

"I wasn't, because I was with you." She leaned forward and kissed his cheek, enjoying the fresh scent of soap on his skin. "Goodnight."

She walked to the sleeping berth, paused, and turned to look at Colin one last time. His figure was illuminated by the moonlight streaming in the window as he gazed back at her.

She shivered under his hot gaze and wondered if Kate had felt this way when she fell in love with Trev.

Chapter 16

The weather had cleared and the sun melted the snow from the tracks, enabling the train to travel steadily over the next twenty-four hours. It made only six stops in towns along the way to drop off passengers and replace them with new ones. They had made it through the worst of the mountains and were now rolling across Nevada, where they would arrive in Reno mid-afternoon of the fourth day of traveling.

Sitting beside Margaret on the love seat, Colin glanced at his other traveling companions. Annie and Percival were rehearsing yet again—it seemed that was all they had done since yesterday morning. Essie had started hobbling about, relieved to be off the couch, which she had proclaimed was "harder than a sailor's pecker after a year-long voyage." Fortunately, she hadn't spouted the little declaration in front of Margaret. Annie, however, heard it and hadn't even attempted to stifle her laughter.

Colin turned his attention to Toby and Alexander, who were playing a card game simple enough that Alexander could participate. As the big man won, Toby grinned in victory as if he himself had triumphed. Fate might have dealt them a bad hand in life, but their friendship was something so rare, Colin was envious of them.

"What do you think?"

Margaret's question brought his attention back to her as she held up the dress she had been altering for the past two days.

"Do you think the neckline is decent enough for Annie?" she asked.

Colin gazed at the ivory dress critically, imagining Annie's voluptuous form filling it—and envisioned the upper slope of her breasts exposed to every hungry pair of male eyes in the theater. His contemplative mood slipped to surly. "No. You need to make it higher."

"Really?"

"No, not really," Essie said, shuffling up beside them. "You make it any higher and people will think she's a nun."

"She's a young woman with a proper upbringing," Colin argued.

"When she wears this she's Katharina, an Elizabethan bride," Essie said. "Not Annie Trevelyan."

"She's right, Colin," Margaret said quietly.

Colin stared at her a moment and shook his head. "I can't believe you and Essie are agreeing on something."

Annie and Percival joined them.

"What are they agreeing on?" Annie asked curiously, then her gaze lit on the dress. "Is it done?" she asked Margaret excitedly.

"Yes."

"No," Colin said at the same time.

"Yes," Essie said firmly, her crossed arms telling them her word was the final one.

"Perhaps Annie should try it on," Percival suggested tactfully.

"Good idea." Annie grabbed the dress and moved behind the privacy screen in the corner.

"You're her chaperone," Colin reminded Margaret. "Do you think Trev and Kate would allow her to wear that?"

Margaret eyed Colin. "If Trev and Kate were here, Annie would not be performing at all. You are the one who allowed her to participate in this play."

Colin clenched his hands into fists of frustration. Maybe Margaret wasn't quite as docile as he had originally thought. "That was before I knew about . . . about that dress."

"Calm down before you hurt something important," Essie said without an ounce of sympathy. "I think you should both just let Annie make her own decisions." She limped over to the chair and sat down with a sigh. "When I was her age, I didn't have a choice."

"What do you mean?" Margaret asked curiously.

"I was fifteen years old and looking more like twenty when my folks threw me out of the house." She shrugged. "I can't blame them; they had a dozen mouths to feed. I would have ended up in a cathouse if this traveling show hadn't been in town. When they asked me if I wanted to join up, I jumped at the chance, and I've never regretted it."

Colin could understand—he too had been pushed into the world at a young age. What if he had been a girl? What choices would he have had then?

However, Annie *did* have other choices, and Colin was determined she make the right decisions.

A wolf whistle from Toby's direction made Colin glance up and Annie's entrance from behind the screen stole the air from his lungs. The décolletage definitely showed the upper swell of her bosom, but fortunately it looked like there would be little chance of her spilling out of the dress. The gown didn't rely on a bustle or layers of petticoats to give it shape, only Annie's curves, which were more than adequate for the task.

She pirouetted slowly and the smooth-textured material clung to her legs and well-shaped derriere. Colin's mouth grew dry and his groin responded to Annie's abundant charms.

Then he spotted the angel on the chain around

her neck, reminding him whom he was lusting after. He cleared his throat and found himself the center of attention.

"Well?" Annie asked impatiently.

It was obvious Colin had missed something. "Well what?"

"What do you think of the dress?" Annie repeated.

I think it should be outlawed in public.

He searched the room and spotted a knot in the wall to focus on. "It's too mature for you."

"Mature?" Annie demanded. She strolled toward him, her hands on her waist and her hips swaying like a porch swing in a brisk wind. Pausing directly in front of him so her breasts were at eye level, she asked in a husky voice, "You don't think I'm old enough to wear this dress?"

Aware of everyone watching him, Colin swallowed and forced his gaze past the tempting mounds of flesh to meet Annie's eyes. "You'll never be old enough to wear that dress."

She laughed, a light tinkling sound that reached deep into Colin and wrapped around his heart. She leaned down and kissed his cheek, and though the touch was fleeting, it seared him.

"Thanks for wanting to protect my virtue, but I think I can take care of that myself." She winked. "Remember the knee trick Papa taught me?"

He deserved that knee, for the inappropriate visions scampering through his head. "All right, lass, you win. But if your father hears about this,

I'm going to have to board the next ship to China."

Laughter filled the car, sweeping away the tension.

After the excitement of arriving in Reno the evening before, Annie had slept well on a bed she had all to herself. Colin had procured her and Margaret a room with two beds. His room was across the hall and she was certain he had listened, guarding it from intruders . . . and ensuring a certain young woman didn't go off exploring by herself.

As she completed her toilette, she watched Margaret braiding her long dark hair in preparation for pinning it into a bun at the base of her neck.

"Your hair is too beautiful to hide," Annie suddenly said.

Margaret's fingers paused momentarily in the middle of braiding. "It's not proper to wear it loose."

"Who says?"

"Why, everyone, of course."

"I don't." Annie gave her wavy blond hair one more swish of the brush. "You shouldn't let other people tell you how to live your life, Margaret."

"If one didn't have rules to follow, civilization would decline."

Annie placed her brush back in her bag and asked Margaret with mock gravity, "So if you don't make that hair bun just so, civilization would decline?"

Margaret's cheeks reddened. "Of course not. All I'm saying is that—" Her voice trailed away. She tied off the end of the braid, but didn't attempt to pin it up. "My husband used to punish me if I didn't follow the rules," she whispered.

Annie frowned and joined the older woman, perching on the bed beside her. "No person has the right to punish another, unless he or she has broken a law. Then it's up to the courts to do the punishing."

Margaret patted the back of Annie's hand. "You're so young and idealistic."

Stung, Annie leaned away from the older woman. "You make it sound as if that's a bad thing."

"Not bad. Merely naïve."

"Because I don't think a woman should have to put up with a man who thinks he owns her?"

Margaret remained silent for a moment, then said quietly, "Essie wasn't the only one who had to make decisions at an early age." She paused and stroked her braid absently. "My father said either I was to marry the man he had chosen for me or I would be thrown out of the house without a penny."

Annie inhaled sharply, then hugged Margaret. "I'm sorry."

"I am, too." Margaret looked past Annie and out the window. "I rejoiced when my husband died. After I was told of his death, I excused myself to be alone. Everyone thought it was so I could mourn behind closed doors. Instead, I jumped up and down, clapping my hands and thanking God he was out of my life forever."

"You had every right to celebrate. The man was a monster."

"Maybe. But he was still my husband."

"He didn't deserve to be," Annie said.

Margaret brushed a hand across her damp eyes. "You've known Colin for a long time."

Though it wasn't a question, Annie nodded. "Ever since I was a child."

"Is he that way? Does he believe a woman should obey her husband's every word?"

Annie worried her lower lip between her teeth. She often teased Colin about his old-fashioned ideas on men and women, but would he actually force a woman to obey him, or punish her when she didn't? No, she could never see Colin lift a violent hand to any woman, no matter the provocation.

"Colin is a kind and decent man," Annie began. "My father and stepmother have known him for years. If he was like your late husband, Papa and Kate wouldn't count him as one of their dearest friends."

Margaret nodded thoughtfully. "I didn't believe Colin was, but I had to be certain."

"Why?" Annie knew she didn't want to hear the answer.

"Before I allowed him to court me further, I had to know."

Annie's heart squeezed painfully. "If he asks you to marry him, what will your answer be?"

Margaret's half smile was enigmatic. "It depends on my choices."

Puzzled, Annie wanted to ask her what she meant. Did she really want to know? Or was ignorance bliss in this situation?

"Are you ready for your performance tonight?" Margaret asked.

Annie didn't know whether to be relieved or annoyed by the change of subject. She didn't want to dwell on tonight any more than she wanted to think about her feelings for Colin. "I feel like I'm not even close to being ready," she admitted.

"Although I was against your doing this in the beginning, I can see that you love acting. It was in your eyes and the way your whole face lit up when you rehearsed." Margaret smiled. "Let me offer this piece of advice, Annie. Attend the finishing school, then follow your heart. If it still tells you to act, then that is what you must do."

What if my heart says it wants Colin but he's married to you?

"I'll think about it," Annie said, unable to promise more. She stood. "Ready for breakfast?"

"Yes."

Annie glanced at the braid which draped over Margaret's shoulder and almost to her waist, and smiled in approval. "Forgive me for saying this, but you look much younger with your hair like that."

"Thank you, I think," Margaret said with a sheepish smile.

The women left the room and strolled down the stairs to the hotel restaurant. Annie was well aware of the admiring gazes they received as they walked arm-in-arm across the lobby. She was accustomed to the masculine attention, but this time it wasn't all directed toward her. A week ago, Annie had seen Margaret as a dull-as-dishwater woman, but in the short time they had been aboard the train, Margaret had blossomed. Now there was no excuse Annie could give Colin not to pursue her.

And the worst part was that Annie *liked* this new Margaret and suspected they could become good friends . . . if only Colin wasn't between them.

Shoving away the cloud of gloom, she looked around the restaurant and spotted Colin already seated at a table with Toby and Alexander.

As they neared the table, Colin stood and Annie was shocked to see Toby and Alexander follow his example.

Toby pushed Annie's chair in for her while Colin did the same for Margaret.

"My, such polite young gentlemen," Margaret said, gazing at Toby and Alexander.

Toby shrugged, embarrassed. "Colin was just tellin' us about manners and stuff. I figgered we could give it a try."

Annie gave his hand a gentle squeeze. "You did very well. Thank you."

She glanced up at Colin, who winked at her. Although flustered, Annie winked back and was rewarded with a smile that made assorted parts of her body curl with desire.

"So what are you having, Alexander?" Margaret asked kindly.

"Me and him are having flapjacks with blueberries and lots of maple syrup," Toby replied.

"That sounds wonderful. I'm afraid my clothes would never fit if I ate all that."

"Me and Alexander can help you finish, Mrs. Mopplewhite," Toby offered. He looked at her as if seeing her for the first time. "I like how you got your hair. It makes you look prettier."

"Why, thank you, Toby," Margaret said.

Annie glanced across the table and found Colin staring at Margaret, his expression unreadable. She quickly looked away, afraid he was thinking the same as Toby.

The waitress brought two more cups of coffee, then took their orders. Half an hour later, the plates were pushed back one by one.

"Can we go look around the town?" Toby asked Colin.

Annie frowned in surprise at the question. Toby rarely asked anyone for permission to do something.

"All right, but make sure you're careful, and remember to meet us at the theater at eleven," Colin said.

"We will." Toby pushed back his chair. "C'mon, Alexander. Let's go explore."

Alexander lifted a hand to the adults, then followed the boy out of the restaurant.

Annie's astonishment changed to outright shock. "So what did you do with the real Toby?"

Colin chuckled. "During our discussion of manners, I also mentioned that you and Margaret wouldn't worry so much about them if you knew where they were."

"Very tricky, Colin," Annie said with a grin that quickly faded. "Although he doesn't act it, he *is* only a child."

"And children like to have someone to answer to as long as they know that person truly cares for them," Margaret added.

Annie didn't miss the pleased look that crossed Colin's face at Margaret's words. With her thoughtful words, the widow had moved up another notch in his estimation of the perfect wife and mother.

"How did you sleep?" Colin asked Margaret.

"Very well, thank you." The older woman looked at Annie. "And I'm sure Annie appreciated not having to share a bed with me. My late husband used to complain about my restlessness all the time. I finally got to a point where I would sleep in another bedroom."

Annie searched Margaret's features and marveled at her composure. She suspected the widow would never confess all the abuse her husband had inflicted upon her for imagined slights, but revealing this much had to have been difficult.

Colin wisely didn't comment, and Annie wondered if he already knew about Margaret's late husband. "Would you ladies like to take a stroll around town before going to the theater?"

"Weren't Percival and Essie going to meet us for breakfast?" Margaret asked.

"They were down earlier, then had a cab take them and the costumes and props to the theater."

"I should have gone with them," Annie said.

Colin shook his head. "Percival said to tell you to 'relax this morning in preparation for your performance tonight.'" He mimicked the actor's speech.

Annie laughed. "You sound just like him." She rolled her shoulders to ease the stress in her tense muscles. "I wouldn't mind. How about you?" she asked Margaret.

"Would you mind terribly if I lay down for a little while? It is heaven to rest without the bed moving beneath me," Margaret said.

Satisfaction and happiness surged through Annie. She would have Colin all to herself. "Of course not. We can stop by and pick you up on our way to the theater. Right, Colin?"

"You aren't getting sick, are you, Margaret?" he asked in concern.

"No, I'm fine. Just a little tired," she replied.

Colin frowned, clearly displeased that she wouldn't be accompanying them, and Annie's heart dropped. He would probably prefer it if

Margaret went with him and Annie stayed behind to rest.

"All right, then. We'll be back here about ten forty-five and we can ride a cab to the theater together," he said.

Margaret and Annie stood, and Colin gallantly came to his feet.

"I have to get my coat. I'll meet you by the door," Annie said to Colin.

Once in their room, Annie asked, "Are you sure you don't want to go with us? Colin seemed truly upset that you wouldn't be accompanying us, and you *are* my chaperone."

"I'm certain," Margaret said firmly. "Besides, I trust Colin with you implicitly. Any fool can see he loves you."

Annie's heart skipped and her fingers trembled. Surely Margaret meant sibling love, not the love between a woman and man. "Of course he does," she said flippantly. "He's known me since I was younger than Toby."

Margaret reached over and smoothed down the collar on Annie's coat. "You and Colin have a good time. I want to be well rested to enjoy your stage debut." She gave the younger woman a gentle shove toward the door. "I'll see you in two hours."

Somewhat baffled by Margaret's odd behavior, Annie decided to enjoy the last time she would be exclusively in Colin's company.

She scurried down the stairs and met Colin at the appointed place.

"Are you ready to 'go explorin',' as Toby would say?" Colin asked.

"Definitely. I need something to take my mind off this evening," Annie replied.

He extended his crooked arm and Annie put her hand through it. He guided her outside and down the boardwalk.

Reno was quite a bit smaller than Denver, but it didn't appear any less busy. People bustled here and there, and horse-drawn wagons rattled over the hard-packed snow covering the street.

Annie enjoyed observing the people they passed. There were some old men dressed in coveralls gathered in front of the barbershop, swapping tall tales. A group of women with children darting in and out of their skirt folds gossiped about what had happened to whom and why so-and-so thought she was so much better than the rest of them.

Annie grimaced, knowing she could never be content living a life like theirs, with only children and the local personalities to discuss. Yet a part of her wondered if she would feel the same way if she was Colin's wife and was raising his children.

But that could never be. Besides wanting to act, there was also her fear of dying in childbirth. Or even more terrifying, losing her mind, if in fact that was what had happened to her mother.

"Did you study your lines any more last night?" Colin asked.

"Twice. Margaret helped me by reading Percival's part." Annie pressed closer to Colin so she wouldn't bump into someone walking in the opposite direction, but didn't move away when they passed. "I had thought Margaret would be completely against me performing, but she's not. If I didn't know better, I would say she even approved of me acting."

"She's a special woman," Colin commented.

Annie's stomach ached. "Are you going to ask her to marry you?"

Colin didn't seem to notice her agitation. "I don't know. Probably. She's exactly the type of woman I've been looking for."

Suddenly the sunny day seemed dreary, cast in shades of gray. She forced herself to put some more space between their bodies as they walked. "I had a feeling you would like her." Annie pasted on a smile. "Will I be invited to the wedding?"

"Would you come?"

She didn't want to, but knew she would. Colin deserved whatever happiness he found and Annie was truly glad for him. "Try to keep me away," she said in a bantering tone.

"I knew I could count on you."

They continued strolling, moving into a busier part of town with more people crowding the boardwalks. Colin drew Annie closer to his side and she didn't complain.

Suddenly she felt Colin stiffen and glanced up at his face. His lips pressed together in a thin line as his gaze surveyed the bustling street.

"What is it?" she asked.

His muscles relaxed and he smiled down at her. "I thought I saw an old friend."

"Who?"

He gave her arm a squeeze. "Nobody you'd know, lass."

In spite of his light tone—or perhaps because of it—Annie suspected he was hiding something. She searched the area, but saw only strangers.

It must have been somebody from his railroad days. Sometimes she forgot how long he had been out of her life and all the years he had been on his own. There were times when she felt she knew him better than anyone else, and then there were times like this, when she realized she hardly knew the man at all.

Chapter 17

◯◯

Foreboding tingled down Colin's spine. He had the feeling they were being watched by unseen eyes, observed from some hidden place.

Had Thomas Morales followed Annie? If he had caught the following day's train, he could easily be in Reno. They had been late because of the snowstorm; the next train wouldn't have had that problem.

Colin kept his worry hidden from Annie, who was already anxious enough about her performance tonight.

Thomas had seemed obsessed with Annie. It could have been he who had fired the shots at the depot in Denver, trying to eliminate Colin, whom he thought was a rival for Annie. He also could have been the one who'd tried to run them down with the wagon, though Colin wasn't certain, since Annie could have been injured or killed as easily as him.

He would just have to keep his guard up and make sure someone was with Annie at all times—preferably him.

Colin spotted a department store ahead and steered her toward it. "Let's take a look in there," he said.

Annie's eyes lit up and she eagerly entered the building. Colin released her in the middle of the women's clothing section, and she wandered around, checking out the items. Colin kept her in sight as he darted searching looks out the window. If someone had been out there watching them, he had now disappeared.

"Look at this," Annie called.

Colin joined her as she displayed a sheer camisole made of lace. His face warmed. "That's nice," he managed to say.

Annie held it up against her chest and though she wore many layers of clothing, Colin could easily imagine her in only the lacy underclothing.

He grabbed it from her and hung it back on the rack. "You're not old enough."

"When *will* I be old enough?" she asked, batting her long eyelashes and looking too damned irresistible.

"The same time you're old enough to wear Katharina's dress."

Annie giggled. "In other words, never."

He crossed his arms, feeling foolish, but better

to look a little silly than to allow her to find out about his attraction toward her. "That's right."

She turned away, but he could feel her sidelong gaze on him. "Maybe you should buy it for Margaret as a wedding present. She could wear it on your honeymoon night."

Colin refused to let her see his startled reaction. "*If* I ask Margaret and *if* she agrees to be my wife, I might consider it."

"So there is a romantic buried under the pragmatic shell," Annie said. "I knew you couldn't be as stuffy as you pretended to be."

She leaned forward, and before Colin even realized what she was doing, Annie was kissing him. Not on the cheek—of course not, this was Annie—but a full-fledged kiss on the lips.

Her pliant lips remained closed but moved subtly across Colin's, at first gentle; then she applied more pressure. Her tongue darted out, urging the line between his lips to open and admit her. Colin, caught in the heat, welcomed her into his mouth as he held her face between his hands. The touch and taste of her filled him and he moaned.

The sound slapped his wits back into place and he forced himself to draw away. His heart pounded in his ears as he tried to get his breathing back under control.

He glanced away, relieved to find no one had witnessed their inappropriate display. "Would you like to continue shopping?"

She wrinkled her nose, but her kiss-swollen lips detracted from the impish expression. "No. I want to explore some more, but I'll settle for seeing the town."

It took a moment for Colin to catch the meaning of her sassy reply and another long moment to talk himself out of further exploration.

Annie grabbed his hand and tugged him back onto the boardwalk. He breathed deeply of the crisp air, concentrating on cooling his blood. What was it about her that made him forget everything but kissing her and touching her and tasting her?

And wanting her . . .

His mind cleared and he remembered the crawling sensation of being watched. Somebody was doing it again, and he suspected it was Morales. There was no other reason the man could be in town.

Toby and Alexander were already at the theater with Percival and Essie when Colin ushered Annie and Margaret in a little after eleven. A painted backdrop of a formal garden had been set up with the other props, to ready the stage for the abbreviated version of "The Taming of the Shrew."

Percival was attired in his costume—knee-length pants with tights and a billowy white shirt tucked into the waistband. Colin noticed how Margaret's gaze moved over the man and he was startled by his lack of jealousy. Perhaps it was because he knew Margaret would never become involved with an actor.

Essie lounged on a fainting couch set offstage, just beyond the edge of the curtains. Some telltale wrinkles in her brow attested to the discomfort of her ankle, but her tongue was in typical form.

"It's about time you got here. I was beginning to think we'd have to send out the dogs to dig up your lazy bones," Essie said.

"We're only ten minutes late," Margaret argued.

"Ten minutes, ten hours. Late is late."

Margaret, who had been so even-tempered in Denver, propped her hands on her hips and marched up to Essie. "Annie is only doing this as a favor to you, so if I were you, I'd shut my mouth."

"Ladies, ladies," Percival broke in. "There's no need for such churlishness. Come, come. We must have at least one dress rehearsal before this evening." He looked over at Annie. "Please don your costume."

Margaret glared down at Essie. "Now there's a person of true breeding who knows how to be courteous." Before Essie could blow up, Margaret took Annie's hand. "Come along, dear. I'll help you into your costume."

With a helpless shrug, Annie followed Margaret to the dressing room Percival had pointed out.

"What was all that about?" Essie asked, staring in the wake of the other two women.

"I think you and Annie are teaching her how to stand up for herself," Colin said.

Percival sighed wistfully. "I must say, such spirit only adds to her beauty."

Did Percival think that he had a chance with a woman like Margaret? The scandal would be too much for a proper widow like her.

While Percival directed Toby and Alexander to move some of the stage items, Colin walked over to the couch where Essie lounged with a playbook.

"What does a dress rehearsal entail?" he asked the actress.

"Everyone in the cast will be completely in character and the performance will be acted in its entirety. Usually we give ourselves two or three days' worth of dress rehearsals, but with our late arrival here, that's impossible," Essie explained. "Why don't you sit down? I promise I won't bite." She paused. "At least, not too hard, or anyplace where it might hurt."

Colin laughed and lowered himself to the wide cushion by her legs. "How do you think Annie will do?"

"She's a natural. The stage is in her blood."

Though Colin had suspected the same thing, he wasn't certain he was ready to accept it. "Having lived the life you have, can you honestly tell me that being an actress is the best thing for her?"

Essie glanced down at the playbook, her expression more thoughtful than Colin had ever seen it. "If she wasn't already determined to become an actress, I'd say no. But Annie's heart is set on the theater. With or without her folks'—and your—approval, she's going to pursue her dream."

Colin took a deep breath and let it out slowly. As much as he desired Annie, there were too many obstacles in their path. He had to be realistic. If he wanted a family, he couldn't have Annie. It was as simple as that.

The sound of footsteps on the wooden stage announced the return of Annie and Margaret. Although Colin thought he had prepared himself for her appearance, his gaze flew to her bosom and slid down the dress which clung to her figure. His fingernails bit into his palms as he fisted his hands.

"She reminds me of me when I was her age," Essie said with a hint of maternal pride. "You'd best go join your girlfriend before she scratches out my eyes."

For a split second Colin thought she meant Annie, but one glance at Margaret dispelled the notion. Margaret did indeed look like she had her fur up.

"Good idea." He stood. "By the way, how does your ankle feel?"

"Like I won't be riding any studs like you in the next week or so."

Colin laughed. "Why do I even ask?"

Essie reached up and clasped his hand. "Because you're a good man and you care about people. Now go join Margaret before I have to fight for your honor."

Colin squeezed her hand fondly and walked over to Margaret. "Let's go sit down."

He guided her down the steps to a couple of seats in front of the stage. "Best seats in the house."

Margaret's smile was a little warmer than the North Pole. "I hope we're doing the right thing by allowing Annie to participate. She is shaking like a leaf."

"From what I understand, theater people are like that, but once they're on the stage, the nervousness disappears."

"I hope so."

"It'll be all right," he said with more confidence than he felt.

For the next three hours, Colin and Margaret learned that acting was an arduous business. Annie stumbled on her lines occasionally and Essie would call the correct ones out in a stage whisper. Colin could see the stress start to play on Annie, but he also saw what Essie had called her natural talent.

There were times when Colin forgot it was Annie up there, seeing only Katharina, the woman she portrayed. However, Colin had to admit, his Annie and Katharina had much in common. Both were independent and stubborn, with sharp tongues to match their spirits.

The final line was spoken and Toby and Alexander drew the curtains closed, only to have to open them one more time to allow Percival and Annie to practice their bows. Margaret and Colin stood and applauded.

"Thank you," Percival said, his gaze on Margaret.

The older woman's face pinkened as she stared at the actor. "You were extraordinary." She blinked and quickly turned to Annie. "Both of you."

"You're too kind, my dear," Percival said with a gallant bow.

Colin shook his head half in humor and half in exasperation. Did Percival speak this way to all his female admirers?

"Although it wasn't perfect, I feel we shouldn't practice any further," Percival said.

"But I'm not ready," Annie said desperately.

"You did a great job," Colin said without hesitation.

Margaret gave her a hug. "Colin's right. You were wonderful. I'm almost envious of you."

For the first time he could recall, Annie was speechless.

"Let us change our attire and find a restaurant. It'll be a long time before we can sup," Percival said.

Annie still appeared somewhat lost as Margaret led her to the dressing room.

"Will she be all right tonight?" Colin asked Percival.

"Annie is a trouper. She'll be fine," the actor reassured.

Colin nodded reluctantly. "Do you remember the young man who accompanied Annie to the play the last night you were in Denver?"

"Yes. Handsome young man. He seemed quite polite, too."

"He's not as polite as he appeared to be. He attacked Annie in her home the day before we left."

Percival gasped. "The poor dear. I hope the young man was arrested."

"Annie didn't press charges and I don't blame her. He apologized and he might have been sincere. If he wasn't, he may have followed her here to Reno. I haven't seen him, but I've had this feeling we were being watched."

"Shouldn't we alert the authorities?"

"And tell them what—that there *might* be a man in town who's *thinking* of trying something with a woman who *used* to be his friend?" Colin shook his head. "The authorities would laugh in our faces. I wanted to let you know so you could help keep an eye on her."

"Of course. I shall also alert Toby and Alexander. They can assist us."

Toby and Alexander knew what Morales looked like and they adored Annie. They would be good allies in protecting her. "All right. But don't tell Annie. I don't want her to worry; she's anxious enough about the play."

"I understand. You shall have my complete discretion."

"Thanks, Percival."

The actor went off to change while Colin remained in the center of the stage. He turned to gaze out at the chairs set up for the evening's audience and tried to imagine what it would feel like to perform in front of them. But he couldn't.

He was a man grounded in reality, in planting roots and having a family to love and care for. Annie's world was as foreign as the moon, which left little common ground between them.

Colin sighed. Better to settle for second best than try to change the woman he really wanted.

For if he succeeded, Annie wouldn't be the woman he had fallen in love with.

Annie peeked through the opening between the curtains. The hundred seats were filling up quickly—the owner of the theater had told Percival there was standing room only.

Her stomach lurched and she crossed her arms tightly beneath her breasts. She closed her eyes and mouthed a half dozen of Katharina's lines, putting herself into character. Breathing deeply, she imagined how Katharina must have felt to find herself the object of men's pursuit simply because of her fortune. She placed herself in Katharina's shoes as Petruchio tried to tame her with his love.

Petruchio's face blurred, then cleared, revealing Colin in his place.

She snapped her eyes open. Good Lord, she couldn't afford to think of Colin now. Her entire concentration had to be on her performance . . . which Colin would be watching.

A touch on her shoulder made her spin around, and she gasped. "You scared me."

"I'm sorry," Colin said. "I just came to wish you luck."

She covered his mouth with her palm. "Don't ever say that. If you want to wish an actor luck, tell him to 'break a leg.' "

He lowered her hand. "That sounds a little dangerous."

"It's tradition."

Colin grasped Annie's shoulders gently. "Break a leg, lass." He leaned over and gave her a sisterly peck on the cheek.

Then he was gone, leaving her alone once more with her insecurities.

Essie hobbled up beside her. "You'll do fine, sweetie. And don't panic if you forget a line. I'll prompt you."

Annie nodded. "Okay. Thank you."

Essie hugged her. "You're welcome. Besides, I think I'm the one who owes you the thanks. If you hadn't stepped into the role, Percival would have been out of luck."

"I'd say it's my pleasure, but I think I'll wait until after the show is over."

Essie stepped back and surveyed Annie's costume and hair. "You look beautiful."

Percival scurried up. "Curtain time, ladies. Let's take our places."

Annie quickly moved onto her mark on the stage, her heart thundering in her chest above the noise of the crowd. She sent up a quick prayer for assistance and took a deep breath.

"Ready?" Percival asked.

She nodded, unable to speak.

"You'll be marvelous, my dear. Relax." Then he moved off the stage.

Alone, Annie stood in the "garden" as Alexander and Toby opened the curtains. Voices faded, a whistle sounded from the audience, then all was silent.

Katharina came to life.

An hour and a half later, clapping and hooting filled the theater. People stood as Annie and Percival held hands and bowed to the audience. Annie blew a kiss to Colin, who sat in the front row with Margaret.

She had done it! She hadn't even needed prompting with her lines. Elation filled her, making the lights brighter and the sounds crisper.

This was the reason she wanted to be an actress. Nothing in her life had ever given her so much satisfaction and happiness—except for Colin's kiss. It encircled her, buoyed her, and made the world so much sweeter. How could she explain this to her parents? How could she describe this euphoria which nearly overwhelmed her?

The curtains closed for the last time and Percival hugged her.

"You are the next Lillie Langtry, my dear," he said.

Annie grinned. "I'd rather be the next Sarah Bernhardt."

"After that stellar performance, others will be wanting to be Annie Trevelyan," Essie said, limping over to join them. She embraced Annie briefly. "You were superb."

"I owe it all to my mentors," she replied graciously.

"You did real good, Annie," Toby spoke up.

Colin and Margaret walked through the opening in the curtains and Annie launched herself at Colin. He caught her in his arms and swung her around.

"So, what did you think?" Annie demanded.

"I think I'm glad you didn't break your leg," he teased.

Annie punched his arm, but she couldn't stop smiling. "It was great, Colin. I didn't make any mistakes and I remembered all my lines."

Colin set her back on her feet. "I've never seen a better actress." At Essie's growl, he added, "Present company excepted, of course."

"Let's go eat. Me and Alexander are starving," Toby said.

"I think we all are," Colin said, ruffling Toby's hair. "What do you say we go have a steak on me?"

Annie shook her head. "That's all right, Colin. You don't have to do that."

"I want to, lass." He took hold of her shoulders and turned her around. "Now, go change before Toby and Alexander faint from lack of food."

"Would you like some help?" Margaret asked.

Annie smiled at her friend. "Yes, please."

As they walked toward the dressing room, Annie couldn't help but ask, "So?"

"So what?"

Annie was about to explain when she noticed the glint in the woman's eyes and laughed.

"You were spectacular, Annie. At first, I thought I wouldn't be able to enjoy the show because I would see you, not the character. But you weren't you anymore. Everything about you changed. I was astounded." Margaret glanced down as if embarrassed by her display of excitement. "I have never known any actors or actresses before. I was brought up to believe that women who acted were no better than harlots." She met Annie's gaze with a teasing smile. "Meeting Essie almost confirmed my opinion."

"She does tend to be a bit outspoken," Annie said carefully.

"That she is, but she is also not the harlot I had believed."

"Except around Colin," Annie added. "But she knows Colin won't take her up on her offer, so she merely has fun with him."

They arrived at the dressing room and Margaret stopped. "May I ask you something, Annie?"

"Of course."

"Are Percival and Essie more than friends?"

So she hadn't been imagining the attraction between Percival and Margaret. "No," she replied firmly. "They're like siblings, always arguing, but they stay together because each one truly cares about the other."

"And they both care for Alexander and Toby."

"That's right." Annie rubbed her chin and asked innocently, "Why?"

Margaret's cheeks grew rosy. "No reason. I was merely curious."

Annie nodded, but she smiled inside. It didn't look like Colin's search for a wife would end anytime soon.

She opened the dressing room door and slipped inside.

A rough hand slapped across her mouth while an arm snaked around her waist. She tried to scream, but could barely breathe.

She heard a vague cry and recognized it as coming from Margaret. Then her captor was dragging her out the door as he gave Margaret a shove with his shoulder. The widow struck the wall, and slumped to the floor.

Terror climbed into Annie's throat.

He'd killed Margaret—and Annie was certain she was next.

Chapter 18

A faint cry sounded from beyond the stage and Colin froze.

Annie.

Fear spurred him into motion and he dashed toward the dressing room. Though his injured leg protested the harsh treatment, he ignored its complaints. He was vaguely aware of Percival, Toby, and Alexander following him, but terror for Annie overshadowed all else.

He skidded around the corner and spotted a body lying in the dim hallway in front of the open dressing room. He raced over to it and squatted down beside Margaret's stirring body.

"Margaret, can you hear me?" he asked.

"He . . . he has her," she murmured.

Colin's heart nearly leapt from his chest. "Who has her?"

"A man . . . his f-face was . . . covered."

Son-of-a-bitch.

He had let down his guard, and now Annie was paying the price for his blunder.

Percival joined them and Colin glanced at him long enough to order, "Stay with her."

The actor nodded.

Colin continued the chase, knowing Alexander and Toby were right behind him. He stumbled, and an arrow of pain shot through his leg. He gasped and was glad for Alexander's hand on his arm, holding him upright.

Then he shook off Alexander's support and skidded around another corner of the hall. He spotted the man dragging Annie behind him. She was shouting at him to stop and slowing him with her struggles. A door opened and Colin realized her captor had found an escape route to the outside. Three seconds later, Colin shoved through the same door with Alexander and Toby close on his heels.

Colin paused, looking down the dark alley, but he could see little. The dank darkness sparked a black memory buried deep within him. The tomblike stillness after the cave-in filled his mind and the remembered helplessness clawed at his sanity.

"There they are," Toby shouted.

His voice brought Colin out of his personal

hell. He cursed and turned in the direction Toby pointed. Silver moonlight glinted off Annie's blond head. Colin started after them, and Annie and her captor stopped abruptly—the alley had angled into a dead end. He halted ten feet from them and was shocked when the man suddenly shoved Annie toward him.

Colin caught her in his arms as the man ran past him. Toby and Alexander chased after the would-be kidnaper.

"Let him go, Toby! Alexander!" Colin shouted. "Get back here."

"M-Margaret," Annie stuttered. "He killed her."

Colin grasped her arms to keep her from escaping in a blind rush. "She's all right. She just had the wind knocked out of her. Percival is with her."

The two youngest members of the troupe returned, their reluctance obvious.

"We coulda caught him," Toby argued.

"He may have a gun," Colin stated. "You could've been hurt."

Though shaky, Annie drew away from Colin to stand in front of Toby. She gripped his thin shoulder. "Colin's right. I'd be very upset if either of you was hurt because of me."

"We shoulda protected you better," Toby said. "What do—"

"Toby, you and Alexander go find a lawman and bring him to the theater," Colin interrupted.

The boy nodded and the two trotted away.

Annie's body was trembling violently, so Colin removed his jacket and placed it over her shoulders. Her slender fingers clutched the lapels and tugged it close around her chest, as if it were a talisman to ward off evil spirits.

He wrapped his arms around her, not surprised she was still shuddering. "It's all right, you're safe now." She sagged against his chest and he rested his chin on her crown. "Shhh, it's all over. He won't touch you again. I promise."

Her shoulders shook with silent sobs and Colin soothed her by rubbing her back gently.

After a few minutes, Annie's cries slowed to hiccups and she pressed away from Colin's chest, brushing her hand across his damp shirt. "I hope I didn't ruin it."

"It'll be fine," Colin assured her. "How are you feeling? Better?"

Annie smiled wryly. "It's amazing how much a good cry can help."

He gently thumbed away the glistening trails of tears. "We should get back to the others."

Another bout of trembling gripped Annie.

A wave of protectiveness washed through Colin and he hugged her close again. "I'm sorry I let you down, lass," he said with a husky voice.

"It wasn't your fault."

He closed his eyes. "Aye, it was." He stroked her long hair, the motion reassuring him that Annie was safe and unharmed. "I had a feeling someone was watching us this morning while we were walking around town."

Annie's body stiffened, but she didn't pull away. "Why didn't you tell me?"

"I didn't have any proof, just a gut feeling. Besides, you were worried about your performance and I didn't want to add to your burden."

Annie's shoulders rose and fell with a deep breath and she eased out of his arms. Gazing up at him, she shook her head sadly. "Don't treat me like a china doll that can be easily broken. Papa and Kate raised me to think for myself and to take care of myself." Her short laugh sounded more like a sob. "Of course, they probably now regret making me so independent." She took a deep breath and pressed her shoulders back. "I want to be an actress and I want to stand on my own two feet. I can't do that if you think you have to protect me from the boogeyman."

"That man wasn't a boogeyman. He was real, and he could have killed you." Colin's voice trembled. What if she had been killed? Or disappeared never to be seen again? He couldn't bear to think of that. "Could it have been Thomas Morales?"

"I-I don't know. He had his face covered." Annie's brow furrowed. "No, I don't think it was him. He was shorter than Thomas."

"Do you have any idea who else might want to kidnap you?"

She swallowed and shook her head. "Why would anyone want to kidnap me? I don't understand."

He hugged her and kissed the top of her head. "I don't either, but I promise I'll protect you." He harnessed his emotions. "Come on, let's get back inside."

With an arm around her waist, he guided her back into the building to rejoin their friends gathered on the stage.

Essie hobbled over to Annie and hugged her. "Don't you be scaring me like that again, sweetie. I have enough gray hairs as it is."

Percival, who stood close to Margaret, smiled warmly at Annie. "Are you all right, dear?"

"I'm fine." Annie reached out to clasp Margaret's hands. "I was so frightened that you'd been killed."

The widow smiled. "I'm a little sore, but nothing some good old horse liniment won't cure."

Annie laughed. Her expression turned to a grimace as she glanced down at her soiled gown. "It looks like the dress is ruined."

"Nonsense. It just needs to be cleaned and one or two small tears mended," Margaret said.

"If you say so," Annie said dubiously.

She glanced up to see Toby, Alexander, and a man wearing a badge walking toward the stage. The lawman introduced himself as Constable John Bell, and listened while Colin explained what had happened with Annie filling in the blanks. Annie and Margaret could give the constable only a vague description of the assailant that could have fit a hundred different men.

"Weren't you the woman in the play?" Bell asked Annie.

She smiled. "Yes, I am."

She answered with such pride and conviction that Colin's own throat swelled with admiration.

"You're a good actress, ma'am," the constable said. "My missus really liked you, too." He glanced at Percival and his expression lost some of its magnanimity. "She thought you did pretty good, too."

Percival bowed at the waist. "Please thank her for me."

Annie's smile grew. "Yes, please."

"I surely will." Bell's expression sobered. "I'll take a look around for your attacker, but I'm afraid it'll be a miracle if he's found."

"I understand," Annie said.

"Will you be around town for a few days in the event we find someone matching his description?"

"We're leaving tomorrow morning," Colin replied.

"There won't be a whole lot we can do once you go since we don't have any witnesses. But we might get lucky tonight." He touched the brim of his narrow-brimmed derby hat. "Goodnight." The lawman left.

Toby's stomach growled and everyone laughed. "Can I help it if I ain't had anything to eat since this afternoon?"

"Why don't you all head over to the restaurant?" Colin suggested. "Annie and I'll be there after she changes her costume."

"I should probably stay and chaperone," Margaret said.

"I'm her chaperone, too, you know," Colin reminded her.

Essie snorted. "In a pig's eye."

Colin stifled a smile even as his face heated with embarrassment. "I've known her since she was four years old."

"A blind man can see she's not four years old anymore."

"I think we should take Colin's suggestion," Percival interrupted. He placed a possessive arm around Margaret and steered her toward the exit. "It is already nine thirty and I believe the restaurant closes at ten o'clock."

Relieved, Colin watched as Toby and Alexander followed Percival. Essie swung her cape on with a flourish and leaned close to Annie. "Don't even think of doing something I wouldn't do."

"I don't think my imagination is up to the task," Annie whispered back.

Essie snickered and waved good-bye as she hobbled out to join the others.

"I'll go change," Annie said.

"I'll walk you to the room."

"The man is probably long gone."

"Humor me."

"I always do," Annie said and added an exaggerated long-suffering sigh.

"I think you have it turned around, imp," Colin teased.

She merely wrinkled her pert nose at him.

He rested his hand against her back and guided her down to the dressing room. She went inside and he leaned against the wall in the hallway with his arms crossed.

"I need some help," Annie called out two minutes later.

Colin straightened. "What do you need?"

"I can't reach some of the buttons in the back."

"Do you want me to get Margaret or Essie?"

She opened the door a crack. "You don't have to bother them. You can do it."

Colin's mouth lost all moisture. "It isn't proper, lass."

"Who cares what's proper and what isn't? You used to put me into my nightgown fifteen years ago."

"If you haven't noticed, you've changed."

"So have you, but it doesn't bother me."

Stung, Colin said, "I didn't say it bothered me. I said it wasn't proper."

Anne swung the door open further and reached out to snag his arm. She tugged him into the room and closed the door behind them. "Do you think I'm going to have my way with you?"

The imp had no sense of propriety.

"Of course not."

"I wouldn't mind," she said thoughtfully, as if he hadn't spoken. "Having my way with you, I mean. We've already got the kissing part down. I figure we could work on the more advanced principles of lovemaking."

Colin's lips moved but no words came forth. He snapped his mouth shut. "That's quite enough. I would never have given in to your request if I'd have known you'd want to extend your education."

Her lips turned into a pout. "I didn't realize the kissing had been so repulsive for you."

"I didn't say that." Colin was getting in way over his head and he had no idea how to swim out of it.

"You didn't have to." She turned around and gathered her long hair up on her head. "Please unbutton me."

Colin's legs became wooden. He stepped forward stiffly and with clumsy fingers worked the small buttons through the buttonholes. With each release of a button, the more her smooth, pale back came into view . . . and the more awkward his fingers became.

"Aren't you done yet?" Annie asked, shifting her weight from one foot to the other.

"Just—" his voice broke. "Just about."

Finally he came to her camisole, which shielded the rest of her creamy skin from his sight—though it was a little like mending the fence after the cows got out.

"I'm done." He would have bolted for the door, but he couldn't get past Annie without touching her. And if he touched her, he was afraid his thin thread of control would snap.

Annie freed her arms from the sleeves and shimmied it down over her waist and hips. He tried to keep his gaze aimed at the wall but the enticing wiggle of Annie's backside was impossible to ignore.

Annie touched his hand and he jerked. "Are you all right?" she asked.

"Fine."

"Are you sure? You seem so tense." Annie rubbed his arm.

He glanced down at her and his gaze fell on the curve of her breasts and the hint of dusky circles beneath the white camisole. His breath caught, then he was struggling for air.

He closed his eyes, but the image of her breasts was burned into his eyelids. "I have to get out of here."

"Why?"

Something in her voice brought his attention back to her. Her wide blue eyes were heavy-lidded, giving her a sultry wantonness.

Flames leapt through Colin's veins. No man could resist such temptation, and Colin was no exception. He lifted a hand and traced her velvety jaw with his fingertip. Annie's nipples peaked against the thin cloth.

With a groan, Colin cupped her face and swooped down to capture her mouth with a fierce kiss that gentled the moment he tasted her lips. He explored the curve of her lips, pressing down, then retreating to feather light touches across her full lower lip.

She moaned and opened her mouth, inviting him inside. Colin accepted the invitation and swept his tongue over her teeth and the roof of her mouth. She tasted like mint and honey and . . . Annie.

Keeping one hand on her cheek, he allowed the

other to roam down her neck and across the ivory skin above her breasts. His fingers skimmed back and forth over her warmth, moving lower and lower.

Annie raised herself on her toes so that his hand slipped beneath the camisole. The warm, soft fullness made him gasp.

He found a pebbled nipple and rolled the flesh between his fingertips. This time it was Annie who gasped in pleasure.

Suddenly her body was flush against his, with his erection trapped between them.

"You're playin' with fire, lass," Colin said hoarsely.

"I like playing with fire," she whispered back.

Desire coursed through Colin, stunning him with its impact. He clasped her shoulders almost roughly and pressed her away from him, putting some space between them and the heat that radiated from their bodies.

Surprise and hurt reflected in Annie's flushed face as she gazed up at him, her lips red and swollen from his kisses. "What's wrong?"

"*This* is wrong, Annie," he said firmly.

"You don't want to be my teacher anymore?"

He imagined them in bed, him instructing her in the pleasures of her own body and his name coming from her lips as she experienced her first passionate climax.

"It's wrong," he reiterated. "Your husband should be the one to teach you these things."

She crossed her arms, but her stubborn stance was lessened by her state of undress. "I'm not going to get married."

"Then you don't need to be learning about things like this." His face was hot with embarrassment as he wondered for the hundredth time how he had gotten himself into this predicament. "Finish getting dressed, then we'll go have something to eat."

"It's probably after ten."

Colin tugged his watch out of his pocket—five minutes past ten. The restaurant would be closed.

"Then we'll just go back to the hotel. It's been a long day."

"It could be a long night, too."

Colin scrubbed his face with his palms. "Just get dressed and we'll go back to the hotel."

He slipped past her and out of the room. Once in the hallway, he tried to bring himself back under control.

How had he allowed things to get so out of hand? Annie was an innocent and he wasn't. He should not have allowed her to tempt him or to let his body betray him. Around Annie, all restraint seemed to desert him.

Five minutes later, Annie came out of the dressing room attired in the conservative skirt and blouse she had worn earlier in the day. The only evidence of their dalliance was her lips, still fuller than normal. He hoped nobody would notice.

He accompanied her out of the theater and down the boardwalk illuminated by street lights.

Annie was uncharacteristically silent as they walked. Colin should have been relieved she didn't want to talk about what they had done, but another part of him recognized the unnaturalness of her silence.

"Are you all right, Annie?" he asked.

They dodged around a man who smelled of stale whiskey.

"I'm tired," she replied simply.

"What did you think of your performance?" Colin asked, hoping to get her to talk.

She glanced at him quizzically. "It was better than I imagined it would be."

"You were nervous." It wasn't a question—he knew.

She huffed a soft laugh. "Scared to death."

"But you got past it, Annie. You overcame your nervousness and succeeded."

She stopped and Colin did the same.

"Do you understand why I love it so much— why I can't forget about ever doing this again?" she asked, entreating him.

Colin nodded slowly. "I understand, though I wish I didn't."

She grabbed his hand and squeezed it, then continued holding it as they walked. "I knew you would."

Colin suspected he should probably tug his hand out of hers, but he couldn't. Besides, the intimacy felt right, like sleeping in his own bed after weeks of staying in hotels.

He knew it would feel the same way if they became lovers—so natural, like one was a part of the other. But he didn't want merely a lover, he wanted a wife: a woman to love him through the night and raise his children during the day.

Although he loved Annie in every way possible, he wouldn't be satisfied with a part-time mistress.

Chapter 19

The next day, Annie found herself and her companions in another private car for the final leg of their journey. She had assumed Colin would buy a regular ticket like the rest of them, since the train wasn't filled this time.

However, she was glad for the comfort of the Pullman he'd taken in spite of his close proximity. He had hardly said two words to her that morning. While they had visited the police station to see if they had any leads on Annie's attacker, Colin had been subdued.

That was her fault. There had been so many emotional ups and downs the previous evening. The play had been a success and she had enjoyed the applause and words of admiration. Then there had been the kidnaping attempt and her terror when he had dragged her out of the dressing room. And finally there was her aborted attempt to seduce Colin.

Why had he refused her? What had she done wrong? She had allowed him liberties she had not permitted any other man. In fact, she had gone even further than she had planned. Her cheeks heated with the memory of his hand upon her bare breast and his hard erection—which she could only imagine—pressing against her. The images and feelings those sensations had wrought had nearly driven her mad to fulfill some need she didn't quite fathom. But she was beginning to.

No wonder wars were fought over love and men killed in fits of passion. Her own passion had been so overwhelming she had been shaken by her loss of control.

But why Colin? She had kissed other men, but none of them had made her throw caution to the wind and forget everything else. Was this love? Or was it merely lust?

She glanced over to see Colin had joined Margaret on the love seat, and jealousy pierced her chest. Would he give Margaret what he wouldn't give her?

Yes, a little voice whispered, because Margaret will be his wife and you won't.

Annie counted to ten slowly. To become a wife meant becoming a mother, and Annie couldn't risk that. No, there was too much she wanted to do with her life—she wouldn't throw it all away.

Percival strolled over to join Margaret and Colin and sat beside the widow so that she was between the two men. Colin didn't look happy about the situation. In fact, he looked downright annoyed.

Good riddance.

Essie plopped down beside Annie and wiped her forehead. "The ankle is hurting like a son-of-a-bitch today."

"Maybe it's because you walked on it too much yesterday."

"Hush, sweetie. I don't need you ganging up on me, too."

"Colin must have scolded you already."

"You know, if God's going to make a man as good-lookin' as him, he ought not to give him a brain. It complicates things."

Annie's laughter echoed around the train car. "It does seem like a waste of a good brain, doesn't it?"

Essie narrowed her eyes. "I wondered why the two of you didn't make it to the restaurant. I suspect it wasn't because you were having trouble getting out of your costume."

Annie glanced away guiltily. "To be honest, I did have some trouble with the buttons down the back."

"So Colin, gentleman that he is, helped you?" The actress smirked.

"Yes," Annie said tersely, determined not to divulge any more particulars.

Essie leaned closer. "So, how was he? Any good?"

Annie clenched her teeth so hard she thought she heard them crack. "We didn't get that far."

"But you wanted to."

"Yes," Annie hissed.

So much for keeping my big mouth shut.

"Damn. I knew he was too much of a gentleman," Essie said with genuine regret.

"That's not a bad thing, Essie." She couldn't help herself—she had to defend his honor.

"It is if you're hot and ready."

Annie grabbed her arm and whispered hoarsely, "Shhhh. Don't let anyone hear you."

"Sorry, sweetie. I forget how naïve you are," Essie said in a quieter voice. "So are you going to let Margaret land and bed him?"

Annie squirmed uncomfortably. "It's not my choice. Colin's going to take me to that stupid finishing school and leave me there."

"Not if you give him a reason to take you with him."

"But I don't want to go with him. I want to act."

"Well, damnation, girl, who says you can't have both?"

"Colin wouldn't stand for a wife of his to be an actress," Annie said bitterly.

"Just because he said that doesn't mean it's true." Essie sighed heavily. "You really are an innocent, aren't you?"

Annie scowled. "Stop calling me that. The stories of your escapades have given me a pretty good picture of what happens between men and women."

"I'm not talking mechanics, Annie. I'm talking about the heart. It pretty much has a mind of its own when it comes to love. Colin may not want an actress for a wife, but any fool can see he's head over heels with you. All you have to do is convince him that you can be both—a wife and an actress."

"No. I don't want to get married," Annie said stubbornly. "My mother died bringing my little brother into the world. I'm small, like she was and I'm not going to take a chance of that happening to me, too."

Essie's expression sobered. "I'm sorry, Annie. I didn't know."

Annie shrugged, embarrassed by her admission. "Only my family and Colin know what happened to her. It's not something I like to talk about."

Essie patted her arm. "I can understand that. It also puts a whole new light on things. Maybe becoming an actress is the best thing for you. With your talent and looks, you'll go far and won't have to rely on any man."

"I can be like you."

"No, not like me," Essie said sternly. "I've warmed the bed of more men than I can remember to get where I'm at. You don't have to rely on your abilities in bed; *you* can make it with your acting skills."

Annie had never even considered that Essie didn't want to sleep with men. She always seemed so forward, wanting to enjoy a man's company.

"Don't you worry, sweetie. I never did anything I didn't want to," the older woman said, uncannily guessing Annie's thoughts.

"But it's not right."

Essie laughed, but it was tinged with bitterness. "Do you think someone merely decided all actresses were whores out of the blue? Hell, no, most reputations have a kernel of truth in them. Most actresses find themselves in my position— unable to work all the time, so they let some nice man take care of them long enough for them to find another troupe and leave again."

"I guess I never really thought about it before," Annie said quietly.

"Don't fret about it. Someday it'll be different; mark my words. Actresses like you will show those bastards that we don't need them to be great. We'll be able to do it on our own—using our God-given talents."

Annie settled her gaze on Colin, who listened intently to Margaret and laughed at something she said. It should be her talking and laughing with him, not Margaret.

She couldn't give him what he wanted— children—without forfeiting her dreams. And he couldn't give her what she needed—her freedom—without giving up his dream. There was no hope for them.

* * *

Annie sat beside a woman who lay on the floor with blood all around her. A tiny bundle of squirming arms and legs lay within the red pool.

She picked up the little body and the baby let out a long wail.

"Get it away from me. I hate it, hate you," the woman screamed over and over.

Then the woman reached for the baby, her hands flexing and unflexing, like an evil witch trying to cast a spell. Annie wrapped her arms around the baby, protecting it from the woman's grasping hands. But the woman somehow snagged Annie's dress and began to pull the girl and the baby toward her.

Annie awakened from the nightmare, shaking and breathless from the terror that gripped her belly. Her nightgown was damp with sweat and she wiped her forehead with a trembling hand.

It had been a long time since the nightmare had invaded her sleep. It was more vivid this time: she had heard her mother's voice, and the words she spoke were hateful and virulent. Was it a memory?

No, Papa had always said her mother had loved them. Why would he lie?

Though the sleeping compartment was dark, she could make out the lump that was Margaret beside her. She appeared to be sound asleep and Annie cautiously slipped out of bed.

She donned her robe and tied the sash, then tiptoed out past the curtain. She was startled to find the dawn's rosy glow lighting the inside of the train car, heralding the sunrise. She glanced over at the chair where she thought Colin would be sleeping, but it was empty. Percival lay on the sofa snoring and Toby and Alexander were sleeping on the floor, blankets piled over and under them.

She spotted Colin sitting by the table, his gaze aimed out the window. One side of his chiseled face reflected the dawn's light, deepening the etched lines of thoughtfulness in his brow. She tried to picture him from the memories of her childhood—him lifting her onto his so very broad shoulders and his eyes laughing more than his lips. Instead she saw the man who kissed her with so much tenderness and passion that her eyes filled with tears at the memory.

If she wasn't so terrified of dying in childbirth, would she fight for him? Would she be willing to give up an acting career to sleep with him every night?

"What're you doin' up so early, lass?" Colin's quiet voice interrupted her reveries.

"I had another nightmare," she replied. "Do you mind if I join you?"

"Not at all." He stood and waited until she slid onto the opposite bench before sitting back down. "Sometimes talkin' about it helps, makes the bad memory go away a little faster."

Colin always did know just what to say to ease her disquiet. She reached across the table and took one of his hands in both of hers. Turning it over, she traced the lines in his palm with a fingertip. "I've always liked your hands, Colin. Even though they weren't as big as Papa's, I always thought they were just as strong." She rubbed a callous on the fleshy pad at the base of his thumb. "What's this from?"

"Mucking out the mines when I was a lad. After the dynamite was blown, we had to go in and shovel the loose rock into rail cars to get it out of the mine."

"How old were you?"

A crease marred the skin between his eyebrows. "I started workin' the mines when I was six. I didn't start muckin' until after my ma died. I was ten then."

Annie's grip tightened. "You were a child."

"I was nearly a man," he stated. He curled his fingers around her hand. "Why all the questions, lass?"

She shrugged. How could she tell him she wanted to know everything about him? That she felt as if she had never really known him?

Instead of trying to answer his question, she said, "I've had this nightmare for as long as I can remember. I'm not sure what it means." She paused, drawing small circles with her fingertip on the back of Colin's hand. "I think it's a memory."

"Of what?"

Her motions stopped and cold dread snaked through her chest. "My mother." She looked up at Colin to see guarded wariness in his face. "I was with her when she gave birth to Brynn, wasn't I?"

Colin pressed his lips together and nodded. "Aye, you were only four years old."

"Papa never told me about it."

Colin leaned across the table. "He only wanted to protect you."

"From what?" Annie swallowed hard. "My own mother?"

Colin glanced away uneasily. "It's not my place to be tellin' you."

Annie's stomach lurched. "What? That my mother hated me? That she died giving birth to a child she didn't want?" Another, more horrifying, thought struck her. "What kind of man makes a woman have his children if she doesn't want them?"

Colin blinked. "What're you talkin' about?"

Annie jerked her hands out of his as the truth became all too clear in Colin's expression. "Why did he get her with child if she didn't want children? Papa killed her as surely as if he'd shot her."

"No! He loved her. He would never have hurt her."

Uncontrollable fury clouded Annie's thoughts. "Then why did he hide the truth from me? Why didn't he tell me my own mother hated me? Why didn't he tell me I was with her when she died?" She noticed Percival looking at her over the back of the couch. She should be sorry she woke him, but she wasn't.

Annie scrambled to her feet. "Why didn't *you* tell me? I thought you were my friend!"

Colin stood and reached for her, but she slipped away from him. "Annie, please, it's not what you're thinkin'. Your da didn't tell you because he didn't want you to remember your mother that way."

"He lied to me. He said she loved me, and that she gave her life for Brynn's."

"She did."

A tear rolled down Annie's cheek and she rubbed it away impatiently. The nightmare *was* a forgotten memory. At four years old, she had been terrified by her mother's screams and all the blood around her. She must have forgotten it on purpose, just as she had stopped talking for months after her mother had died.

"No! She told me right before . . . before she died. She said she hated us."

Colin grabbed at her and caught her arms. "She was ill, Annie. She missed her parents' home and hated livin' in Orion. Her mind—" He took a deep breath. "Her mind wasn't strong."

Annie stared at him as the blood drained from her face, her greatest fear becoming all too real. "My mother was crazy, wasn't she?"

Colin shifted uncomfortably. "I don't know, lass. Maybe she was just hurtin' so bad she took it out on those she loved."

Annie's mind raced. What if dying in childbirth wasn't her only worry? What if her mother's insanity had been passed down to her? Is that why they hadn't told her?

Her stomach roiled. "Let me go."

He continued to hold her a moment longer, then released her. She took a step away from him.

"Are you all right, lass?" Colin asked gently.

Nothing was all right. Maybe it never would be.

"I'm going to go lie down," she said.

Colin looked like he wanted to say more, but he remained silent.

Annie returned to the berth to find both Margaret and Essie awake. It appeared that everyone in the car had gotten an earful.

"Are you all right?" Essie asked.

Annie shook her head. "No. I'm going to lie down."

Margaret patted her arm. "I'm getting up, so you can have the bed to yourself. If you want to talk . . ."

"Thank you." Annie crawled up into the bed and lay down on her side facing the wall. She didn't want to talk to anyone. She just wanted to sleep, and when she woke up, she wanted everything to be just as it had been.

Margaret and Essie's hushed voices drifted to Annie, but it took too much energy to make sense of their words. Misery settled over her. All these years she had imagined her mother as a loving woman who made cookies with her daughter and read her stories and sacrificed her own life for her son's.

It had all been a lie. Her mother was nothing like she'd imagined her.

Annie stared at the dark wall and wondered why she couldn't cry.

Maybe some grief went too deep, where even tears couldn't touch it.

"We're almost there," Toby said. He glanced uneasily at the sleeping compartment. "Ain't Annie gonna come out?"

Margaret paused in her mending task and smiled gently at the boy. "She'll be out soon."

"You said that an hour ago."

"It was only fifteen minutes ago," Colin corrected him. Though his worry wasn't as obvious as Toby's, he was extremely concerned about Annie. In all the years he had known her, he couldn't remember a time when she had retreated from a problem. Annie was one to stand up and fight, not slink away to lick her wounds.

Trev's decision had finally come back to haunt them. After Annie's speech had returned, Colin had thought the young girl should have been encouraged to talk about the day her mother had died. He also believed that once Annie was old enough, she should have been told the truth about her mother's melancholia. However, she was Trev's daughter and he had the final word.

Colin rubbed his aching brow. Annie and her father hadn't been on the best of terms while Colin had visited them in Denver. This deception would only serve to widen the breach between them.

Not to mention the strain it put on Colin and Annie's relationship. He recognized his guilt in the deceit. He knew the truth, but when she had asked, he had repeated the same lie Trev had created.

He glanced out the window as the train slowed its approach into the San Francisco depot. The engineer blew the whistle twice.

A movement from the sleeping compartment caught his attention. Annie slipped out from behind the curtain and even from where he sat, he could see the dark smudges beneath her eyes. His heart lurched as he realized he was responsible for them.

Margaret rose and walked across the slowing train car to her side. "How are you feeling, Annie?"

The younger woman smiled, but it was a pale imitation of her usual bright expression. "I'm fine. Thank you."

"We were talking." Margaret glanced down nervously. "Would you like to spend the night in a hotel, then go to the school tomorrow?"

Annie shook her head vehemently. "I just want to get it over with."

"But—"

"No." Annie touched Margaret's arm in apology for her sharp tone and spoke in a more composed voice. "I would prefer to go straight to the school and get settled in."

Colin wanted nothing more than to convince her to stay at the hotel with them one more night, but he doubted she would listen to anything he said right now.

Essie elbowed him in the ribs. "Tell her how you feel about her," she muttered.

Colin's mouth gaped. "What?"

"If you don't tell her you love her, you're going to lose her. Is that what you want?" Essie hissed.

Colin's shock ebbed. "No, but it's not what *I* want. It's what *Annie* wants."

"You're both idiots."

The train came to a complete stop and Alexander and Toby headed for the door, their bags in hand. Colin sighed. Nothing about the trip had gone as planned. He had spent most of his time in Annie's company, even as he'd half-heartedly courted Margaret, and had gotten to know the acting troupe.

He was going to miss everyone, but especially Annie.

Definitely Annie.

His gaze followed the back of her head as she left the Pullman between Margaret and Percival. She hadn't even glanced at him.

Colin stood and grabbed his bag. He exited the train and shivered from the onslaught of cool, damp air coming in from the bay.

Annie stood off to the side, separate from the others, and stared into the distance. Her uncharacteristic melancholy nearly undid his shaky control, and his fingers tightened around the suitcase handle. She didn't want his comfort—not after his betrayal.

He stepped over to Margaret. "Will you be going to the school with us?"

Margaret shook her head. "I shall catch a cab to my brother's home. Maybe it's better you take her by yourself."

Colin didn't think so, but he didn't argue. "May I call on you at your brother's?"

Margaret studied him, her expression pensive. "Do you love me, Colin?"

Stunned by the unexpected question, he took a step back. "No," he replied honestly.

"Do you think you ever will?"

Colin scowled in frustration. "I don't know. Maybe someday."

She smiled, but there was regret in her eyes. "No, you may not call on me at my brother's. Thank you for making the journey a pleasant one."

Margaret was rejecting *him*? He was looking for a wife and she was looking for a husband. What had gone wrong?

She patted his arm and leaned closer. "Why don't you court the woman you really love?" Then she kissed his cheek. "Good-bye, Colin."

Still in shock, he watched her say her farewells to the theater troupe. Although he loved Annie, he knew without a doubt nothing could come of his feelings. And if he was foolish enough to convince Annie to marry him, he knew it wouldn't be long before she regretted being tied down. She would be miserable being the wife of a horse rancher, and her fear of having children would deny him his heirs.

He sighed and reined in his musings. Annie wanted to go directly to the school and get settled in, and Colin couldn't blame her. She needed time to sort through all her feelings—about her mother, being so far from home, and her dream to become an actress.

And maybe her feelings for me.

If she has any left.

Chapter 20

Annie gazed at the two-story school. It didn't look like the prison she had imagined all these weeks; too bad she wasn't planning on staying around long enough even to see the inside of it.

She lifted the bag from the floor of the cab. "Well," she began awkwardly. "This is it."

Colin nodded from his seat across from her. "I guess so."

Silence resonated between them.

"Thank you for getting me here," Annie said. Thanks to her acting abilities, she actually sounded like she meant it.

"It was my pleasure. Your trunks should be arriving by wagon shortly."

No, they wouldn't. She had given the porter revised directions when Colin had been occupied elsewhere. She should have alit from the coach then, but made the mistake of looking into his eyes.

"I'm sorry I didn't tell you about your mother, Annie," Colin said quietly.

Her throat tightened at the sincerity in his voice and face. She looked away, unable to bear his sadness and guilt. "It wasn't your fault."

"It doesn't matter. You were hurt because we hid the truth from you."

More like devastated. "But now I know," she said, more harshly than she had intended.

The silence in the cab grew suffocating.

"Come on. I'll help you get settled," Colin said, starting to rise.

Annie grabbed his arm. "No. I can do this the rest of the way by myself. You did your duty. You got me here."

"But—"

"I'm an adult, Colin, not a little girl you can order around and lie to."

He flinched. Annie should have felt satisfaction, but she only felt disgust at the spiteful blow.

"Aye, you're a grown woman now, Annie." He lifted his hand to her neck and fingered the angel on the gold chain. The whisper-soft touch sent an arrow of awareness straight to Annie's heart.

"I hope someday you'll be able to think of me without hating me, lass," he said quietly.

"I-I don't hate you, Colin. I'm only angry and disappointed."

He sighed. "You have every right to be."

"Yes, I do—but a part of me understands why you kept the truth from me." She looked back at the imposing school. "I suppose you'll be going to find your ranch now."

"Aye. It's my dream, lass."

"I know."

Feeling like her heart was splintering in two, Annie rose from her seat. Colin opened the cab door and alit, then gave Annie a hand down.

"Are you sure you want to do this by yourself?" he asked gently.

No, she wasn't certain, but she knew Colin wouldn't understand—she had to pursue her dream no matter the cost. "I'm sure."

They stood facing one another for a long uncomfortable moment. Annie's heart beat a wild tattoo in her chest. She hadn't expected the farewell to be this difficult.

"Good-bye, Annie," Colin said.

The two words pierced her and hurt more than saying good-bye to her parents in Denver. Annie dropped her bag on the ground, wrapped her arms around his neck, and kissed him. His lips opened beneath hers and she traced the contours of his mouth and played tag with his tongue. She wanted to memorize the feel of him and the taste of him.

Colin drew away first, his eyes wide and his nostrils flaring as he struggled to catch his breath. "Was that just another rehearsal?" he asked with a tinge of bitterness.

"No," she replied softly. "That was good-bye."

Before he could say anything, Annie grabbed her suitcase and hurried away toward the school. She could feel Colin's gaze on her, but she didn't dare look back. If she did, she might not have the strength to leave him behind.

She entered the building and closed the door, but didn't go any farther down the long hallway. Instead, she peeked out a window and watched Colin return to the cab. As the carriage rolled away, she sniffed and tears threatened. She was finally alone—truly alone. She'd never imagined she would feel this . . . lonely.

Taking a deep, quavering breath, she slipped back outside. She had a destination and the determination to get there. Everything was proceeding as planned.

After sending three telegrams, including one to Trev and Kate telling them Annie was safely at the school, Colin found a hotel in which to spend the night. It felt odd to be alone, which was strange since Colin had spent most of his life alone.

He ate in the hotel restaurant, missing the company of his companions of the past week. Afterward, he went outside and found a bench where he could sit and enjoy a cigar.

Only his dark thoughts didn't let him take pleasure in the little indulgence.

His broker had found a ranch about a hundred miles south of San Francisco. The description had sounded exactly like what he was looking for. He would go look at the property, and if he liked it, make an offer.

He would ensure his corrals and barns were ready for the prized Andalusians he had already purchased. He only had to contact the rancher who was caring for the horses and have them delivered.

Then what?

Start a family.

How?

Colin pulled the cigar from his lips and stared at it crossly, as if it were the cigar's fault that he didn't have any wife prospects. What had Margaret been thinking to turn him away?

That she wanted to marry for love and I couldn't give that to her.

Damn.

What about Annie?

She was at school and Colin suspected she would stay in San Francisco afterward to become an actress in spite of Trev's disapproval.

He ground out his cigar and tossed it in a tin can beside the bench.

I miss her.

There, he'd admitted it. So why didn't he feel any better?

Because I want her but can't have her.

Maybe he should have just asked her flat out to marry him. What was the worst that could happen?

She could say no.

Well, he would visit the property his broker

had found for him, then return to San Francisco to see Annie one last time to make sure she had settled into the school without any problems.

He might even get up the courage to ask her.

Annie had known they would welcome her with open arms and keep her secret. Now that Percival was thinking about buying his own theater, he was looking for another actor and actress to add to the troupe. Though he was delighted to have Annie join them, she had to convince him nobody would be looking for her.

To be certain the school wouldn't miss her, she sent the headmistress a telegram explaining that Annie Trevelyan would not be attending the school because of a death in the family. Then Annie had written her parents a letter to let them know she had settled right into the school life, even including some creative little stories about her first day. She wasn't certain how long her ruse would last, especially if Colin came to visit her at the school, but it would buy her some time.

Annie threw herself into her new character. Though it was a smaller role than her part in "The Taming of the Shrew," she didn't complain. She was gaining experience.

And it was only at night, as she lay in her cot in the tiny room behind the stage, that she could admit she missed kissing him and teasing him and holding his hand.

*   *   *

Colin climbed down from the rented carriage and tugged at his new jacket, then straightened his collar for the umpteenth time. Maybe he was on a fool's errand and would make a complete ass of himself, but he had to know if he had a chance with Annie.

In the two weeks since he had seen her enter this building, he had bought his ranch and ordered his five Andalusians delivered. The one thing he hadn't been able to do was look at another woman without comparing her to Annie. None of them had even come close.

When he had stood on the porch of his ranch house, it had been Annie he had imagined standing next to him. At night it had been Annie he had dreamed of in bed with him.

So now he stood outside Miss Sally Langford's Finishing School and felt like he was seventeen years old again.

"Buck up, McBride," he said aloud.

Pressing his shoulders back, he strode to the front door and used the brass knocker to announce his presence. A minute later the door was swung open by a tall, skinny woman whose hair was tied back so tightly, her eyebrows were hiked upward as if she were constantly surprised.

"May I help you?" she asked with a coolly polite voice.

"I'm here to see Annie Trevelyan."

A frown flittered on the woman's thin lips. "We received a note that she would not be attending because of a death in the family."

Colin flung out a hand to brace himself against the door frame. "Who died?"

"The note didn't say. It merely said not to expect her."

Though Colin's heart still pounded out of control, he heard something in her words that didn't make sense. "But she was here already."

The woman shook her head. "She never arrived."

"I dropped her off personally two weeks ago. I saw her walk inside this very building."

"You're mistaken. Annie Trevelyan is not enrolled here, nor did she ever register for her room." She began to close the door, but Colin planted his foot against it.

"I brought her here. Are you telling me she never showed up?" Colin demanded.

"That's correct, sir. Now remove your foot."

Too confused to argue any further, Colin did as she'd said. The door banged shut in his face.

Annie had never arrived here. But she had.

I was with her. I saw her go inside.

She must have waited inside until he was gone, and then run away.

Fury overtook his shock. She had never planned to attend the school.

His fingernails dug into his palms. Where would she have gone? Who did she know here?

Margaret? No. The widow wouldn't allow her to leave the school.

Percival and Essie? Colin ground his teeth together. If she wanted to act, they were the perfect choice. But where was the troupe?

There were too damned many theaters in San Francisco.

He stalked back to his rented carriage and climbed into the driver's box. When he found Annie, he was going to give her a piece of his mind.

She already had his heart.

Annie bowed with Percival and Essie as the audience clapped and shouted their approval. Though the theater was small, the enthusiasm of the spectators made up for it. Toby and Alexander tugged the curtains closed for the last time.

"For opening night, I thought it went quite well," Percival said.

"It most certainly did."

The familiar woman's voice made Annie spin around only to see Margaret walking toward Percival with a smile on her face and her long hair loose around her shoulders. He opened his arms and she entered without hesitation and they kissed.

Annie's mouth gaped. "What—"

"Holy shit," Toby said at the same time.

Margaret turned in Percival's embrace to gaze at Annie. "I made him and Essie promise not to tell you. I wanted to surprise you."

"Well, you did," Annie said, unable to articulate anything more intelligent.

"We are getting married," Percival announced.

"That is one of the reasons I chose to buy a theater."

" 'We' bought a theater," Margaret corrected him.

Annie groaned inwardly. Had Percival taken advantage of Margaret to get the money to buy the theater?

"He wouldn't take the money at first," Margaret said, as if reading her mind. "In fact, he asked me to marry him before I even offered."

"It's true," Percival said with a tender smile. "I have loved her since the moment I laid eyes on her."

"But wasn't Colin courting you?" Annie asked.

"He didn't love me and I didn't love him," Margaret said, then smiled at Percival. "But Percy and I love one another."

Annie's mind was still trying to assimilate the odd couple when another worry occurred to her. "Have you known about my being here?"

Margaret nodded. "Percy told me."

"Did you—"

"He convinced me not to contact your parents. I'm not certain that was right, but I can see you're happy here. And your talents would be wasted in a finishing school." Margaret smiled warmly at all of them, including Toby and Alexander. "Besides, everyone seems to be taking good care of you."

Annie's eyes filled with tears. A month ago she would never have believed Margaret could change so much. Or maybe the real Margaret had finally broken out of her shell. "Thank you."

"No, I should be thanking you. If not for you, I wouldn't have met Percy."

The adoring look Percival gave her brought a stab of pain to Annie's heart. Colin had looked at her that way. Did he love her like Percival so obviously loved Margaret?

"We must go celebrate the success of our opening night," Percival announced.

Three hours later, they returned to the theater. Alexander and Toby insisted on escorting Annie to her room in spite of her insistence that she would be fine. They had become almost as endearingly protective of her as Colin had been.

"Did I ever tell you I love you, both of you?" Annie suddenly asked.

Toby grinned. "Yep."

She smiled back. "Good. Because I do."

Alexander nudged the boy and Toby's cheeks reddened. "Well, we like you, too, Annie."

Alexander nodded in agreement.

She gave them each a hug. "Goodnight." She closed the door and turned and even in the dimness she recognized the familiar figure. She stumbled back, her eyes wide.

"You just couldn't wait, could you?" Colin asked.

"Laddie."

"Colin," he corrected, stalking over to her. "You've been drinking, Annie."

She had had only one glass of wine, but maybe

she could use his incorrect assumption to her advantage. She drew her shoulders back ... and
pretended almost to fall over backwards. Colin
caught her arms and she allowed herself to sag
against his chest. Oh, yes, this act definitely had
its advantages. She put her arms around his waist
and snuggled close. With her ear against his
chest, she could hear the steady thumping of
his heart. She could have listened forever. "This is
nice."

"Why did you run away?" he asked quietly.

"Didn't wanna go there," she said, slurring her
words enough to make him believe she was tipsy.

"You never planned to go, did you?"

"Stupid school. Who wants to be a lady, anyhow?" She wriggled against him and felt his muscles grow taut. "I wanna be an actress." She
raised her head and breathed close to his bare
neck, "And a courtesan."

Then she stood on her tiptoes and kissed
him. Hard. "Make me *your* courtesan, Colin," she
whispered.

His eyes darkened, and he swooped down to
devour her lips. Annie met his tender assault
with her own, learning the shape and feel of his
lips beneath hers. When he asked for entrance,
she granted it willingly.

Annie threaded her fingers through his thick
hair as their tongues dueled in desire. She felt his
hands moving up and down her back, then lower
to cup her buttocks and tug her closer to him.

She couldn't have imagined anything feeling

this good, this exciting. Colin stole her breath and gave his own back to her. He shifted his attention from her lips to her face, feathering kisses across her cheeks and eyebrows and around to her earlobes and down her neck.

She tipped her head back, granting him further liberties which he didn't hesitate to seize. His teeth grazed her skin, sending delicious tingles through her.

Suddenly, he drew back and gazed at her. His eyes were hooded with desire but a frown marred his features. He was breathing heavily and Annie, with a little thrill of discovery, realized she had done that to him. Just as he had made her breathless.

"You've been drinking. I won't take advantage of you, lass," Colin said, his voice low and husky, as if he were restraining his lust by sheer will.

She managed to pull her chaotic thoughts into some manner of order. She knew the consequences, but this was her only chance to be with Colin—the man she loved. If someone was going to teach her how to love, it had to be him.

"I only had one glass of wine." She wound her arms around his neck and he instinctively put his arms around her waist. "I know what I want, Colin; I want you."

He gazed down at her as if ascertaining her sincerity. Then he leaned down to kiss her, and spoke with his lips close to her cheek. "Love me, Annie."

His emotion-laden words were like a physical caress, and her body melted into his. She felt his fingers on her chest, unbuttoning her bodice. Cool air swirled in, but it was quickly replaced by the heat of Colin's hand palming her breast and his fingers rolling an already-hard nipple between them.

She gasped and leaned forward, kissing and sucking at the pulse point on his neck. His rough whiskers and the taste of salt and shaving soap inundated her, bringing a heavy ache to her belly and lower. She'd never known anything could feel so good . . . so overwhelming.

Annie wanted to touch and taste all of him. She whimpered as she tried to pull his jacket off his shoulders. Colin released her and she leaned toward him, not wanting to lose the contact.

"I'm not goin' anywhere, lass," Colin said gently, a smile in his voice. "I'm just goin' to get rid of a few things."

Annie's greedy gaze refused to leave him as he removed his coat, then his shirt. Her fingers grazed his smooth chest and the muscle flexed beneath her fingertips. "You're beautiful, Colin."

"Women are beautiful, lass. Men are—" He shrugged. "Men."

She shook her head and took a step closer. "You are a man and you're beautiful, Colin. I never imagined, never thought . . ." She leaned forward and shamelessly kissed the center of his chest, then continued brushing her lips across his smooth skin until they settled on a nipple.

Colin gasped sharply. "Are ye tryin' to kill an old man?"

She raised her head long enough to toss him a saucy grin. "You're not old, Colin, just experienced." She went back to paying homage to his broad chest.

Even through her layers of skirts, Annie could feel his erection against her. Her own breathing became more labored and her clothes constricting. Pulling her hands away from him, she began to undo the rest of the buttons on her dress to tug the garment off.

Colin reached up to help her, then slid her petticoat and drawers down to her ankles. Almost frantic, Annie jerked her camisole off over her head and dropped it to the floor, leaving her breasts bare to Colin's hot gaze.

She stared into his eyes, feeling fire burn between them like a living entity. No man had ever seen her like this and she knew deep down no other man would. Only Colin—her best friend and now her lover.

Colin led her to the narrow bed. The back of her knees hit the frame and she dropped onto the mattress. He knelt on the floor in front of her. As he unlaced her shoes with trembling fingers, Annie rested her hands on his shoulders, kneading the warm flesh beneath her palms. Her world narrowed to Colin and what he was doing to her.

After removing her shoes, he rolled her black stockings down. Little arcs of heat darted through her. Naked now, she felt the first tickling of self-consciousness and crossed her arms over her breasts.

Colin leaned back on his heels and laid his hands on her thighs. "If you've changed your mind, lass, we can stop." He huffed a nervous laugh. "I may not be able to walk for a few minutes, but I won't do anything you don't want me to."

She stared into his eyes, overflowing with tenderness and affection. How could she even think of stopping now? She wanted that "something" that danced on the periphery of her awareness.

Keeping her gaze locked with his, she lowered her arms. "I want *you*, Colin."

Her husky declaration was nearly his undoing as he struggled to move slowly, to ensure Annie's pleasure came first. He stood and was shocked when Annie's fingers fell to his trouser buttons. Her hand brushed across his engorged penis and it jerked against its confines.

Annie raised her head to look at him, a question in her uncertain expression.

Colin stroked Annie's glossy hair as he gazed down into her brilliant blue eyes. "It's all right, lass. I want you, too."

She swallowed and nodded. She finally undid the buttons of his trousers and drew back, seemingly afraid, now that she had come this far.

Colin stepped back and removed his boots, pants, and socks, which left him in only his underwear. His hard masculinity was outlined against the thin material and Annie caught her breath as she stared at it. For a moment, Colin thought she would call an end to their lovemaking, but Annie did the unexpected again. She reached out and pushed the underwear down his hips, releasing him.

With a light touch, she grazed his length with her fingertip and he jerked from the erotic sensation. Afraid he would lose what little control he had, Colin pressed her back on the bed and joined her. Heat emanated from her body and he closed his eyes to struggle with his desperate need. He had to go slow or he would scare her.

Then Annie pounced on top of him and Colin realized she wasn't frightened and she had no intention of going slowly. She wanted him as badly as he wanted her.

With his arms around her waist, he rolled them over so she lay beneath him. He straddled her hips and peered down into her flushed face. He lowered his head and kissed her, then made love to her neck and breasts with his lips and tongue. She squirmed beneath him, arching upward to meet him.

"Please, Colin," she whispered hoarsely.

Retaining some lucidity, he shook his head. "We need to go slow, lass, or I could hurt you."

"Forget slow. I want you now."

Her lower lip thrust out and Colin couldn't resist leaning over to drag his tongue across the pout. He smiled against her mouth. "Always so impatient, imp."

"Please," she pleaded. "I want you inside me."

Colin's breath caught in his throat and blood pulsed through his brain, obliterating all rational thought. When he moved between her legs she opened to him without hesitation. Her musky scent rose around him, making him grow even harder.

He leaned over to suckle her nipple as he began to enter her. Her hot flesh closed around him and he had to stop before he was overwhelmed. But Annie wasn't to be denied and she wrapped her legs around his waist, urging him to complete their joining. Gritting his teeth to hold himself in check, he continued until he came up against her virginity.

He raised his head from her chest and kissed her. "This will hurt, but I promise it'll get better, lass."

Her body tensed around him but she nodded. "Please."

With one thrust, he broke through and was fully sheathed within her. She groaned once but gamely hung on, trusting him to show her the pleasure.

He remained still, waiting for her body to grow accustomed to him. When her flesh pulsed around him, Colin withdrew slowly, then pressed back into her.

"Oh, Colin," Annie breathed.

Her husky words unleashed his passion and he began to move in and out. Annie arched up to meet him, her motions settling into a rhythm that met each of his thrusts with equal force. Her low moans merged with her slick heat to quickly bring him over the edge.

With a shout of completion, he emptied his seed within her. Annie's answering cries and clenching muscles told him she wasn't far behind. As her climax washed through her he dropped bonelessly over her, his arms holding his weight so he wouldn't crush her.

Their panting filled the small room as Annie ran her hands up and down Colin's back.

"That was . . . wonderful, magnificent, beautiful, stupendous—"

Colin kissed her, then gazed down at her swollen lips and pink cheeks—she looked like a woman who had just been thoroughly loved. "Yes, it was," he said softly. "And more."

With a sigh of regret, he rolled off her and pulled her into his arms. Her head rested on his chest and her long hair tickled his arm, which curved around her shoulders.

Annie giggled. "Now I understand why Essie likes doing this so well."

Colin grinned as he rested his chin on Annie's crown. "I have to admit, it's much better when you do this with someone you love."

"You love me?" Her childlike surprise made his smile grow.

He kissed her head gently. "Yes, I love you, imp."

She tilted her head back to gaze at him. "I love you, too."

Though he had suspected she felt the same way, her profession still astonished him. Now was his chance. "Will you marry me?"

Annie stiffened as sadness replaced happiness. "I can't."

Colin had half expected her refusal, but he also had confidence he could persuade her to accept his proposal. "Why not?"

"You know why. I want to be an actress."

"You can be an actress and be my wife."

She gazed up at him, her eyes glistening. "At first you wouldn't mind, but after a while you would want me to quit." She paused. "And you would want children. I won't take that chance, Colin. I don't want to die."

"Your mother died because she didn't take care of herself, Annie. She had you without any problems," Colin argued.

Annie shook her head and pushed away from him. "You don't know that." She slid out of the bed, taking a blanket with her to wrap around her nakedness. "This was wonderful, Colin, but I still don't want to get married."

"I hoped you would change your mind."

She shook her head.

Frustrated anger rushed through Colin and he jumped to his feet. "So you're just going to walk away and become a courtesan?"

"Please, Colin, don't make this any worse than it is."

He gathered his clothes, jerking them on. "I

think *you've* done that." With his shirt hanging out and his shoes untied, he stalked to the door. "Break a leg, Annie," he said sarcastically.

As he strode out the door, he heard her yell, "Thanks for the experience. I'm sure it'll come in handy."

Her words matched his, cruel hurt for cruel hurt.

Chapter 21

Colin awakened with a headache and a mouth that tasted like cotton. He brought his fingers to his lips and grimaced slightly at the soreness. Then the previous night's activities penetrated his sleep-hazed brain.

Annie. He had taken her virginity and she had thanked him for the experience.

She thanked me, for God's sake.

He sat up and drew his knees up to prop his elbows on them. Some part of his mind had been convinced that if he took Annie to bed, she would jump at the chance to marry him.

But Annie had turned him down flat. There was nothing else for him to do here in San Francisco. It was time to go to his new ranch and start his life there—his lonely life. If he couldn't have

Annie, he didn't want any woman. Even the thought of not having children didn't bother him as much as living without Annie.

Glancing at his pocket watch on the stand by the bed, he was surprised to see it was nearly noon. When he looked outside he saw gray clouds and a light drizzle coming down. No wonder it was so dark in his room.

He kept his mind blank as he washed, shaved, and dressed. After packing his bag, he looked around the room one last time for anything he might have forgotten. But the only thing he would be leaving behind was his heart.

He would send a telegram to Trev explaining what Annie was doing and how he had let his friend down. But Colin wouldn't force Annie back to the finishing school—his lass was all grown-up now.

Thanks to me, he thought bitterly.

A knock on the door startled him and he opened it. A boy not much older than Toby held out a folded piece of paper. "Message for you, mister."

Frowning, Colin took it and handed the boy a nickel. With a grin, the kid dashed off, and Colin closed the door to read his note.

If you want Annie Trevelyan back alive, meet me at two o'clock at the old Penny Mine three miles south of the city. Come alone.

Colin read the message two more times, but there was no clue to the identify of the kidnaper.

"Damn it!" He should have known the bastard in Reno would follow them and try again. Instead, Colin had blithely gone on his way after dropping her off at the school.

He dug his watch out of his pocket: one o'clock. He had just enough time to stop by Annie's room at the theater and see if the kidnaper had left any clues before going to the meeting place. Leaving his bag behind, he quickly went down to board a cable car for the theater.

Half an hour later, Colin stood in Annie's open door. The bed was still mussed and Colin remembered too vividly what had happened there last night. Shaking himself free of the memories, he walked around the small room, touching her hairbrush, a blouse she had thrown across the chair, and finally the pillow where her head had lain. He could smell the faint scent of her perfume and he clenched his jaw.

Who the hell had taken her? Somebody who obviously knew she meant a great deal to him. Somebody who knew he would do anything to save her.

Somebody who was after *him.*

Colin had been his target all along. The realization staggered him. It was his fault Annie's life was in danger. Some protector he turned out to be.

"Where's Annie?"

Colin whirled around to find Toby and Alexander standing in the doorway. It took a few moments for his heart to slow its rapidfire pulse. "Have you seen her today?"

Toby shook his head. "We just come down to see if she wanted to go eat. Percival and Essie are waiting for us out front." Eyes too sharp to belong to a nine-year-old searched the room. "Where is she?"

"Somebody kidnaped her."

Toby's eyes widened. "Just like in Reno?"

Colin pulled the note out of his pocket and held it up. "Only this time they succeeded," he said grimly. "Let's go see if Percival or Essie saw anything."

Tucking the note back in his coat pocket, Colin closed the door softly behind him and followed Toby and Alexander.

"Colin," Percival said in surprise in the lobby of the theater. "What are you doing here?"

"Annie's been kidnaped," he said without preamble. "Have you seen anyone hanging around here lately?"

Percival and Essie, their faces revealing their shock, shook their heads.

"Has anybody been asking questions about her or about me?" Colin pressed.

"No, nobody," Percival said. "Last night was our opening night and nothing untoward happened that I'm aware of. After the performance we all went out to eat, then came back to sleep."

"When did you find out Annie was here?" Essie asked.

"Last night," Colin admitted. "I went to the finishing school to visit her and found she had never shown up. Since you and Margaret are the only people she knows here, I tracked you down."

"So you saw her after she got back here last night," Essie said matter-of-factly. "How do you know she was kidnaped?"

"A note was delivered to my room an hour ago. It told me where and when to meet if I didn't want to see Annie killed," he explained.

"Where?" Percival asked.

Colin shook his head. "It said I had to come alone."

"But—"

"I won't risk her life. If my hunch is right, the kidnaper's after me, not Annie." He pulled out his watch. "I have to get going." He took a deep breath. "If neither Annie nor I come back, can you contact her parents and let them know what happened? Margaret knows them."

"If it's necessary, we shall take care of it," Percival said somberly. "Good luck, Colin."

Colin nodded solemnly. "Hopefully both Annie and I will be back in time for dinner."

He bade farewell to Percival and Essie. Toby and Alexander were gone, though they had been almost on top of him two minutes ago. He frowned, but had a more important thing to worry about—saving Annie's life.

Annie glared at her captor from her unladylike position on the mine's hard ground. She had been trying to remember where she had seen him before, but her sluggish mind couldn't come up with the answer. "If we're just going to sit here, why don't you untie me so we can play poker? I might even let you win a few hands."

The man barked a laugh. "You're telling me you know how to play poker?"

Feigning indignation, Annie narrowed her eyes. "I do have a brain, not that it takes much intelligence to play poker. I mean, look at you."

"If you're trying to insult me, you're going to have to try harder than that."

Annie slumped. So he wasn't as stupid as he looked. Darn. "Can you at least tell me why you kidnaped me? If it was for money, I'll have you know my parents are not wealthy people. I mean, my father insisted I go to this stupid finishing school and he was paying for it, so I suppose he has some money, but he's not rich."

"Shut up."

Annie kept her fear hidden. *Don't let the audience see how terrified you are.* "You don't enjoy stimulating conversations?"

"I enjoy peace and quiet." The man shifted on the rock he was using as a chair.

"Then you shouldn't have kidnaped me. You ask anyone and they'll tell you that if you want peace and quiet, don't kidnap Annie Trevelyan. She can talk the ear off a preacher."

Her captor closed his eyes and shook his head. Annie grinned to herself. Maybe she could talk her way out of this one.

"Even my parents will tell you that once I get going, nothing can stop me. I guess that's one of the reasons I want to be an actress—so I can talk to a whole audience of people."

The man groaned.

"When I was really young, I didn't talk for six months. Everyone figures I'm making up for lost time now." She shrugged, a difficult thing to do with her hands tied behind her back. "They could be right. I don't remember much from that time. I was only four or five then."

"All right, that's enough." The man stood and Annie clamped her mouth shut. Had she pushed him too far?

He removed a white handkerchief from his pocket and quickly wrapped it around her mouth to gag her. He tied the ends and she snarled when he tore out some strands of hair with the knot.

He stepped back and observed his handiwork while Annie put all her fury into a glower. He chuckled, further infuriating her.

"I should've done that right away. It would've been a whole lot more peaceful," he said. He squatted down in front of her. "You want to know why I kidnaped you?"

She didn't give him the satisfaction of an answer.

"Your boyfriend McBride killed my brother."

Shock filled Annie, followed by disbelief. Colin would never hurt anyone, unless he was protecting himself or someone he cared for. She shook her head vehemently and tried to speak, but the gag made her words come out like a two-year-old's garble.

"He made a mistake when he set the charges and one of them didn't go off until my brother was inside. He was killed, but McBride lived. Damn him!" The man's hand curled into a fist, which he rested on his thigh. "I'm going to get him in here with you and blow the mine. Hopefully he'll live long enough to see you die and then he'll follow you."

Annie trembled with terror and helplessness. She knew of Colin's fear of caves and tunnels. He had also told her his suspicions about the Jenkins brothers being the ones who had made the mistake with the explosives. Colin had felt sorry for the man because of his loss and had never told anyone of his suspicions. Colin had even helped Jenkins get the job he held now.

Annie's eyes widened as she recognized her kidnaper—he had been at the Denver railway station after the shooting of Mr. James. Leonard Jenkins must have been the sniper. There had been enough time between the shooting and the time he had joined them for him to hide his rifle.

Her head swam in dizziness and her stomach rolled. He was probably the one who had tried to run them down in Denver and tried to kidnap her in Reno.

Jenkins smiled. "I see you remember me."

Annie shivered and this time she couldn't hide

it from her captor. Colin was going to die because of her.

Jenkins lifted a hand and she drew back, but he only laughed and skimmed his fingertips down her cheek. "It's a shame I have to kill you, too. We could've had some fun together." He pulled his watch out of his pocket. "Time to welcome McBride."

The man stood and stared down at Annie for a long moment. "I really am sorry I have to kill you, too, but I want McBride to know how I felt when he killed my brother."

Jenkins tipped his hat and left her alone in the darkness lit only by a single candle.

She struggled against her bonds, but he had tied them well and she succeeded only in getting rope burns on her wrists and ankles. Maybe if she could stand, she could hop out and warn Colin. She rocked her upper body and managed to get her feet under her, but her long skirt was caught under her heels and kept her from rising.

One helpless tear trickled down Annie's cheek and anger dashed away any others that considered falling. She couldn't let him murder Colin. Her breath caught in her chest and turned into a sob. He had said he loved her, and she had admitted to loving him in a moment of weakness.

Could marriage to Colin take the place of the joy she experienced while performing on stage? And what if she became pregnant? Could she take the chance of dying in childbirth?

The answer crystallized within her—yes, she could, if it was his child . . . *their* child. Another tear trailed down her face.

Her choices became clear: a lifetime—however long that might be—with Colin, or years performing in different cities all over the world. Without Colin, it would be a hollow life.

If a choice had to be made, she would choose Colin, even if they had only a year or two together. He was her best friend and the man she loved . . . and he was going to die unless she could escape.

She increased her struggles until she heard somebody approaching. She froze and listened intently. Someone was drawing nearer—her heart threatened to leap out of her chest.

I'm sorry, Colin.

Holding a lit candle, Colin halted at the entrance to the Penny Mine. The dark tunnel both beckoned and terrified him. His breathing turned into desperate gasps and his palms moistened with sweat. When he received the note, he should have realized what he would be facing. Or maybe subconsciously he had, and refused to acknowledge it until he was faced with the actuality.

Pitch darkness . . . thick silence . . . smothering dust.

His choking echoed in the stone chamber, as loud as the explosion that had ripped through the same space only moments earlier. Air flowed a little more easily into his lungs. He bent his right leg and excruciating pain shot up the limb. He swallowed his scream, but the whimper that escaped him was even more frightening.

He had to get out of here . . . escape before the air ran out.

His heart thundered in his chest, thumping like a stamp mill. He would die in here and nobody in the world would mourn his passing. Thirty-odd years came down to this—dying alone in a black hole beneath the earth.

The reason-stealing hysteria clouded his mind, invaded his body until he couldn't even lift a foot to take a step forward. He couldn't go in there.

He *had* to go in there. Annie's life depended on it.

He closed his eyes, picturing five-year-old Annie playing with her dancing doll on that Fourth of July so long ago. Then he remembered her as an awkward adolescent with an embarrassing crush on him during one of his rare visits.

Memories of last night eclipsed those of her as a girl. His love for Annie had evolved through the years to what he felt for her now—love for a woman he wanted to spend the rest of his life with. If she wanted to act, he would follow her wherever her performances took her. As long as she was in his arms at night, it didn't matter where they were.

He took a deep breath and opened his eyes. The black adit yawned in front of him. For Annie's sake, he could do this. He *had* to do this.

Trembling, Colin managed to lift his right foot and move it forward. He set it down and raised his left foot. Another step, and another, until he was inside the cave. His breath roared in his ears and his head pounded, but he was still alive.

With every step deeper into the tunnel, Colin's hysteria faded and his heartbeat slowed. He had spent most of his life in places like this. There was nothing to fear except the fear deep within him.

The terror dissipated, replaced by determination. Annie had too much to live for—he couldn't let her die because of him.

"Hello, McBride."

The familiar voice shocked the remaining apprehension from him. He held out the candle and peered into the darkness, able to make out a man's shape. "Jenkins?"

The kidnaper stepped out of the shadows into the candlelight. He held a gun. "Surprised to see me?"

"Yes, but I guess I shouldn't be." Colin studied the man he had run into only a few weeks ago. "You were aiming at me when you hit Rudy, weren't you?"

Jenkins nodded. "You moved at the last minute. I felt bad about shooting Rudy."

A droplet of sweat rolled down Colin's face. "It was you who almost ran us down with the wagon in Denver, and tried to kidnap Annie in Reno."

"You always were smart, McBride. Until you made the mistake with those explosives."

Colin shook his head slowly. "That wasn't my fault, Leonard. That was the string I gave you and your brother to take care of."

"No. You were the boss. It was your fault it didn't detonate with the others." Jenkins's voice was·calm. Too calm.

"Where's Annie?"

"Come on back and see for yourself." He motioned with his gun for Colin to walk ahead of him.

As much as Colin wanted to ensure Annie was all right, he knew the deeper into the cave they went, the less chance they had making it out of this alive. "I want your word that Annie will be released unharmed."

Jenkins smiled coldly. "As long as you cooperate, she'll be fine. Enough stalling, McBride. Let's go."

Colin followed the order, exaggerating his slight limp. If Jenkins thought he was less of a threat, he might not be prepared when Colin made his move. But with Jenkins at his back, it would be nearly impossible to get the gun from him. He had to bide his time.

They walked in silence for about a hundred yards. Colin saw the glow of light up ahead and figured Annie was being held there. He turned his head slightly to see where Jenkins was—four feet behind him. Too far to get to him before he pulled the trigger.

If he didn't try something soon, he might not get a chance.

Colin pretended to stumble, falling to one knee. As Jenkins approached, he jumped up and spun around. He swung a fist at the kidnaper, but Jenkins jerked back and Colin's fist only grazed the man's jaw.

Jenkins cocked the pistol. "Hold it, McBride!"

Colin froze, his heart plummeting into his stomach. He had failed. He raised his hands as he glared at his captor.

"That was stupid," Jenkins said.

Colin clenched his teeth as rage and helplessness churned in him.

"You try something like that again and I won't be so forgiving. Move it."

Colin lowered his hands carefully and when Jenkins's finger didn't twitch on the trigger, he continued walking. The tunnel curved slightly and opened into a larger area. Annie sat on the floor, her hands behind her back and a gag in her mouth. He quickly moved to her side and hunkered down beside her, leaving Jenkins to catch up.

"Are you all right, lass?" Colin asked anxiously.

She nodded and an odd gleam in her eye puzzled him. She deliberately looked at his face, then to a place over his shoulder.

Colin turned to see Alexander and Toby hugging the mine's wall behind him. He stood quickly to draw Jenkins's attention. Swaggering, Jenkins passed Alexander and Toby's hiding place.

"As you can see, your girlfriend is all right. Though if I hadn't gagged her, she might not be. I don't know how you put up with her mouth."

Annie made an indignant sound in her throat.

"Now what?" Colin asked. Three lives other than his own hung in the balance.

"I figure it's only fitting that you die the way my brother did."

Colin's blood froze. "That was an accident. You know as well as I do that our job was a dangerous one."

"If you had done your job, he'd still be alive!"

Suddenly Alexander leapt out and grabbed Jenkins around the chest, pinning the man's arms to his sides. Although Alexander was stronger and bigger, Jenkins was wiry and he wiggled out of his arms and raised the gun.

Colin charged Jenkins, his head catching the kidnaper in the side. They fell to the hard ground, Colin on top of Jenkins, then rolled. A rock jabbed into Colin's kidney as he fought to keep the gun barrel away from him.

Using one hand to hold the wrist of Jenkins's gun hand, Colin threw a punch at his adversary. They rolled again and Colin jabbed his knee into the other man's groin.

" 'Oomph," Jenkins groaned.

Colin dug his fingertips into Jenkins's wrist and a shot exploded. Annie screamed and Colin flinched, terrified the bullet had hit her. With fury and fear surging through him, he swung his right fist and knocked Jenkins out.

He pushed himself up and his gaze sought Annie. Now freed, she stood over Toby, who was kneeling beside Alexander. Colin rushed over to Annie and pulled her into a tight embrace as her arms slipped around his waist. He nuzzled her soft hair. "Thank God, you're all right."

He wasn't ever going to let her out of his sight again.

"Is Alexander all right?" Annie asked, keeping a firm hold on Colin.

"His leg is bleeding," Toby replied, his eyes round and making him look like the nine-year-old he was.

Colin squatted down to examine the wound and breathed a sigh of relief. He rested a hand on Alexander's broad shoulder. "It's only a flesh wound. You're going to be fine."

Jenkins moaned.

"I'd better tie him up," Colin said.

Annie slipped away to pick up the ropes that had been used to bind her. "Here."

Colin smiled. "Thanks, lass."

While Colin trussed Jenkins up, Annie ripped a long strip of cloth from her petticoat to wrap around Alexander's shallow wound.

"Does anyone want to tell me how Alexander and Toby got here before me?" Colin asked, once he was done with Jenkins.

Annie stood and pressed close to Colin's side, and he put his arm around her shoulders. She fit perfectly, her head resting against his chest. "I was wondering the same thing," she said and gazed at the boy sitting beside Alexander. "Toby?"

He squirmed a little but Alexander's big hand on his shoulder made him stop. "I picked your pocket while you were talking to Percival and Essie. I read the note and put it back so you wouldn't know. Then me and Alexander came here."

Colin tried to keep his expression serious, but knew his eyes twinkled. "So besides being a cardsharp, you're also a pickpocket?"

"Don't punish them, Colin. If they hadn't shown up, who knows what might have happened?" Annie pleaded.

"It seems to me that if Toby and Alexander didn't live in a city, they wouldn't be picking up such bad habits. I think maybe moving someplace else might help," Colin said, keeping his voice stern.

"Me and Alexander won't go to no home," Toby said fiercely.

"What if it was *my* home?"

Toby frowned and exchanged a look with Alexander. "What do you mean?"

"I have a ranch with five very special horses, and I need somebody I can trust to make sure they're taken care of properly," Colin said thoughtfully.

Alexander snagged Toby's arm and gave it a tug. He was smiling and nodding.

"We like horses," Toby said, but the wariness was still there.

"How about that, Annie? They like horses." Colin glanced at Annie, who appeared to be completely bewildered.

"That's good," Annie said tentatively.

"Definitely, because I will trust both of them to take care of my horses when I'm not there." Colin turned to gather Annie in his arms and gazed down at her shining blue eyes. "You see, I'll be away frequently because I'll be with my wife, who's an actress."

"I-I can't let you do that," Annie stuttered. "The ranch . . . it's your dream. What you've always wanted."

Colin shook his head as he smiled. "You're my dream, lass. I don't need children or a ranch. I only need you."

"I can't let you make that big a sacrifice." Her eyes filled with moisture but she smiled a smile so full of love it would have stolen Colin's heart if that hadn't already been captured. "I want to be your wife and have your children. I don't have to be an actress to be happy."

"But that's *your* dream."

"For Pete's sake, why don't you two stop being so stupid?" Toby interrupted. "Stay at the ranch part of the time and act part of the time."

Colin and Annie turned their heads toward the boy, then looked back at each other.

"Out of the mouths of—" Colin began.

"Smart young men," Annie finished.

"Will you marry me, Annie?"

"That depends. Will you marry me, Colin?"

"Yes," he replied.

"Then I guess I'll have to marry you, too."

Colin smiled and bent down to kiss his lass—his unexpected wife-to-be.

Alexander pulled a paper horse out of his trouser pocket and held it between two large fingers. He glanced at Colin and Annie, then shared a secret smile with Toby and slipped the horse back into his pocket where it belonged.

Epilogue

The curtains opened once more to the thunderous applause of the audience. Annie stood between two other actors as they took another bow. She gazed out across the sea of faces in the London theater and knew some of the royal family stood out there, clapping for her, Annie Trevelyan McBride.

Flowers were tossed onto the stage—expensive roses and bouquets of rare lilies—but she ignored all of them. Instead, she walked to the edge of the stage to accept a bouquet of wilting daisies from the small hand that held them up to her.

Annie leaned over and kissed Katie, her four-year-old daughter. Another wildflower bouquet from the English countryside was offered by her eight-year-old son, Casey. Joy filled her at the sight of her two precious children and her husband, who held Katie in his strong arms.

"You 'broke a leg' good," Colin whispered, and brushed a kiss across her lips. "Congratulations, imp."

"I love you, Colin," she said, her voice trembling.

"I love you, too, lass. Now take your final bow. You deserve it."

Holding the two small bouquets, she straightened and looked beyond to her father and Kate, who had come all the way across the ocean to see her perform.

It had been difficult in the beginning. Her father's disapproval of her acting and her own anger that he had hidden the truth about her mother had opened wounds that had taken a long time to heal. But Colin's support and Kate's had aided in the healing process. Besides, now that Annie had children of her own, she knew that despite everything, her own parents had never stopped loving her.

She blew a kiss to her papa and Kate, then stepped back into the line and took her final bow. As the curtains began to close, she kept her gaze on her family, the only dream that truly mattered.

Tomorrow they would begin the journey back home to the ranch in California. Annie looked forward to spending time with Colin and the children, as well as Alexander and Toby, who had taken care of the place while they had been in England. She would invite Percival, Margaret, their four children, and Essie to come down to visit for a few days. It had been too long since she had seen them.

The curtain closed completely and the actors and actresses hugged each other good-bye. Tears were shed, but none were from Annie.

She was going home.

Dear Reader,

Warm up with Avon romance! There's something for everyone . . . and I guarantee these books will heat you up on a cold winter's night. And, if you live in a balmier climate, you'll just have to turn up the A.C. . . .So, if you like the Avon romance you've just finished, check out what we have next month.

Let's begin with January's Avon Romantic Treasure, *Too Wicked to Marry* by Susan Sizemore. Lord Martin Kestrel can have any woman he desires . . . but the only woman he'd ever deign to marry is the woman he knows as Abigail Perry. But as a woman in the service of the queen, Abigail has deceived Martin, and when he discovers her ruse she must handle the consequences . . .

Remember that rhyme you said as a kid? "First comes love . . . then comes marriage . . ." Well, sometimes it's the other way around, as we discover in Christie Ridgway's *First Comes Love*, an Avon Contemporary romance. What would *you* do if you found out you were accidentally married? I know, it sounds crazy, but in a romance by Christie anything is deliciously possible!

If you love romances by Lisa Kleypas, you're going to love Kathryn Smith's sensuous and dramatic Avon Romance, *A Seductive Offer*. Lord Braven has saved Rachel Ashton's life once . . . and when she accepts his offer of a marriage in name only, she knows he has actually saved her yet again. But what happens when her passion for him turns to true love?

A bride sale! How can it be? But in *The Bride Sale*, an Avon Romance by Candice Hern, Lord James Harkness stumbles upon this appalling practice, and stuns himself by bidding on a beautiful gentlewoman being auctioned off. James knows he's not fit to be a true husband, but how can he resist her?

I promised these would be hot! I hope you enjoy them,

Lucia Macro

Lucia Macro
Executive Editor

REL 1201

Captivating and sensual romances
by *New York Times* bestselling author
Stephanie Laurens

A SECRET LOVE
0-380-80570-7/$6.99 US/$9.99 Can

A ROGUE'S PROPOSAL
0-380-80569-3/$6.50 US/$8.50 Can

SCANDAL'S BRIDE
0-380-80568-5/$5.99 US/$7.99 Can

A RAKE'S VOW
0-380-79457-8/$6.99 US/$9.99 Can

DEVIL'S BRIDE
0-380-79456-X/$6.99 US/$9.99 Can

CAPTAIN JACK'S WOMAN
0-380-79455-1/$6.99 US/$9.99 Can

ALL ABOUT LOVE
0-380-81201-0/$6.99 US/$9.99 Can

ALL ABOUT PASSION
0-380-81202-9/$6.99 US/$9.99 Can

And Coming Soon in Hardcover

THE PROMISE IN A KISS
0-06-018888-X/$18.00 US/$27.50 Can

Available wherever books are sold or please call 1-800-331-3761
to order.   LAU 0601

Avon Romances—
the best in exceptional authors
and unforgettable novels!

THE LAWMAN'S SURRENDER   by Debra Mullins
0-380-80775-0/ $5.99 US/ $7.99 Can

HIS FORBIDDEN KISS   by Margaret Moore
0-380-81335-1/ $5.99 US/ $7.99 Can

HIGHLAND ROGUES: by Lois Greiman
THE FRASER BRIDE
0-380-81540-0/ $5.99 US/ $7.99 Can

ELUSIVE PASSION   by Kathryn Smith
0-380-81610-5/ $5.99 US/ $7.99 Can

THE MACKENZIES: ZACH   by Ana Leigh
0-380-81103-0/ $5.99 US/ $7.99 Can

THE WARRIOR'S DAMSEL   by Denise Hampton
0-380-81546-X/ $5.99 US/ $7.99 Can

HIS BETROTHED   by Gayle Callen
0-380-81377-7/ $5.99 US/ $7.99 Can

THE RENEGADES: RAFE   by Genell Dellin
0-380-81849-3/ $5.99 US/ $7.99 Can

WARCLOUD'S PASSION   by Karen Kay
0-380-80342-9/ $5.99 US/ $7.99 Can

ROGUE'S HONOR   by Brenda Hiatt
0-380-81777-2/ $5.99 US/ $7.99 Can

A MATTER OF SCANDAL   by Suzanne Enoch
0-380-81850-7/ $5.99 US/ $7.99 Can

AN UNLIKELY LADY   by Rachelle Morgan
0-380-80922-2/ $5.99 US/ $7.99 Can

Available wherever books are sold or please call 1-800-331-3761
to order.   ROM 0801

Experience the Wonder of Romance
LISA KLEYPAS

SOMEONE TO WATCH OVER ME
0-380-80230-9/$6.99 US/$8.99 Can

STRANGER IN MY ARMS
0-380-78145-X/$6.99 US/$9.99 Can

MIDNIGHT ANGEL
0-380-77353-8/$6.50 US/$8.50 Can

DREAMING OF YOU
0-380-77352-X/$6.99 US/$9.99 Can

BECAUSE YOU'RE MINE
0-380-78144-1/$5.99 US/$7.99 Can

ONLY IN YOUR ARMS
0-380-76150-5/$5.99 US/$7.99 Can

ONLY WITH YOUR LOVE
0-380-76151-3/$6.50 US/$8.50 Can

THEN CAME YOU
0-380-77013-X/$6.99 US/$9.99 Can

PRINCE OF DREAMS
0-380-77355-4/$5.99 US/$7.99 Can

SOMEWHERE I'LL FIND YOU
0-380-78143-3/$5.99 US/$7.99 Can

WHERE DREAMS BEGIN
0-380-80231-7/$6.99 US/$9.99 Can

SUDDENLY YOU
0-380-80232-5/$6.99 US/$9.99 Can

Available wherever books are sold or please call 1-800-331-3761
to order.   LK 0901

America Loves Lindsey!
The Timeless Romances of
The New York Times Bestselling Author

Johanna Lindsey

KEEPER OF THE HEART	0-380-77493-3/$7.99 US/$10.99 Can
THE MAGIC OF YOU	0-380-75629-3/$7.50 US/$9.99 Can
ANGEL	0-380-75628-5/$7.50 US/$9.99 Can
PRISONER OF MY DESIRE	0-380-75627-7/$7.99 US/$10.99 Can
ONCE A PRINCESS	0-380-75625-0/$7.99 US/$10.99 Can
WARRIOR'S WOMAN	0-380-75301-4/$6.99 US/$8.99 Can
MAN OF MY DREAMS	0-380-75626-9/$7.50 US/$9.99 Can
SURRENDER MY LOVE	0-380-76256-0/$7.50 US/$9.99 Can
YOU BELONG TO ME	0-380-76258-7/$7.50 US/$9.99 Can
UNTIL FOREVER	0-380-76259-5/$6.99 US/$9.99 Can
LOVE ME FOREVER	0-380-72570-3/$6.99 US/$8.99 Can
SAY YOU LOVE ME	0-380-72571-1/$6.99 US/$8.99 Can
ALL I NEED IS YOU	0-380-76260-9/$6.99 US/$8.99 Can
THE PRESENT	0-380-80438-7/$6.99 US/$9.99 Can
JOINING	0-380-79333-4/$7.50 US/$9.99 Can
THE HEIR	0-380-79334-2/$7.99 US/$10.99 Can
HOME FOR THE HOLIDAYS	
	0-380-81481-1/$7.99 US/$10.99 Can

And in hardcover

HEART OF A WARRIOR
0-380-97854-7/$25.00 US/$37.95 Can

....

Available wherever books are sold or please call 1-800-331-3761
to order.   JLA 0901

America Loves Lindsey!
The Timeless Romances
of #1 Bestselling Author

GENTLE ROGUE	0-380-75302-2/$6.99 US/$9.99 Can
DEFY NOT THE HEART	0-380-75299-9/$6.99 US/$9.99 Can
SILVER ANGEL	0-380-75294-8/$6.99 US/$8.99 Can
TENDER REBEL	0-380-75086-4/$6.99 US/$8.99 Can
SECRET FIRE	0-380-75087-2/$6.99 US/$9.99 Can
HEARTS AFLAME	0-380-89982-5/$6.99 US/$9.99 Can
A HEART SO WILD	0-380-75084-8/$6.99 US/$9.99 Can
WHEN LOVE AWAITS	0-380-89739-3/$6.99 US/$8.99 Can
LOVE ONLY ONCE	0-380-89953-1/$6.99 US/$8.99 Can
BRAVE THE WILD WIND	0-380-89284-7/$7.99 US/$10.99 Can
A GENTLE FEUDING	0-380-87155-6/$6.99 US/$8.99 Can
HEART OF THUNDER	0-380-85118-0/$6.99 US/$8.99 Can
SO SPEAKS THE HEART	0-380-81471-4/$6.99 US/$9.99 Can
GLORIOUS ANGEL	0-380-84947-X/$6.99 US/$8.99 Can
PARADISE WILD	0-380-77651-0/$6.99 US/$8.99 Can
FIRES OF WINTER	0-380-75747-8/$6.99 US/$8.99 Can
A PIRATE'S LOVE	0-380-40048-0/$6.99 US/$9.99 Can
CAPTIVE BRIDE	0-380-01697-4/$6.99 US/$8.99 Can
TENDER IS THE STORM	0-380-89693-1/$6.99 US/$9.99 Can
SAVAGE THUNDER	0-380-75300-6/$6.99 US/$8.99 Can

Available wherever books are sold or please call 1-800-331-3761
to order.

JLB 0901